Brigid stared at Utu with green glints of suspicion shining in her eyes

"You expect us to believe you don't have similar ambitions? If as you say, Africa is your ancient territory, you'll need armies to reclaim it."

Utu's face registered scorn. "I am the god of the dark people of this land as I was thousands of years ago. But now, as in the old days of the Anunnaki empire, I work for the good of the superior race, the ancient masters of humanity to reassert our rule over Earth. When we mount our thrones, the only humans will be slaves, regardless of their skin color."

"Obviously you think the Collar of Prester John will help you achieve that end," Brigid said curtly, sounding not the least intimidated by the overlord's statement of policy. "So why shouldn't we take it out of Africa altogether?"

Pakari swiveled her head toward Brigid, eyes widening with horror. "You can't—"

Other titles in this series:

James Axler
Outlanders®

RIM OF
THE WORLD

A GOLD EAGLE BOOK FROM
WORLDWIDE®

TORONTO • NEW YORK • LONDON
AMSTERDAM • PARIS • SYDNEY • HAMBURG
STOCKHOLM • ATHENS • TOKYO • MILAN
MADRID • WARSAW • BUDAPEST • AUCKLAND

First edition May 2006

ISBN 0-373-63850-7

RIM OF THE WORLD

Special thanks to Mark Ellis for his contribution to
the Outlanders concept, developed for Gold Eagle.

Copyright © 2006 by Worldwide Library.

"Ye who have seen the Snake," came the voice, "on you is the vow of silence and peace. No blood shall ye shed of man or beast, no flesh shall ye eat till the vow is taken from you. From the hour of midnight till sunrise on the second day ye are bound to God. Whoever shall break the vow, on him shall the curse fall. His blood shall dry in his veins, and his flesh shrink on his bones. He shall be an outlaw and accursed, and there shall follow him through life and death the Avengers of the Snake. Choose ye, my people; upon you is the vow."

—*Prester John* by John Buchan

The Road to Outlands—
From Secret Government Files to the Future

Almost two hundred years after the global holocaust, Kane, a former Magistrate of Cobaltville, often thought the world had been lucky to survive at all after a nuclear device detonated in the Russian embassy in Washington, D.C. The aftermath—forever known as skydark—reshaped continents and turned civilization into ashes.

Nearly depopulated, America became the Deathlands—poisoned by radiation, home to chaos and mutated life forms. Feudal rule reappeared in the form of baronies, while remote outposts clung to a brutish existence.

What eventually helped shape this wasteland were the redoubts, the secret preholocaust military installations with stores of weapons, and the home of gateways, the locational matter-transfer facilities. Some of the redoubts hid clues that had once fed wild theories of government cover-ups and alien visitations.

Rearmed from redoubt stockpiles, the barons consolidated their power and reclaimed technology for the villes. Their power, supported by some invisible authority, extended beyond their fortified walls to what was now called the Outlands. It was here that the rootstock of humanity survived, living with hellzones and chemical storms, hounded by Magistrates.

In the villes, rigid laws were enforced—to atone for the sins of the past and prepare the way for a better future. That was the barons' public credo and their right-to-rule.

Kane, along with friend and fellow Magistrate Grant, had upheld that claim until a fateful Outlands expedition. A displaced piece of technology…a question to a keeper of the archives…a vague clue about alien masters—and their world shifted radically. Suddenly, Brigid Baptiste, the archivist, faced summary execution, and Grant a quick termination. For

Kane there was forgiveness if he pledged his unquestioning allegiance to Baron Cobalt and his unknown masters and abandoned his friends.

But that allegiance would make him support a mysterious and alien power and deny loyalty and friends. Then what else was there?

Kane had been brought up solely to serve the ville. Brigid's only link with her family was her mother's red-gold hair, green eyes and supple form. Grant's clues to his lineage were his ebony skin and powerful physique. But Domi, she of the white hair, was an Outlander pressed into sexual servitude in Cobaltville. She at least knew her roots and was a reminder to the exiles that the outcasts belonged in the human family.

Parents, friends, community—the very rootedness of humanity was denied. With no continuity, there was no forward momentum to the future. And that was the crux— when Kane began to wonder if there *was* a future.

For Kane, it wouldn't do. So the only way was out— way, way out.

After their escape, they found shelter at the forgotten Cerberus redoubt headed by Lakesh, a scientist, Cobaltville's head archivist, and secret opponent of the barons.

With their past turned into a lie, their future threatened, only one thing was left to give meaning to the outcasts. The hunger for freedom, the will to resist the hostile influences. And perhaps, by opposing, end them.

Prologue

The Southern Congo

The drums spoke of the coming of the god.

In the village at the edge of the Usumbur Tract, the Waziri people stopped their work to listen. They cast uneasy glances at one another as the pounding rhythm increased in volume, seeming to seep from the tree line.

The double rows of giant eucalyptus trees stood like silent sentries at the border of the tract. The Julaba River flowed close by, curving away toward the eastern savannahs, but it didn't run through the tract itself. There was no movement of clean life within it, only the feeble and aimless slosh of stagnant waters, the drapery of liana-enshrouded boughs, the sulphurous stench of bog holes and the slither of the venomous snakes infesting the mire between the veldt and the deep jungle. In the twisted boles of the Borassus palm trees, no birds sang.

The sun sank slowly in the purple African sky and dusk rose up from the land itself, as if to smother its last glow. As twilight spread across the Usumbur Tract like the unrolling of a carpet, the drums reached a thunderous and frantic beat. The Waziri had heard the drums before and knew what the rhythm portended.

The village rose from a low escarpment. All the bee-hive-shaped houses were made of dun-colored mud brick topped by reed roofs, both materials provided by the tract. The structures enclosed a large hollow square and from the center blazed a communal cooking fire. The flames cast red streaks on the great oval shields of elephant hide held by the guardsmen and glinted from the points of the long spears angled over their chests. The faint breeze ruffled the shaggy dyed lions' manes that comprised their headdresses.

They stared up at the sky, dark faces impassive. The villagers followed their gazes uneasily, moving together toward the fire. An old man stripped to the waist threw more logs into it and the flames blazed up higher, turning the square into an oven despite the heavy humidity of the night.

A short distance away at the edge of the village, a young woman stepped out on the verandah of a bungalow much larger than the other huts. The flame of a torch affixed to a corner post cast dancing orange highlights over her slender arms and legs.

She was a tall woman, with the proud and erect carriage of Waziri nobility. Big gold hoops glinted at the lobes of her ears and several more encircled the slim column of her throat. Her eyes, a beautifully strange blending of pale brown and deep yellow, held an aureate hue, picking up the gleam of the golden bangles and baubles on her naked limbs.

Her complexion was a rich brown, her hair a thick black mass, caught back and confined by a golden fillet. From the apex rose the gilded tip of an elephant's tusk, giving her the aspect of a unicorn. Other than the feather anklets on her legs and the thin antelope-skin cups partly covering her taut breasts, her only garment was a brief kilt of leopard pelt about her loins.

Her features were bold and cleanly chiseled with a full-lipped mouth and strong chin. Unlike her subjects, Princess Pakari gazed up at the sky with no fear in her eyes or bearing, even though she knew the drums heralded the arrival of the god.

The booming drumbeats ended, replaced by the god's summons, a sound like a long, mournful wail. It rose and fell, echoing through the twilight and out across the grassland and seemingly deep into the Usumbur Tract. The call rose steadily in pitch, becoming as sharp and as piercing as a knife. Several people in the square clapped their hands over their ears and a number of children ran squalling toward their huts.

Then the god's eye appeared high in the sky, a glinting silver orb which at first seemed to be one of the new stars of the evening. Then the eye plunged straight down and braked to an abrupt halt, hovering directly above the leaping flames of the communal fire. A featureless disk of molten silver, the eye was twenty feet in diameter. Perfectly centered on the disk's underside bulged a half dome, like the boss of a shield.

A funnel of incandescence washed from the dome beneath the disk, its glare dazzling the cowering people of the village. The eye floated in the air as if suspended on a long string of screaming sound that filled the dark sky.

Princess Pakari gripped the rail of the verandah and

stared unblinkingly toward the village square and the cone of light flowing down from the disk, interweaving with the tongues of fire.

At the same time the nerve-scratching wail faded, a giant figure suddenly shimmered in the midst of the flames. A fearful murmuring arose from the villagers and they moved away from the fire, toward the opposite side of the square. The guardsmen remained in place, their impassive faces registering no emotion, but they gripped the shafts of their spears very tightly.

The god towered nearly fifteen feet tall. Elaborate body armor tinted a deep magenta with flaring shoulder epaulets and an iridescent gem-encrusted breastplate encased his gaunt frame. The armor was scrawled over with writhing dragons and snarling devil faces. He was clad entirely in metal except for his head.

The skin of his face, drawn tightly over strong, high-arching cheekbones and brow ridges, was of a pale crimson hue. His fierce, lusting eyes gleamed like molten brass, bisected by black, vertical-slitted pupils.

A pattern of scales glistened with a metallic luster on the flesh of his visage, and a back-curved crest of red spines sprouted from his hairless skull. The god, despite his inhuman characteristics, had a terrible, arrogant beauty about him, but there was something viscerally revolting about him, too—his aspect suggested a pampered, depraved child, not an entity touched with divinity.

Princess Pakari whispered in English, "It's him...returning exactly when he said he would."

A shadow stirred from within the house just inside

the doorway. A woman's voice, soft but underscored with tension, said, "I want to see."

Pakari cast a swift glance over her shoulder, saying sternly, "Stay out of sight, Doctor."

Taking a deep breath and composing her face, Pakari stepped off the verandah with plumed head held high and marched single-mindedly across the open ground toward the village square. The murmuring people parted for her, like water before the prow of a ship.

The firelight winked dully on the underside of the silver disk hovering in midair. As she approached, the god stepped majestically out of the fire, his giant, armored body rippling like the surface of a disturbed pond.

The god spoke. "Princess."

The god's voice didn't boom, but reverberated with an echoing, metallic whisper overlaid by a smooth, oily texture. "Again you do not order your subjects to kneel in my presence."

Pakari's lips twisted as if she contemplated spitting at him. "The Waziri do not pay homage to tricksters, Utu."

"*Overlord* Utu," the looming figure corrected her.

Pakari ignored the remark. "I told you when you visited last that I will not give you the sacred Great Snake, the Collar of Prester John. It is not fit for your hands."

Utu's eyes flashed, glowing a bright yellow and Pakari felt her breath catch in her throat. She told herself it was merely a trick of the flickering firelight. Flexing his metal-shod fingers, he intoned grimly, "My hands crafted it aeons ago, long before your people even existed. I created it and I am its rightful owner. I merely demand what is mine. It is a small thing your god demands."

"You," Pakari said calmly but contemptuously, "are not a god. I have it on good authority you are only a fraud with a bag of tricks."

Utu's expression didn't alter. "Kneel."

Pakari shook her head. "No."

Utu's lipless mouth writhed back over his teeth in a fierce snarl. "Kneel to me, Princess…and pray that you and your people will die easily when I have no further use for you. *Kneel.*"

Drawing in a long breath through her nostrils, Pakari tilted her head back so she could stare directly into Utu's eyes. "Never."

For a long, tense moment, there was no sound in the village except for the pop and hiss of the flame-eaten logs. Then, from the underside of the hovering disk stabbed forth a short needle of white light. It pierced one of the guardsmen, punching through the tough hide of his shield with a small puff of smoke.

The needle penetrated the man's broad chest, exited his back and impaled the Waziri soldier standing directly behind him. Both men continued to stand, blinking down in confusion at the cauterized pinholes in their bodies. The whiff of cooked meat joined with the odor of wood smoke. Then life vanished from their eyes. Knees buckling, they crumpled together to the ground without uttering so much as a grunt of dismay.

"Kneel of your own accord," Utu said, a twist of

cruel laughter lurking at the back of his voice, "or I will compel all of you as I compelled those two fools."

Crying out in terror, all of the villagers including the other guardsmen prostrated themselves before the shimmering image of the god.

Utu's features creased in a smile. "Your subjects show far more survival sense than you, Princess."

Utu's voice rose. "I command the priest to come forth."

After a moment the lean figure of a man shuffled toward the fire. Like most of the Waziri, he was tall, but his great age bowed his shoulders. A long white beard fell from his jawline and over his chest. Over his back lay a *kaross* of leopard skin. His dark brown face bore deep creases and crisscrossed lines. He looked as old as time itself. His eyes, covered by a milky film, were blind, and he felt his way forward by means of a wooden staff topped by the likeness of an elephant's head, with the trunk curled.

"I am Inkula," he announced in a surprisingly vibrant tone.

"You are the keeper of the Great Snake, the Collar of Prester John." Utu didn't ask a question; he made a flat, declarative statement.

The old man nodded. "It is in my care and will remain so until the rightful heir stands upon the rim of the world."

"Your god bids you to bequeath the inheritance of Prester John to whom I choose. I will return at the waning of the Moon and then you will deliver the collar to the heir."

"And who is that?" Pakari demanded. "All Waziri are the heirs of the collar."

Utu gestured negligently with his right hand. A rainbow-colored borealis suddenly shimmered beside him and swiftly coalesced into the image of a young Waziri man. Naked to the waist, his massive pectoral muscles showed an intricate pattern of ritual scarring. He wore an ostrich-plumed headdress above a fierce, scowling face. He wore a duplicate of Pakari's gold-tipped elephant-tusk fillet, and like her, his only clothing was a leopard-skin kilt.

"Laputara!" Pakari shrilled in angry incredulity. "Even from exile you betray your people to this monster?"

Utu chuckled patronizingly. "Your half brother cannot hear your recriminations. This is but the prince's likeness, wafted here by the winds at my command—"

"It's a hologram," Pakari broke in impatiently, "like you are. How did you buy him?"

"Unlike you, the prince recognized and accepted his true god."

Pakari clenched her fists so tightly her nails bit into her palms. "Only because Laputara believes your lies, that he stands to gain complete power over Africa. I knew he was ambitious and vain, but I didn't know he was a traitor! Don't you know he dreams of reviving the days of Shaka—invasions, massacres, whole tribes wiped out?"

Utu shrugged. "If he wishes to emulate a long-dead Zulu conqueror, then once he wears the collar he has the right."

"But first," Pakari snapped, "he must do your bidding."

Utu smiled crookedly. "Isn't that always the way of

mortals who seek boons from the gods? You can prevent Prince Laputara from reenacting the role of Shaka
simply by acceding to my request to accept the collar...and obey me—at least for a time."

"I can do the one," Pakari declared darkly, "but not
the other."

The smile fled Utu's face. He gestured toward the
sky. "When the Moon wanes, Princess. Laputara will
arrive before that and make preparations."

The image of Utu rippled, shivered and burst apart
into millions of tiny, multicolored motes that then
swarmed up into the belly of the disk like a cloud of
fireflies. Despite the way her heart trip-hammered painfully within her breast, Pakari forced herself to remain
standing, staring defiantly upward at the silver craft.

It slid soundlessly across the sky and within seconds
was lost from view in the deepening African twilight.

Slowly, Princess Pakari unclenched her fists and
her respiration became less labored. Wheeling around,
she said sharply, "On your feet! The Waziri bow to no
fakers!"

Carefully, eyes on the sky, the villagers rose from the
ground. They murmured apprehensively, shuffling
away from the corpses of the guardsmen. Pakari gestured toward them. "Attend to their bodies and be respectful. They at least died on their feet."

Head held high, Pakari marched purposefully across
the square, ignoring the pleas and hands reaching for
her. Inkula the priest called to her querulously, "Princess—"

She strode past the old man. "Later. We will talk later."

Pakari entered her house, striding into a dimly lit foyer where lion skins carpeted the floor. Once out of sight of the villagers, she sagged against the wall, running a trembling hand over her sweat-filmed brow.

Aware of a presence in the doorway to her private chambers, she demanded in English, "Did you see?"

A sturdily built woman stepped out of the shadows. Her bronze skin was a shade lighter than that of Pakari's, but her eyes were a deep, liquid brown. She was clad in a colorful, intricately dyed cloth shift of the type favored by the Waziri women. A bright red turban was wound about her head. Her full bosom strained at the thin fabric of the shift. A square case dangled from her right hand.

"I did, Princess," the woman replied quietly. "It was just like you described. He even scared me, and I knew what to expect. Don't be too hard on your subjects."

Pakari sighed and shook her head wearily. "They are not my subjects yet, not technically. Whoever wears the Collar of Prester John will hold that honor."

"We'll see what we can do about that." The woman reached up and pulled away the turban. Her hair fell in an ash-blond stream to her bare shoulders.

Pakari straightened up and eyed her challengingly. "When you came here to administer to my people, you also said you could help us against Lord Utu, that you knew who—what—he really was."

Reba DeFore nodded, lifting the case containing the satellite transcomm system. "All I have to do is make a call. Show me where I can set this up."

Princess Pakari gestured across the room to a doorway that opened onto a shrubbery-enclosed garden. DeFore followed her hand-wave and stepped out into the humid night, unlatching the case.

She glanced up into the sky at the big, bright full Moon, gleaming like an orb of cold fire overhead. She wondered briefly if Brigid, Grant and Kane were able to appreciate its beauty.

Chapter 1

The Sudan

Kane silently cursed the steady silver glare of the full Moon. He moved cautiously, circling to the right to put his back against the canyon wall. A small edge, but under the circumstances he was willing to accept anything he could get.

Yusef mirrored his movements. The goateed man was slightly shorter than Kane's six foot one, but younger by at least a decade. He looked immensely strong from a lifetime of eking out an existence in one of the harshest environments on Earth.

Naked to the waist, Yusef's brown torso was roped with heavy muscle. He stood poised on the balls of his feet, his eyes squinting from beneath heavy black brows as he studied his adversary. With a thumb he absently caressed the hawk-headed pommel of the curved *jambiya* dagger in his right hand.

In turn, Kane calculated, considered and discarded half a dozen strategies for engaging the younger man. Like Yusef, he was stripped down to pants and boots. He was built with a lean, long-limbed economy, with most of his muscle mass contained in his upper body, much like that of a wolf. A wolf's cold stare glittered in his blue-gray eyes, the color of dawn light on a sharp steel blade.

His musculature was long and flowing, like stretched-out bundles of sinew covered by a tan lacquer. The smooth symmetry of the lacquer was spoiled by a number of scars, from the stellated puckers of bullet wounds to the thin, jagged lines inflicted by edged steel. A faint hairline scar showed like a white thread against the sun-bronzed skin of his left cheek. Unlike the man he faced, he was clean-shaven.

Kane's dark hair was damp with perspiration, despite the comparatively cool breeze that had begun to waft over the Nubian Desert with the arrival of night. He heard the rustling whisper of the sand slithering across the outcroppings of red-gray rock rearing from the ground.

Djebel Kif, a black pillar of basaltic stone loomed three hundred feet above the tumbled crags and the humans clustered at its base. The fourteen-inch combat knife in Kane's right hand felt as effective as a child's toy against the eternal hostility of the desert—but he didn't intend to use it against the desert, only against one of its spawn.

"Which one of you silly sods is going to make the first move?" Suliedor Entwhistle asked impatiently.

Without taking his eyes off Yusef, Kane retorted flatly, "Let's make it a surprise, how about."

The eight wiry men in burnooses and girdled caftans murmured among themselves, not really understanding Kane's words but comprehending his disrespectful tone to their chief. Angrily, they clutched at their firearms. The guns were crude, home-forged affairs, twin barrels with large, funnel-shaped bores. They were antiques, but ones as deadly as Sin Eaters in the right hands, with the right ammunition, as had already been proved. They were all sturdy desert men whose faces were as flint-hard as the rocky wasteland around them.

Suliedor Entwhistle turned his head toward Kane, but the mirrored lenses of his sunglasses turned his face into something blank and even a little inhuman. A hook-nosed man of medium height with a spade beard, he was clad in Arabian elegance. His turban was of rose-colored silk, his boots stitched with gilt thread and his girdled *khalat* was gaudily embroidered.

He said, "I don't like surprises, Kane. That is why you and your *feringhi* friends are in this unfortunate predicament. I thought that might have occurred to you by now."

The man spoke with the clear, concise enunciation of the upper-class British. Whether his mode of speech was an affectation, as was his very Anglo-Saxon surname, or he was an Englishman in exile he had not explained.

"It definitely occurred to me," rumbled Grant, straining against his bonds. "More than once."

"Me, too," Brigid Baptiste said sourly. "At least three times."

"Silence, woman," Entwhistle spit. "You befoul this holy spot with your very presence, let alone your voice."

Brigid exchanged a quick questioning glance with

Grant and he shook his head slightly, indicating that she should do as the sheikh ordered, at least for the moment. Both she and Grant stood between tall wooden posts driven deep into the ground. Their arms were raised at the shoulder, their wrists lashed tightly to crossbars fitting into Y-shaped notches atop the posts.

The guttering firelight gleamed on Grant's coffee-brown face. Standing four inches over six feet tall, his musculature was heavy, accentuated by exceptionally broad shoulders. His short-cropped hair was touched with gray at the temples, but it didn't show in the gunfighter's mustache that swept out fiercely around both sides of his tight-lipped mouth.

His face displayed no particular emotion, but his brown eyes were black with repressed rage. Grant's right pant leg was dark with blood that had oozed from a bullet wound in the meat of his upper thigh. The injury was more unsightly than critical, a bruised bleeding gash.

Brigid Baptiste wasn't hurt, but the expression on her face registered a degree of inner pain, one that derived from self-anger. She felt responsible for leading her two friends into the ambush that had resulted in their capture.

A tall woman with a fair complexion and big eyes the color of polished jade, Brigid's high forehead gave the impression of a probing intellect, whereas her full underlip hinted at an appreciation of the sensual. Her mane of red-gold hair fell down her back in a long, sunset-colored braid to the base of her spine. Her delicate features had a set, almost feline cast to them.

Like Grant and Kane, she wore tricolor desert-camouflage BDUs, although the lightweight field jacket had been ripped from her by the clansmen. The military-gray T-shirt beneath only accentuated her willowy, full-breasted figure and her bare arms rippled with toned muscle.

The BDUs were departures from the skintight black shadow suits they usually preferred to wear on dark-territory missions, but Lakesh had suggested such clothing would make them appear less sinister to the bedouin tribespeople—and in Brigid's case, a little less revealing and therefore not quite as offensive to Muslims. Diplomacy, turning potential enemies into allies against the spreading reign of the overlords, had become the paramount tactic of Cerberus over the past year. Lessons in how to deal with foreign cultures and religions took the place of weapons instruction and other training.

Over the past three years, Brigid Baptiste and former Cobaltville Magistrates Grant and Kane had tramped through jungles, ruined cities, over mountains, across deserts and they found strange cultures everywhere, often bizarre recreations of societies that had vanished long before the nukecaust.

Due in part to her eidetic memory, Brigid spoke a dozen languages and could get along in a score of dialects, but knowing the native tongues of many different cultures and lands was only a small part of her work. Aside from her command of languages, Brigid had made history and geopolitics abiding interests in a world that was changing rapidly.

She and all the personnel of Cerberus, over half a world away atop a mountain peak in Montana, had devoted themselves to changing the nuke-scarred planet into something better. At least that was her earnest hope. To turn hope into reality meant respecting the often alien behavior patterns of a vast number of ancient religions, legends, myths and taboos.

Now the concept of violating a religious taboo seemed so irrelevant as to be ridiculous. Sheikh Suliedor Entwhistle had sprung the treacherous attack without warning. One moment, the outlanders were engaged in friendly conversation with Entwhistle and his men about a campfire—and in the next instant, guns blazed and the clansmen rushed in from all directions, bowling them over.

A rifle barrel used as a bludgeon slammed hard into Kane's back and he went down on his knees, his Sin Eater stuttering in his hand. The bullets kicked up sand in little plumes, intersected with the fire and sent sparks and embers exploding in all directions like miniature novas.

Grant fired a triburst with his own Sin Eater at a white burnoose and the face framed within it vanished in a red mass of splintered bone and punctured flesh.

Kane struggled to his feet and started to fire again, then checked his finger on the trigger stud. Into a patch of moonlight emerged Brigid with two men crowding close to her, heavy *jambiya* blades in their hands.

One of the men grabbed for Brigid and her TP-9 autopistol came from beneath her jacket. A single shot blew away the man's right kneecap. As he fell, scream-

ing and plucking at his maimed leg, the other Arab
turned and ran away, squalling in fear, overwhelmed by
the sight of a mere woman dispatching a male warrior
so quickly and efficiently.

The metal-reinforced butt of a rifle slammed into
Kane's left rib cage and sent him sprawling, knocking
the wind from his lungs. As he tried to struggle to his
knees he saw Suliedor Entwhistle standing over him
with the weapon in his hands and he saw his own features reflected in the sheikh's mirrored sunglasses.

He heard a sharp report and a brief outcry from
Grant, more anger than pain. He glimpsed the big man
fall, clutching at his thigh. Immediately he was surrounded by three men, hammering at him with the
stocks of their rifles.

"Enough!" Brigid cried, throwing her pistol toward
the fire. *"Pashita watta!"*

Kane reluctantly holstered his own weapon and
raised his hands. Howling with delight, the bedouin
ran forward to seize them. In the process of turning over
his Sin Eater, Kane struck Suliedor Entwhistle with an
open left hand and then spit in his face.

Brigid grasped Kane's strategy of slapping the chief-
tain with his "unclean" hand and spitting on him—he
meant to force the man into single combat, since such
insults could only be expunged from his honor by personally killing the aggressor. For Entwhistle to simply
order Kane's execution was tantamount to an admission
of cowardice on his part. If he failed to accept the challenge and redress Kane's insult, then his position as
sheikh would no longer be secure.

At least, that was the code of the bedouin desert warrior as contained in the Cerberus database. With a sinking sensation in the pit of his stomach, Kane realized adjustments had been made to the code after Suliedor appointed his own, much younger champion to answer to the challenge in his stead. None of the clansmen objected to the substitution of Yusef for their sheikh. Instead, they appeared very happy about it, if for nothing else but to see the looks of dismay on the faces of three outlander infidels.

"Yusef!" Suliedor barked impatiently, then spoke in a rapid-fire dialect. *"Imshi ta'al feringhi!"*

Instantly, Yusef bounded at Kane as if shot from a cannon.

Chapter 2

Yusef dived in low, throwing himself down to pivot swiftly on his left hand, the knife in his right lashing out toward the tendons at the back of Kane's left knee. Kane leaped straight up, and the man's blade shaved a little curl from the sole of his boot.

Kane stomped down as he landed, hoping to break Yusef's hand, but the muscular bedouin was an eye blink too fast. He rolled backward and came smoothly to his feet, then plunged forward, the *jambiya* raised high, arcing up, then down, the polished blade flashing in the moonlight.

Kane dived in under his swinging arm, trying for a crippling slash through Yusef's Achilles tendons. The Arab danced away, stabbing downward, and Kane felt the knife point rip across the back of his shoulders. Tucking and rolling, he came up on his toes as Yusef wheeled around, hacking with the blade.

Still off balance, Kane clumsily jerked his combat knife up in a defensive gesture. The blades met with a loud clash of steel against steel and a brief flare of sparks at the impact point. Kane winced as a streak of pain zigzagged through his metacarpals and up his right arm. He staggered backward, his hand losing almost all feeling. His fingers lost their grip on the Nylex handle of the knife and it slipped from his grasp.

At the same time, Yusef cried out in pain and dismay as his *jambiya* dropped from numbed fingers. Baffled, surprised and not a little frightened by their unexpected disarmament, the two men stared at each other in silent surmise. The Arab's eyes were feral, narrowed. Both Kane and Yusef reassessed their situations, then simultaneously closed in on each other. The clansmen lifted their voices in ululating howls of bloodthirsty delight.

Yusef launched a roundhouse kick, and Kane dodged away, but the heel of the man's left boot clubbed against his hip. A new wave of pain joined the throbbing in his right hand and wrist. Even as he stumbled backward, he caught Yusef's ankle and dragged the bedouin with him. Kane swung him around in a semicircle, released him and slammed him face-first against an outcropping, but Yusef managed to cushion the collision with his forearms.

As he whirled around, Kane met him with a triple-hammer blow, the side of his left fist beating in a fast, furious rhythm on Yusef's midriff. The Arab grunted, but continued lunging for him. Kane ducked between his arms and glided behind him.

Yusef wheeled around and Kane pistoned his left fist forward in two short, jabbing blows that rocked the younger man's head back and split his lower lip. Blood started trickling from his nostrils.

A growl of fury humming in his bull throat, Yusef swung at Kane's face with two knotted fists. Kane dodged back and then sidled in. Tingling sensation returned to his right hand, and he delivered a right hook to the man's diaphragm. Yusef responded with a lightning-swift left cross. Kane shunted aside the fist driving toward his jaw and chopped with the edge of his stiffened hand at the base of Yusef's corded throat.

Although the heel of his hand rebounded from the thick mass of muscle there, Yusef uttered a choking cry and half staggered away in a tangle-footed backpedal, massaging his neck. The moonlight glinted for an instant from his eyes, and Kane glimpsed a mixture of respect and fear gleaming there.

As Kane figured, Yusef had grown accustomed to allowing his size, strength and most likely his reputation to intimidate opponents. Facing a skilled martial artist like Kane was a completely new and even frightening experience for him. Kane's trained reactions and speed offset his adversary's massive build and greater strength.

Yusef definitely possessed ability, but Kane had lived longer and harder and faced a more diverse set of challenges as both a Magistrate and an exile. He knew far more about the rudiments of pitting talon against fang when the situation was strictly kill or be killed with no niceties about the means. He had fought for his life many times in his far-ranging career as both Magistrate and insurrectionist, and he knew every trick of close-quarters fighting, especially the dirty ones.

Kane also knew when he had been manipulated into playing a rigged game. Regardless of who won the trial by combat, he and his friends would be the losers unless he figured out how to change the rules. He hoped he could find a way to do it. He deliberately didn't look in the direction of Brigid and Grant.

The two men circled the campsite, a slow, shuffling orbit about the cookfire. Kane managed to keep the rocks at his back, but the light shed by the full Moon was almost as bright as day so little refuge lay in the shadows.

Yusef launched a sudden spin-kick at Kane's head. Kane had been expecting it, even hoping for it. Rather than move into the arc and latch on to the Arab's leg as his instincts urged him, he evaded it and slapped the man's foot as it whistled past, forcing him to turn a complete, clumsy circle.

Yusef staggered as he regained his footing, the expression on his face registering embarrassment. Kane smiled at him thinly, condescendingly, but made no move. Magistrate doctrine taught never to be defensive when any opportunity presented itself to go on the attack, but Kane had learned painful lessons in his post-Mag years about the importance of impulse control.

"Yusef!" Suliedor snarled. "Don't ease up on him, you lazy git! Wear him down! *Qawam bilajal!*"

The young man threw the sheikh an angry glare, then obeyed, closing in on Kane, kicking, punching, pounding. Kane stood his ground, balanced lightly on the balls of his feet, parrying and blocking the driving blows of his opponent with his legs, forearms and hands. It wasn't easy, but he maintained a slightly mocking smile as if Yusef were a child swatting at him in a tantrum, despite the fact the man's fists felt like blocks of unfinished oak. He called on all the hard-won experience that had saved him so often in the past.

Magistrate martial-arts training borrowed shame-
lessly from every source—from tae kwon do to savate
to bushidokan. The style was down-and-dirty, focusing
primarily on the aspects of offense rather than defense,
but Kane restrained his impulses to react with killing
blows. A single *teisho* punch to the young man's nose
would end the combat decisively, but Kane didn't want
to kill him—at least not yet.

Yusef's breath came in labored rasps and his face
grew pinched from exertion and frustrated fury. Panting, he doubled his efforts, pummeling wildly. One of
his fists crashed through Kane's guard and pounded solidly into his stomach.

Air whistled out of his lungs, but he managed to
keep from doubling over. Kane stabbed out with a left-
handed thumb-and-forefinger thrust to Yusef's throat,
but not hard enough to crush his larynx. He jabbed the
nerve clump just above the base of his neck.

Yusef stumbled backward, coughing, snarling and
wheezing. He strained to suck in air, his hand clutching reflexively at his throat. His left foot came down on
the handle of his *jambiya* knife and he lost his balance,
collapsing to one knee.

Kane swept around him as swiftly as El Borak, the
desert wind. He slid one arm up to lock beneath the
man's chin, his hand grasping his other forearm to complete the vise to jam Yusef's head hard against his right
shoulder. The hammerlock was a killing hold if carried
through. The bedouin cursed breathlessly.

Kane drove a foot into the back of Yusef's right knee
and his leg buckled. Only Kane's grip kept him erect.

Over the man's agonzied, strangulated gasps, Kane heard the faint creak of strained vertebrae.

Into Yusef's ear, he whispered, "I know you can understand me…it's not necessary for you to die."

In a guttural grunt, Yusef replied, "I won't surrender, you filthy *feringhi*—"

The insult died as Kane tightened his right forearm against the younger man's windpipe. Yusef struggled, biting at air. "Don't be an asshole," Kane grated. "You don't want to die, your old man doesn't want you to die. You don't even have to formally give up. Just quit."

Yusef clawed at his arms, trying to prise away the flesh-and-blood vise strangling him. Kane bore down remorselessly, damning and admiring the young man's pride. With the base of his thumb he applied steady pressure against Yusef's carotid artery and the man's struggles weakened.

Blinking back the sweat dripping into his eyes, Kane glanced over at Suliedor Entwhistle. His eyes still masked by the mirrored lenses, he gazed at him expressionlessly, but his fists were clenched so tightly the knuckles stood out in stark relief, almost as if they were about to split the skin.

Kane suddenly released his grip and sprang back. Yusef, gagging and gasping, fell face first to the ground. Reaching down, Kane snatched up the *jambiya* knife and whipped the blade down in an overhand, decapitating loop. At the last microinstant, he checked the movement and lightly placed the curved edge against the back of Yusef's neck.

Staring levelly at Suliedor, Kane demanded, "Do you accept your son's defeat as your own?"

Suliedor Entwhistle stiffened, eyes fixed on Yusef as he struggled to draw air into his lungs. "How did you know he was my son?"

Kane smiled crookedly. "You wouldn't let just anybody avenge my insult. I figured a traditionalist like you would make it a matter of family honor."

The sheikh shrugged as if the matter was of little importance. "He did not yield, outlander."

"But he's beaten anyway," Kane snapped, pressing down with the knife. The razored edge sank slightly into the flesh and a trickle of blood oozed around it. Yusef drew in his breath through clenched teeth. "Do you prefer him dead? If your honor, your code demands it, I can finish the job and behead him. That's still the preferred method of execution hereabouts, I understand. What will it take to satisfy you?"

Suliedor hesitated, then gestured behind him at Grant and Brigid. Several clansmen turned, aiming their rifles at the two people. Between bared, discolored teeth, he hissed, "I can have these two sods killed and spare you—how about that? That might satisfy me."

"I've got a better idea," Kane retorted. "I'll let Yusef live and you let all of us go. That way everybody stays alive and happy."

Enwhistle shook his head. "You will invade the holy Djebel Kif, the abode of the jinn and the afreet. I cannot allow that."

"This was all a misunderstanding," Kane declared. "We have no intention of invading any part of your land."

"It is not my land," Suliedor shot back, "but that of the old gods. We were warned you might appear. Three of you, perhaps more, seeking entrance to the ancient crucible of creation."

Kane scowled at him. "Who did the warning?"

"That is not your concern, *feringhi.*"

"I think I can guess," Kane replied. "An overdressed snake-face who talks all big about doom and bowing and yielding, right?"

The sheikh's face locked in a tight, hard mask of anger. "You blaspheme!"

"Fluently," said Kane dryly.

For a long, stretched-out tick of time, Kane and Suliedor Entwhistle stared at each other in silent surmise. The only sound was the crackle of firewood. Then, an electronic trilling, rising-and-falling warble, cut through the night. Brigid Baptiste jerked in surprised reaction to the signal of her transcomm.

Angrily, Suliedor whirled toward her. "What is that?"

"Oops," she said with feigned shame, extending her right leg. The warble emanated from the pouch pocket. "I should've let my service know I wasn't accepting calls during the trial by combat."

Snarling a torrent of enraged Arabic, Suliedor marched toward her, reaching out for the pocket. As he bent over, Brigid jacked her knee up against his bearded jaw with a sound like an ax chopping into wood. The sheikh hadn't expected an aggressive move from a woman and was taken completely by surprise.

As Suliedor stumbled back a pace, she whipped up

her legs, bending her knees at her chest. Hands wrapped tightly around the crossbar, she straightened out her legs, pistoning them forward like a pair of horizontal pile drivers, the thick treads of her boots smashing full into the man's chest.

The belled sleeves of his robe flapped like the wings of an ungainly bird as Suliedor Entwhistle catapulted backward into the fire.

Chapter 3

As the sheikh tumbled into the flames, Kane wasted no time gaping at the spectacle—unlike Suliedor's followers. None of them caught the blur that was the lightning-quick motion of Kane's right arm. Firelight flickered on polished steel.

The man holding a rifle on Grant staggered backward as if he had been struck a blow. Gurgling and choking, his eyes bugging, he tilted his head back, his chin forced up by the hilt of the *jambiya* knife jutting from his throat.

With a dying effort, he lifted his rifle with both hands, struggling to trigger it with fumbling fingers. He sank to his knees as the twin bores of the rifle gouted thunder and flame. A clansman attempting to render aid to Entwhistle cried out in agony, jackknifing violently over a belly wound.

Suliedor Entwhistle hurled himself out of the fire, his clothes aflame. Leaping to his feet, he performed a whirling-dervish dance, beating at the hem of his robe. A man shifted to one side, trying to get out of his sheikh's way. His attention was focused on Suliedor's spark-spewing contortions and he didn't realize that he moved directly in front of Grant.

Clutching at the posts, Grant sprang up and closed a leg-scissors lock around the clansman's neck. He devoted all of the strength in his powerful leg muscles to choking the life out of the man. Knots and ropes of sinew rippled along his massive legs, as well as a flow of blood.

A drawn-out, gagging gasp burst from the man's lips as he clawed frantically at Grant's boots, then grasped his ankles and tried to wrench them apart. Grant continued the relentless pressure.

Simultaneously, Brigid Baptiste tightened her body like a bowstring and surged up and over, her hands using the crossbar as an axis. She somersaulted over it, her flying feet catching an Arab in the face, knocking him backward. Arms windmilling as he tried to regain his balance, the man fell against one of his companions and both of them went down heavily.

With a whiplash motion of her body, Brigid wriggled atop the crossbar, then planted both feet on top the posts, standing spraddle-legged. She jerked the wooden shaft free of its sockets, and though her wrists were still bound to it, she used the length of wood as a club, whacking a bedouin atop his burnoose just as he struggled to his feet.

Dazed, he fell onto his back. Brigid jumped lithely from atop the posts, her feet slamming solidly against the man's torso. All the air left his lungs in an agonized, grunting whoosh.

She wheeled around toward Grant and the man locked fast between his ankles. The Arab's legs thrashed as if he were running in place as Grant continued to apply the lethal pressure. The man's eyes distended, his tongue slowly protruded as he clawed for the dagger sheathed in the sash girding his waist. Dragging it free, he held it as if to stab Grant through the calf of his left leg.

Brigid was faster, leaning forward to drive the blunt end of the pole against his sternum, then using it to flick the knife from his suddenly slack fingers. The blade spun end over end twice before she was able to catch it by the pommel with both hands. Grant relaxed his scissors hold and the man slid limply to the ground.

With the knife's razor-keen edge, Brigid sawed through the thongs. They parted just as a clansman rushed her, the firelight glinting dully from the tip of the two-foot-long *khanjar* blade in his fist.

Brigid stepped away, the wooden pole in one hand, the dagger in the other. Over the past three years, she had been involved in any number of life-threatening situations, and she still wasn't sure if she'd survived them through luck, divine intervention or simply the proper management and application of skills to circumstances. Now she let her instincts and the intensive training she had received from Kane and Grant take over.

The Arab slashed out with his knife, growling deep in his throat. Brigid blocked the blow with the crossbar, then punched the butt forward from her shoulder in a fast, flat trajectory. The end impacted like a battering ram against the bottom tip of the man's nose.

There was a very faint, mushy crunch of cartilage. The man's head snapped back, his legs flying out from under him. His crushed nose spewed blood as bone splinters pushed through his sinus cavities and into his brain. The bedouin was dead before his body settled.

With wordless, wolfish yells, four of the bedouin converged on Kane. Yusef managed to shamble half-erect, and Kane maneuvered himself behind the young man. He swept his right leg out in a reverse heel-kick, catching the man just behind the knees. Yusef's legs buckled and he fell directly in the path of the clansmen. One of the men tripped over him and slammed full length to the ground. Kane snap-kicked him almost casually in the head.

The three men milled around him, trying to crowd him against a rock formation. A *jambiya* sliced through the air toward his face. Kane sidestepped, blocked the blow with a forearm, locking the man's right wrist in the crook of his left elbow. He wrenched back and up violently, breaking the man's wrist with a dry crunching sound. The man uttered an animal scream and his eyes rolled up in his head. He sagged to his knees in Kane's grasp.

The knife thumped to the sand and Kane kicked it out of reach. At the same time he used his left arm to shunt aside a fist driving toward his jaw. Spinning on a heel, he dropped the bedouin with a back-handed ram's-head punch between the eyes.

The third man managed to bore in from the other side, knocking Kane off balance just long enough to outmuscle him and secure a full nelson.

The man he had snap-kicked staggered to his feet, spitting out blood and teeth splinters. Snatching up the fallen *jambiya,* he lunged forward, the point of the knife on a direct line with Kane's belly.

Using the man holding him as support, Kane bunched the muscles in his legs and sprang upward, the thick soles of his boots catching the blade-wielding clansman squarely between the legs. There was a sound as of a butcher's cleaver chopping into a side of beef.

The bedouin doubled up, croaking in agony, clawing at his crotch. He fell over on his side, jets of vomit spewing from between his lips.

The clansman holding Kane in the full nelson jerked in response to the maneuver, bleating wordlessly in fear and confusion. Planting his heels firmly on the ground, Kane bulled himself backward, slamming the bedouin hard against the outcropping and pounding the back of his skull several times into the man's face. Teeth and vertebrae gave way with grisly crunches.

The clansman's grip loosened and Kane fought his way out of it. Even as he sagged to the ground, the Arab who had received the backhand staggered to his feet, drawing his own knife.

Brigid stepped up behind him and broke the length of wood over a burnoosed head. The man dropped limp limbed and unconscious to the sand. Kane pivoted on a heel, muscles tensed, looking for another enemy.

Suddenly, a blinding flash of fire and a deafening detonation rocked everyone to unsteady halts.

Standing among the fallen bodies, Yusef hefted a rifle in his arms, plumes of smoke curling from the bores. The echoes of the double reports rolled across the desert like the reverberations of a gong.

Stunned into silent immobility, the combatants all stared at Yusef, even Suliedor Entwhistle, who was in the process of stamping out the flaming hem of his robe.

"Enough!" Yusef roared hoarsely. "Enough of this madness!"

Suliedor patted out his smoldering beard. Half of the man's whiskers were no more than charred, stinking stubble, the surrounding flesh swollen with leaking blisters. He had lost his sunglasses, and his blue eyes were bright with rage and humiliation. "*I* decide when enough is enough!" he snapped.

"Not if I'm fighting your battles!" Yusef pitched the rifle over his shoulder. It clattered and clanked loudly against the rock-littered base of Djebel Kif. "I will be the one to say when there has been enough of it!"

He swept an arm around the campsite, toward the many motionless men and the ones who stirred feebly, moaning with pain. "The outlanders have cut us down by a third because you lured them here with the false promise of friendship. This is Allah's punishment for your treachery!"

"We had not shared the salt," Suliedor barked. "They are *feringhi,* foreigners, and they are infidels. Did the god not warn us about them?"

"A false god!" Yusef shouted. "There is no god but Allah, and the creature that spoke to you was as unholy as the jinn that you believe dwell there!"

He stabbed a finger at the towering black basalt pillar. "You are my father, and I do not want to oppose your will but—"

Yusef's words trailed off and in a far less formal, even plaintive tone he said, "Come on, Dad. You're a smart man. You know it was no damn god who spoke to us and there's no nest of damn jinn up there. We both know it's some old lab or military outpost built a couple of hundred years ago."

Suliedor stiffened. Kane and Brigid exchanged swift, startled glances. Gusting out a sigh, Yusef turned to face Kane. "This has been all bollocks and bullshit from the beginning. How about we try starting over?" His English accent was unmistakable.

Kane, feeling blood trickle from the shallow laceration across his upper back, decided to restrict his response to a simple nod.

Grant was not so restrained. Struggling against his bonds, he bellowed angrily, "How about we try cutting me loose before we try anything else?"

WHEN BRIGID SLICED through the thongs binding Grant's wrists to the crossbar, he growled ruefully, "I'm glad I could be of such help."

The man whom Grant had leg-throttled into unconsciousness had regained his senses and he glared balefully at him, massaging his neck.

After Grant was cut free, he took a limping step forward, rubbing his wrists to restore circulation. The bedouin hissed something in his own language. The words were incomprehensible, but the tone was unmistakable. Without altering the expression on his face, Grant turned and smashed his right fist into the belly of the man. He grated, "That's for shooting me, then trying to hamstring me."

The clansman folded in the middle, clutching at his

midsection, a gassy wail escaping his lips. Grant strode on without a backward glance, one hand clapped over the wound in his thigh.

"How do you know he was the one who shot you?" Brigid inquired.

"Because he's wearing a white burnoose on his head."

Brigid started to point out that all the men wore white burnooses, but decided Grant wouldn't appreciate the observation.

While Yusef and Suliedor ministered to their dead and wounded, the three outlanders tended to their own injuries with the contents of the medical kit confiscated by the bedouin. Kane retrieved their weapons, glaring defiantly at the clansmen who muttered resentfully about it. He hadn't received official permission from either the sheikh or his son that they could recover their guns, but Kane didn't care. He wanted to be armed just in case the mercurial nature of the desert men changed from sullen resignation to homicidal fury.

While Kane held his Sin Eater and a Copperhead subgun in both hands, slitted eyes fixed on the Arabs, Brigid examined Grant, who sat down on a rock on the opposite side of the campsite. He cradled his own Copperhead in his big brown hands. She cut open the fabric and saw his wound was little more than a scrape where the heavy bullet had gouged the flesh of his thigh, bruising the muscles during its passage.

As she methodically cleaned the raw, two-inch-long furrow, Brigid asked quietly, "Do either of you have any idea of what might be going on here?"

Kane shrugged, then winced at the sharp sting in his shoulders. "Seems pretty apparent to me. One of the overlords, most probably Utu, since we already have a report of him operating here on the African continent, must be trying to reclaim a local holding. He's using the bedouin as ready-made guardians and cannon fodder."

Voice tight with the effort of repressing pain as Brigid swabbed out the blood congealed around the gouge in his flesh, Grant said, "I thought there was supposed to be an Overproject Excalibur cell inside this pile of rocks. That's the information we got from Aten, right?"

Brigid nodded, continuing to work. "Right."

Over a year before while visiting the hidden city-kingdom of Aten, the Cerberus warriors had come into possession of a computer file that purportedly contained all the data pertaining to the inner workings of Overproject Excalibur and its many subdivisions.

Excalibur was a major division of the Totality Concept, which itself was the umbrella designation for predark American military supersecret researches into many different, yet at the same time, interconnected programs. The spin-off experiments were applied to an eclectic combination of disciplines, most of them theoretical—artificial intelligence, hyperdimensional physics, genetics and new energy sources.

The primary division of the Totality Concept was Overproject Whisper, which in turn spawned Project Cerberus and Operation Chronos, both of which focused on expansions and applications of quantum physics.

Conversely, Overproject Excalibur was a branch of the Totality Concept that dealt with genetic engineering and advances in human biology. One of the Excalibur subdivisions, Mission Invictus, was devoted to altering human DNA so a new breed of Homo sapiens could survive and even thrive in the postholocaust environment. The Invictus mandate was to create the missing link, the biological bridge between predark and postdark man, an invincible superhuman designed to claim the world created by the atomic Armageddon.

The computer file from Aten had identified a Mission Invictus–related base as being located in the Sudan, hidden within the mysterious megalithic rock formation known as Djebel Kif. This particular base bore the code name of Conception: Beowulf. The Cerberus warriors learned a couple of years before that Beowulf had refined the researches of Mission Invictus to create a superhuman.

The scientist who oversaw Conception: Beowulf had found a means to increase the size, muscular capability and intelligence of a human being. As far as the three outlanders knew, the undertaking had created only one superhuman—Ambika, the self-styled pirate queen of the Western Isles in the Pacific.

They had assumed Ambika was merely an isolated, freakish phenomenon and not the avatar of a strategy to release scores, perhaps hundreds of extremely powerful, mutagenically engineered humans into the world. After coming across the Conception: Beowulf entry in the computer file, they began to think they had jumped to a premature conclusion.

"What now?" Grant asked impatiently, shifting position.

"You'll sit still until I tell you to move," Brigid said peevishly.

After the blood was swabbed away, Brigid sprayed the gouge with disinfectant from a small aerosol can. Grant gritted his teeth against the bite of it, but said nothing.

He silently admired the deft ease with which Brigid tended to the wound. Reba DeFore, Cerberus redoubt's resident medic, had done a good job teaching her field medicine. But Brigid's bedside manner was superior to that of her mentor, which Grant reminded himself wouldn't be too difficult.

The bandage Brigid applied came from a can, too. She used an aerosol spray to apply a liquid bandage. A skinlike thin layer of film formed over the bullet scrape in his leg. The substance contained nutrients and antibiotics and would be absorbed by the body as the injury healed.

When she was done with Grant, Brigid rose and strode over to Kane. "Your turn."

Kane obligingly turned around so she could examine the shallow cut scored by the point of Yusef's knife. She didn't react to the sight of the swirling weal of scar tissue between his shoulder blades. It was from an injury he had sustained in the Black Gobi over three years before, when he rescued Brigid from the Tushe Gun's genetic mingler.

He had shielded her unconscious body from the mingler's wild energy discharges with his own. Only the tough, Kevlar-weave coat he had worn at the time saved his life. Brigid had suffered wounds of her own, far subtler and emotionally devastating. Her exposure to the energy of the machine and to an unknown wavelength of radiation had rendered her barren.

Still keeping a watchful eye on Suliedor and his bedouin, Kane only grimaced when he felt the tart pinch of the antiseptic spray on the raw knife cut. The cooling touch of the liquid bandage followed a moment later.

"You're all right," Brigid said curtly, handing him his black T-shirt. "Both of you were very lucky—again."

She took the Copperhead from Kane as he pulled on his shirt. "Suliedor has become a lot more agreeable," he commented.

"He's a businessman first," Brigid replied. "He reminds me of Mohammed bin Sayed, the master slave-trader of nineteenth-century Africa. He was educated and charming but also a robber baron of the most brutal kind. I think our Sheikh Entwhistle is modeling himself after Sayed."

Yusef warily approached them from the cluster of bedouin, a robe thrown carelessly over his shoulders. He kept his hands open and hanging loose at his sides to show he was unarmed.

"I guess it's too late for an apology," he said, "from either side."

Grant pushed himself to his feet and limped over to stand beside Brigid and Kane. "It's about one bullet, one knife-cut and an ounce of blood too late," he growled.

Yusef nodded as if he expected the response. "If you want to go climbing around Djebel Kif, my dad said to go ahead. Nobody feels like trying to stop you anymore. Even if we did, we don't have the numbers."

Brigid raised an ironic eyebrow. "Oh? Does your father hope the jinn up there will eat our souls or something?"

Yusef tried to smile, but it wasn't easy with a swollen and split lip. "Dad doesn't really believe there are jinn up there and neither do I. No, it's busy with strange men and stranger machines, and from what I've heard, they're worse than any soul-stealing devils."

The young bedouin saluted the looming pillar of black rock, now silvered by the full Moon. "But, hey—you're more than welcome to see for yourselves."

Chapter 4

They stared up at the black bulk of stone stretching into the sky above the tumbled crags. On the very summit, they could barely make the out the ruins of an old structure. They saw only a collapsed roof, a few support posts and several stretches of crenellated and buttressed walls outlined against the gleam of the Moon. Through compact binoculars, Brigid, Grant and Kane silently studied the stronghold.

"What the hell is that up there on the top?" Kane inquired.

"An ancient Byzantine monastery," Yusef answered. "Don't be deceived. It may look deserted, but it isn't." A strip of bandage showed whitely on the back of his neck, covering the superficial knife wound inflicted by Kane.

"The jinn have claimed it," Suliedor announced flatly, crossing his arms over his chest.

Lowering his binoculars, Grant cast the man a sour glance. The sheikh's burned face glistened with analgesic ointment applied by Brigid. "What the hell are jinn anyway?" he demanded.

Suliedor's lips curved in a superior smirk. "I don't expect infidels, *feringhi* no less, to know anything about our beliefs—"

"The jinn," Brigid stated in a crisp tone, "are creatures that are half human and half demon from pre-
Islamic times. Originally, they were spirits of nature
that caused madness in humans. They differ not much
from humans—they reproduce, they have the same
bodily needs and they die, although their life span is
much longer.

"The Arabic word jinn, which means 'spirit,' is neutral—some of the jinn serve Allah, while others do not.
There are five orders of jinn—the Marid, the most powerful, the Afreet, the Shaitan, the Jinni and the Jann.

"All the jinn are capable of good and evil acts.
They're mischievous and enjoy punishing humans for
wrongs done them, even unintentionally. Accidents and
diseases are considered to be their work. They are composed of fire or air and they can assume both animal and
human form. They exist in air, in flame, under the earth
and in inanimate objects, such as rocks, trees and ruins."

She waved a hand in the direction of the top of
Djebel Kif. "So I can understand how a superstition
could arise about the place being haunted by jinn."

No one gaped at Brigid in astonishment, but Kane
repressed a laugh at the disconcerted expression crossing Suliedor's face. A trained historian, Brigid had
spent over half of her thirty years as an archivist in the
Cobaltville's Historical Division, but there was more to
her storehouse of knowledge than simple training.

Almost everyone who worked in the ville divisions
kept secrets, whether they were infractions of the law,
unrealized ambitions or deviant sexual predilections.
Brigid Baptiste's secret was more arcane than the com-

mission of petty crimes or manipulating the baronial system of government for personal aggrandizement.

Her secret was the ability to produce eidetic images. Centuries ago, it had been called a photographic memory. She could, after viewing an object or scanning a document, retain exceptionally vivid and detailed visual memories. When she was growing up, she feared she was a psi-mutie, but she later learned that the ability was relatively common among children, and usually disappeared by adolescence. It was supposedly very rare among adults, but Brigid was one of the exceptions.

Since her forced exile, she had taken full advantage of the Cerberus redoubt's vast database, and as an intellectual omnivore she grazed in all fields. Coupled with her eidetic memory, her profound knowledge of an extensive and eclectic number of topics made her something of an ambulatory encyclopedia. This trait often irritated Kane, but just as often it had tipped the scales between life and death, so he couldn't in good conscience become too annoyed with her.

Recovering from his surprise, Suliedor said doggedly, "That may be, but it is no superstition."

Yusef sighed. "Ah, come on, Dad—"

The sheikh ignored him. "Only six months ago some bedouin of another clan wandered up there, looking for an old well rumored to be at the top. Only one of the men came back, and everyone thought he had been struck mad by exposure to the sun, judging from the tales he told. When I heard of this, we came into this region and looked for this man. I found out he had died, but I was told he never stopped babbling about the jinn that haunt Djebel Kif."

"And at what point," asked Kane, "did you meet up with the false god who offered you a job as a night watchman? Before or after you heard about the babbling man?"

When Suliedor didn't immediately respond, Kane cut his pale eyes over toward his son. "I may not know what a jinn is, but I damn well know your old man didn't come here to find out if the stories about devils were true."

Yusef nodded slowly, reluctantly. "You're right. The man raved about the jinn but he also talked of men and of machines up there."

"And guns, I'll bet," drawled Grant.

"And guns, yes."

Kane glanced over at Brigid. "Like you said...he's a businessman first."

Gazing directly Suliedor, Brigid Baptiste challenged, "You thought the man might have found a predark stockpile, didn't you?"

Suliedor blinked, perplexed. "How did you know?"

"It's a major vocation in our country," Brigid answered. "Or it used to be."

Looting the abandoned ruins of predark villes was not only an Outland tradition; it had become a family business. Many generations of outlanders had made a career from ferreting out and plundering the secret stockpiles the predark government had hidden in anticipation of a nation-wide catastrophe.

Finding a well-stocked redoubt, one of the many underground military installations seemingly scattered all over the nuke-ravaged face of America, assured a trader a life of wealth and security, presupposing he or she didn't intersect with the trajectory of a bullet that had his or her name on it. Most of the redoubts had been found and raided decades ago, but occasionally one hitherto untouched would be located. It stood to reason there would be rumors of such hidden caches of pre-dark wealth in other countries.

"What about the god who charged you to guard this place?" Kane asked. "When did you come across him...or was it a her?"

"Him," Yusef said. "There are secret ways into the cliff and though no man of our tribe came here because they thought it was an accursed place, we found the entrance. And that's when the 'god' showed up." The young man crooked his fingers to indicate quotation marks and rolled his eyes in exasperation.

"I take it you weren't as impressed as your old man," Grant observed snidely.

"Neither one of us was born here," Yusef said, ignoring the hostile glare directed at him by his father. "My mom was Arabian and she had been kidnapped by privateers working for the Imperium Britannia and brought to England when she was just a girl. She taught my dad her language and then me.

"We sailed here from England when I was about ten, to join a trading colony set up by the Imperium in Khartoum. The colony didn't get the support we were promised and most everybody left. But we stayed and were accepted into my mom's bedouin clan. She died seven years ago."

"I became the sheikh, the *hetman,* when the old chief died," Suliedor put in, his tone and expression registering irritation. "Okay, so maybe I'm laying it on a little thick about devils and gods, but some kind of entity appeared, warning us not to defile the holy tabernacle of the Annunaki—"

"Figures," grunted Grant.

"—and that we would reap great rewards if we safeguarded it from infidels and interlopers."

Kane nodded as if he had expected to hear nothing else. "What was the entity's name?"

Yusef shrugged. "He never said."

"You saw him, too?" Brigid inquired.

The young man sighed heavily. "Yeah…or I saw a clever bit of trickery. I think the old term used to be… holograms? Is that the word?"

Brigid, Kane and Grant all exchanged swift glances. "It is," Brigid confirmed. "But a hologram of which overlord, I wonder?"

The transcomm in her pocket suddenly warbled and everyone jumped. She fished out it out, murmuring in embarrassment, "I forgot we'd been called—"

"*You* forgot?" Kane asked with wide-eyed mock incredulity. "I can't wait to put that in my diary."

Ignoring him, Brigid put the palm-sized comm to her ear, flipping open the cover and opening the channel key. "Baptiste here."

For a few seconds she heard only a faint hiss of static and then a discordant squeak, which told her the signal was being relayed from a distant handset to the Comsat in high orbit, then to the tight-beam receivers in the pair of Manta TAVs, hidden beneath camouflage tarps several miles away. She knew there would be a short lag in response time.

"Brigid?" came Reba DeFore's husky, worried voice. "I tried reaching you earlier—"

"We were a little preoccupied," Brigid replied wryly. "What's the situation, Reba?"

A couple of seconds later, DeFore said, "I saw him, just like Princess Pakari said. It's Utu."

Brigid stiffened, feeling a cold finger of dread brush the buttons of her spine. "In the flesh?"

She waited impatiently for the reply. "Not exactly," the medic answered at length. "A hologram projected from one those disk-ships that Enlil used to attack Cerberus. The ship killed two of the Waziri as an example."

"What does he want with the Waziri?"

Static filled Brigid's ear and she almost repeated the question and then DeFore stated, "Something called the Collar of Prester John. Does that mean anything to you?"

Brigid's eyebrows knitted at the bridge of her nose as she hastily flipped through her mental index file. "Only a little," she admitted. "I'll have to get back to you on it."

"Pakari's half brother Laputara has thrown in with Utu, for some reason, too."

"He's not there in the village, is he?" Brigid asked.

"No, but according to Utu he'll be arriving shortly."

Brigid started to reply, but Kane caught her eye and tapped his wrist chron meaningfully.

Nodding to him, Brigid asked, "Are you all right there for the moment, Reba?"

"For the moment," DeFore retorted a bit peevishly. "At least until Utu comes back, which won't be for a few days. I'd very much like *not* to be here when he does."

Smiling, Brigid stated, "Understood. I'll contact you when we're on our way. It'll probably be just a couple of hours. Until then, call Cerberus. Lakesh can probably tell you more about the Collar of Prester John than I can right now. We have our own overlord problem."

Folding the transcomm and returning it to her pocket, Brigid turned toward Grant and Kane. "Reba confirmed Princess Pakari's story," she announced flatly. "It's Utu, or at least his hologram."

Grant scowled. "What the hell does a reborn Sumerian god want with native Africans?"

Brigid gestured to the sky, to the rock formations all around them. "Keep in mind that the Annunaki established their first colony on the African continent nearly half a million years ago. The Supreme Council divided the mines, agricultural outposts, even scientific monitoring stations among the overlords. It stands to reason Utu would have had some of his own holdings here."

"What are you talking about?" Yusef demanded impatiently.

"It's complicated," replied Kane distractedly. "The false god you saw is an enemy…one of nine enemies, actually. We've been fighting them for several years in one form or another."

For the past three-plus years, Kane, Brigid and Grant as part of the Cerberus resistance movement had struggled to dismantle the machine of baronial tyranny in

America. They had devoted themselves to the work of Cerberus, and victory over the barons, if not precisely within their grasp, didn't seem a completely unreachable goal. Then unexpectedly, nearly a year before, the entire dynamic of the struggle against the nine barons changed.

The Cerberus warriors learned that the fragile hybrid barons, despite being close to a century old, were only in a larval or chrysalis stage of their development. Overnight, the barons changed. When that happened, the war against the baronies themselves ended, but a new one, far greater in scope, began.

The baronies had not fallen in the conventional sense through attrition, war or coups d'état. No organized revolts had been raised to usurp the hybrid lords from the seats of power, nor had insurrectionists met in cellars to conspire against them.

The barons had simply walked away from their villes, their territories and their subjects. When they reached the final stage in their development, they saw no need for the trappings of semidivinity, nor were they content to rule such minor kingdoms. When they evolved into their true forms, incarnations of the ancient Annunaki overlords, their avaricious scope expanded to encompass the entire world and every thinking creature on it.

The Cerberus warriors had hoped the overweening ambition and ego of the reborn overlords would spark bloody internecine struggles, but in the months since their advent, no intelligence indicating such actions had reached them.

Of course, the overlords were engaged in reclaiming their ancient ancestral kingdoms in Mesopotamia. They had yet to cast their covetous gaze back to the North American continent, but it was only a matter of time.

Before that occurred, Cerberus was determined to build some sort of unified resistance against them, but the undertaking proved far more difficult and frustrating than even the cynical Kane or the impatient Grant had imagined. Even long months after the disappearance of the barons, the villes were still in states of anarchy, of utter chaos with various factions warring for control on a day-by-day basis.

Speculatively, Grant eyed the black craggy tower of Djebel Kif. "Can you show us the way up there?"

"It is death," Suliedor said gravely. "You are brave people, but that courage might be an affront to Allah."

Kane regarded him with a mocking smile. "I thought you were more worried about offending this false god of yours."

Suliedor glowered at him. "I was only trying to warn you. Yes, there are secret ways into the mountain."

"I'll go with you," Yusef volunteered. "I'll show you the way, if for nothing else but to prove there are no such things as jinns and devils."

Kane nodded. "Thanks."

Despite Suliedor's earlier treachery, he found himself liking the English rogue and his straight-talking son. "We're ready to go now, if you are."

"Djebel Kif is my responsibility!" Suliedor protested.

"Then come with us, Dad," Yusef said in irritation.

"It is the home of Shaitan."

"Dad," Yusef said in exasperation, "the only devils up there have feathers and wings and live in a nest."

Suliedor Entwhistle nibbled at his lower lip contemplatively, then shook his head in resignation. "I can't let you go alone, Yusef. You might need me to bail you out of the vulture's nest."

Chapter 5

Less than hour later, as the five people walked around the boulder-littered base of Djebel Kif, the Moon burned in the sky with such a silver brilliance they didn't need to use the Nighthawk microlights they'd taken from their war bags.

No animals or insects stirred among the rocks. The only sound was the crunching of their feet as they moved over a thick layer of shale. Kane felt small and insignificant in the wasteland, made even more oppressive by the suspicion that madness and egomania waited for them on the summit, far more evil than any creatures spawned from Islamic myth.

Nor did he care to trail after Yusef and Suliedor—walking point was a habit he had acquired during his years as a Magistrate because of his uncanny ability to sniff out danger in the offing. He called it a sixth sense, but his pointman's sense was really a combined manifestation of the five he had trained to the epitome of keenness. When he walked point, Kane felt electrically alive, sharply tuned to every nuance of his surroundings and what he was doing.

The sloping sides of Djebel Kif weren't as steep as they appeared from a distance. Narrow paths, little more than goat runs curved up between out-croppings of stone and beneath overhangs. Yusef and Suliedor led the three outlanders toward the nearest trail.

Before they fell into step behind the bedouin, Grant and Kane made sure their Sin Eaters were secure in the rather bulky holsters strapped to their forearms beneath the right sleeves of their field jackets. The Sin Eater, the official side arm of the Magistrate Divisions, was an automatic handblaster, less than fourteen inches in length, with an extended magazine carrying twenty 9 mm rounds. When not in use, the butt folded over the top of the blaster, lying perpendicular to the frame, reducing holstered length to ten inches.

When the weapon was needed, a flexing of wrist tendons activated sensitive actuator cables within the holster and snapped the pistol smoothly into the waiting hand, the butt unfolding in the same motion. Since the Sin Eater had no trigger guard or safety, the autopistol fired immediately upon touching a crooked index finger.

Clipped to the outlanders' combat harnesses were abbreviated Copperhead subguns. Less than two feet long, with a 700-round-per-minute rate of fire, the extended magazines held thirty-five 4.85 steel-jacketed rounds. The grip and trigger units were placed in front of the breech in the bullpup design, allowing one-handed use.

Optical image intensifier scopes and laser auto-targeters were mounted on the top of the frames. Low recoil allowed the Copperheads to be fired in long, devastating full-auto bursts.

Brigid Baptiste carried a Copperhead, as well as her TP-9, snugged in a slide-draw holster at her hip. The war bags each one of them had slung over their shoulders contained Nighthawk microlights, night-vision glasses, extra magazines, as well as a variety of grenades, and as added insurance, a single block of C-4 explosive.

Brigid brushed back her fall of hair and touched the Commtact attached to the mastoid bone behind her right ear, making sure it was adjusted to identical units worn by Grant and Kane. Steel pintels embedded in the bones connected to tiny input ports on the small curves of metal. The Commtacts had been found in Redoubt Yankee and were state-of-the-art multiple-channel communication devices.

Their sensor circuitry incorporated an analog-to-digital voice encoder. The transmissions were picked up by the auditory canals, and the dermal sensors transmitted the electronic signals directly through the cranial casing. Even if someone went deaf, as long as they wore a Commtact, they would still have a form of hearing.

In conjunction with a sophisticated translation program within the PDAs all of them carried, the Commtacts analyzed the pattern of a language and then provided a real-time translation. Some foreign phrases and words wouldn't be exact translations, but the program recognized enough words to supply an English equivalent. Conversely, the program would supply them with the appropriate responses in the language it heard.

As the three Cerberus warriors struggled up the steep

path, Kane felt as if eyes watched them. Despite the little bristling sensation at the nape of his neck, he continued to climb up the slanting parapet.

The pools of shadow lengthened and darkened as they climbed farther. The path became more rugged with sharp, zigzagging upward turns. They squeezed between and clambered around a litter of huge boulders that had broken off from the megalith's upper rim.

Yusef, Suliedor, Brigid, Grant and Kane crept along a sharp-edged causeway butting up against a rock wall on their right and a sheer drop on their left. A rock turned under Kane's foot and he staggered, arms waving as he tried to regain his balance. A miniature avalanche started under his boots, pebbles and gravel cascading down the path and over the edge. Grant snatched out for him, but his groping hand missed his partner's arm. Whirling around, Brigid latched on to his wrist with a surprising strength and anchored him in place.

When he was steadied, he husked out, "Thanks, Baptiste."

"My pleasure," she responded, releasing him.

Rubbing his wrist where she had secured a grip, Kane commented, "You've been working out."

"Quiet back there," Yusef called in an annoyed tone. "Save the muscle admiration for when we're safe."

Kane and Brigid raised ironic eyebrows at one another but said nothing. They started climbing again. Kane couldn't help but reflect that Brigid Baptiste was quite possibly the toughest woman—and one of the toughest people, for that matter—he had ever met.

For a woman who had been trained as an archivist—an academic—and had never strayed more than ten miles from the sheltering walls of Cobaltville, her resiliency and resourcefulness never failed to impress him. Over the past few years, she had left her tracks in the most distant and alien of climes and waded through very deep, very dangerous waters.

She, Grant and Kane had come a very long way in distances that could not be measured in mere miles from the day they had escaped from Cobaltville. As veterans of the Magistrate Division, both Kane and Grant were accustomed to danger and hardship, but nothing like what they and Brigid had been exposed to since their exile.

Kane occasionally wondered how his and Grant's regimented, ville-bred minds had managed to adapt to all the new situations they had found themselves in over the past three years. But somehow he and his friends had not only adapted but also learned an entirely new set of superior skills.

Superior skills were certainly needed after the nuke-caust of 2001. The world lay wasted, nature violated and outraged, transformed overnight into a contaminated shockscape littered with the shattered aspirations of human civilization.

Much of the United States became a hell on Earth where vast tracts of deserts replaced green fields, lakes either boiled away or became toxic inland seas and great cities were reduced to towering, vine-hung ruins. The passage of time had not cleansed the first-strike targets of hideous, invisible poisons. The African subcontinent had been spared much of the scorching radioactive hellfire.

The five people climbed farther until they reached a rampart of heaped-up boulders. Panting from exertion, the muscles of their legs aching, Kane, Brigid and Grant stared at the semicircular doorway cut in solid rock. It was about eight feet high and twice that wide.

Suliedor Entwhistle glanced over his shoulder and said softly, "This is where the god appeared to me."

He stepped through the cleft and the darkness beyond shimmered with a lurid glow. With a multicolored rainbow effect the three Cerberus warriors might have appreciated under other circumstances, a human-shaped but not exactly human figure took form. Little pools of molten light that might have been eyes gazed at them. A ghostly voice, speaking in Arabic intoned, "Do not intrude on the crucible of creation if you value your immortal soul."

CLAD IN THE ELABORATE armor fashioned after the ancient warrior kings of Sumeria, the figure gazed down at them with an austere yet blood-chilling calm. Its skin, showing a delicate pattern of scales, seemed to shimmer. Brigid noted the red spines curving back on the hairless head and murmured, "Utu."

In a soft voice, like the liquid sibilance of a serpent's hiss muffled by velvet, Utu said, "This is the holy tabernacle of the old gods who ruled this land long before the birth of Mohammed. This is the sacred ground of the Annunaki, Those-Who-from-Heaven-to-Earth-Came. If you transgress, you will die in shrieking agony, your soul shredded and divided up among the jinn and the afreet."

"Oh, *please*," Kane sidemouthed to Grant in exasperation. "Why do they have to talk that way?"

Suliedor fell to his knees, clutching at Yusef's hand, trying to pull him down beside him. The young man's expression registered fear, but he steadfastly refused to kneel before the shimmering image of Utu.

"However," Utu continued, "if you safeguard this most holy of tabernacles from foreign infidels, then I will reward you and ensure your spirit's place in Paradise."

"Oh, mighty one," Suliedor moaned, covering his face with shaking hands, "please spare my son. He has his doubts as to your divinity."

"Your mighty one's name is Utu," Brigid declared contemptuously, stepping forward. "And he's not really here. He's an artificial vision, an illusion, nothing but a projection. Watch."

Bending down, Brigid grabbed a fistful of dust from the ground and threw it before her into the cleft. The dirt particles swirled through the air then lit up with thready light beams crisscrossing from various hidden apertures on the rock walls. Peeking through his fingers, Suliedor uttered a wordless cry of surprise.

"We call it a hologram," she said matter-of-factly. "This one is a pretty good example as far as those things go, but it's still just a trick."

"If you wish to earn the rewards," Utu continued sententiously, "then I bid you watch for three outlanders in particular. A pale-eyed killer, a dark-skinned giant and an arrogant woman with hair like the sunset."

"That sounds like us, all right," Grant grunted.

Brigid eyed him resentfully. "You're about half right."

"Kill them," Utu stated, "and all who accompany them. But be careful. They are dangerous, they are deceitful, they are liars. If you heed their words, you will put your immortal souls in jeopardy."

Suliedor cast a surreptitious, suspicious glance toward Brigid. Sensing that the sheikh was reconsidering the hologram's reality, Kane took a long deliberate step forward, and strode right through Utu. The image rippled as he passed through it, like the surface of a pond disturbed by a stone.

"He's not really here, see?" Kane waved his arms through the figure, extending two fingers of his left hand and poking them through the image's eyes. "The scaly son of a bitch recorded this hologram and then programmed it to play when a motion detector was triggered."

"Obey my edicts," Utu droned on. "And you will enjoy peace, prosperity—"

"Oh, shut the fuck up," Grant growled, stiffening his wrist tendons. The Sin Eater sprang from the holster, slapping solidly into his palm, his index finger depressing the trigger stud.

The report of the pistol was like a thunderclap within the cleft. Sparks spurted from a lens inset into the ceiling. The image of Utu wavered and disappeared with the suddenness of a candle being extinguished.

A stretch of silence followed the gunshot, broken by Grant saying in rough whisper, "Not much of a god if one bullet can blow him out."

Yusef threw Grant a fleeting, appreciative smile. He tugged on Suliedor's arm. "You can get up now, Dad."

Suliedor allowed himself to be pulled to his feet, his lips shaping whispered words of astonishment. Turning toward Brigid, he asked, "But what about the jinn?"

She smiled at the way the man now sought out her counsel. "I imagine they are as fraudulent as Utu. Shall we move on?"

The five people walked through the cleft and entered a plaza surrounded by crumbling ruins. Kane commented wryly, "Interesting how Utu expected that we three might show up. I guess the overlords don't underestimate us the same way they did when they were barons."

"I wouldn't be too proud of that if I were you," Brigid admonished. "When they were barons, we were able to get over on them because of the element of surprise. Their arrogance blinded them to what we could accomplish. They never expected inferior humans, us apelings, to be so daring. As overlords, they appear to have learned their lessons."

The Byzantine arches of an ancient cloister reared black against the mercury brightness of the Moon. Part of one tower still stood intact, forming a gateway at the head of the treacherous path they had followed. The archway gaped open like a black maw.

As they came closer to the opening, the feeling of being watched doubled in Kane. His Sin Eater slid out of its power holster into his hand. They halted at the arched entrance, gazing into a blackness—darker than any night—that waited to swallow them.

Grant swept the narrow amber beam of the small Nighthawk microlight into the deep pool of shadow. Brigid, Kane, Suliedor and Yusef followed the beam of the flashlight, their eyes narrowing as they tried to penetrate the indigo pit. A shape shifted within it and a pair of red, slit-pupiled eyes glared out of the murk, hellish orbs staring into their own.

Brigid turned on her own flashlight. A clicking, as of claws clattering against wood and a rustle like leather reached their ears. They caught only a fragmented glimpse of a small figure skittering across the ground, half running and half hopping with a blurring speed. A pair of thick hind legs propelled it in quick, rapid motions as the creature scuttled out of the light. For an instant, the flashlight haloed an oval head that seemed to be all eyes, brow ridges and a wetly hissing open mouth.

The beam gleamed briefly on needle-pointed teeth. Two disproportionately small arms ended in three-fingered hands tipped with curving talons. Leathery membranes stretched out beneath the creature's arms, as if it were a nightmarishly distorted flying squirrel.

Then, as suddenly as it appeared, the creature was gone, as though the gloom reached out and swallowed it. Somewhere in the murk, they heard the bang of a door slamming shut.

Limbs shaking, voice hitting a shrill note of panic, Suliedor demanded, "What was that? What in the name of Allah *was* it? If it was not a jinn, then what the bloody blue hell could it have been?"

Neither Brigid, Kane nor Grant had moved. "Whatever it was," Kane said, "it didn't look very fraudulent to me, Baptiste."

Calmly, Brigid intoned, "I stand corrected."

"Do you know what it is?" Grant demanded.

She nodded. "I've seen pictures. I suppose you could call it a jinn. Two hundred years ago, in another place, it was best known as El Chupacabra."

Chapter 6

"El Chupacabra!" Kane echoed in disbelief. "The goatsucker?"

."So you do remember the briefing," Brigid said, forcing a smile. "I'm impressed. It was a couple of years ago, after all."

"I remember it, too," rumbled Grant.

El Chupacabra was a semilegendary creature that terrorized Puerto Rico a few years before the nuke-caust. First found draining the blood from a goat, the entity was dubbed the goatsucker.

Brigid Baptiste's research in the Cerberus database provided sufficient evidence that the monsters were genetically engineered, failed experiments of a subdivision of Overproject Excalibur, brought into the postnuke world through tampering with Operation Chronos technology.

"Goatsucker?" Yusef demanded incredulously.

Brigid nodded distractedly, eyeing the blackness on the other side of the archway. "The name is a misnomer. They sucked just about anything they could get their tongues into—dogs, cats, cows, even people. Apparently, some experiments with the creatures were performed here…sightings of them among superstitious bedouin were attributed to the jinn."

Yusef and Suliedor stared in astounded disbelief at Brigid. Kane didn't blame them. Clearing his throat, Yusef asked, "You're joking, having fun with us, right? That was a monkey or something, no?"

"No," Brigid answered flatly.

"So it really was a jinn?" Suliedor's voice quavered.

"What you call the jinn are genetically engineered creatures," answered Brigid, "using chimeric gene combinations."

"What?" Yusef asked raggedly.

"DNA taken from one organism and transplanted into another. Shake well, let ferment and see what surprise monster you've made."

"What?" Yusef demanded again. He turned to Grant, a beseeching expression on his face.

"There's a little more to it than that," Grant told him wryly.

Brigid, Kane and Grant put on dark-lensed glasses. The electrochemical polymer of the lenses gathered all available light and made the most of it to give them a limited form of night vision.

A flagstone path on the other side of the crumbling arch led them within the walls of the monastery. Kane took the point and his companions followed him past an old well and a high heap of rubble bordered by squat, bulbous columns. They strode past vaulted, dust-filled chambers that Brigid guessed had once been the cells of the Byzantine monks.

The five people walked along a narrow gallery that dead-ended before a heavy door, at first glance made of bound-together timbers. A tentative tap of knuckles produced a faint metallic clank. Carefully, Kane pushed the door open with the toe of a boot. It swung open almost silently on oiled hinges, revealing an empty cell. The shafts of moonlight slanting in through the broken roof cast a checkerboard pattern on the debris-littered floor.

"There's nothing there," Suliedor husked.

Kane didn't answer, stepping slowly and cautiously into the bare room. The narrow floorboards bent slightly, creaking, beneath his weight. He detected a faint difference of sound when he moved farther into the corner. Bending low, he lightly stamped on the smoothly sawned planks with the sole of a boot.

"What are you doing?" Suliedor asked anxiously.

Kane didn't reply. He cleared shards of pottery away from the corner. He saw only bare floorboards at first, then the beam of the microlight revealed a thread-thin outline of the trapdoor.

Running his fingers along the edges and tugging, he said, "The jinn or goatsucker or whatever you want to call it went through here and locked the door behind it."

"Is it smart enough to do that?" Yusef inquired haltingly.

"Apparently," Brigid answered in a monotone.

Drawing his combat knife, Kane jammed the long tungsten steel blade into the tiny crack between the edge of the trapdoor and the floorboards. He tried prying it open, but it refused to budge, held fast by a catch on the underside.

He put his back against the wall and launched a straight-leg kick at the knife's handle. Metal snapped sharply as the catch broke, and a three-by-three square of flooring popped up. A faint, foul odor rose from the opening, carrying with it a charnel-house reek.

Yusef and Suliedor murmured something and covered their noses and mouths with one hand. Brigid moved closer, face registering worry. Kane put a finger to his lips and gestured for her and Grant to stay put. He returned the knife to its belt sheath and carefully shone the light down into a dark shaft. The metal rungs of a ladder ran down one side of the shaft into the dimness. The walls were made of heavy, mortared concrete blocks. The shaft was a perfect square, six feet wide and fifteen feet deep.

Kane signaled for Grant and Brigid to follow him, eased over the edge and began to climb down. Brigid waited until Grant had descended halfway before swinging her legs over and out. She motioned for Yusef and Suliedor to follow her.

At the bottom of the shaft, on the facing wall, was a slab of steel set tightly in the concrete blocks, a wheel lock jutting from the rivet-studded, cross-beamed mass. When Brigid dropped from the ladder, Grant went to the door. He put his hands on the wheel lock, giving it a counterclockwise twist. It didn't budge. Taking and holding a deep breath, he threw all of his considerable weight and upper-body strength against the lock.

With a tortured screech of solenoids, the wheel turned. Slowly and resistantly at first, then Grant was able to get a hand-over-hand spin going.

Kane pushed his shoulder against the steel door and there was the sticky, sucking sound of old rubber seals separating. The door opened inward. The charnel-house odor crowded into the shaft like a tidal wave of stink. Grant uttered a gagging noise, Brigid covered her mouth and Kane fought down a rise of bile, forcing himself to breathe through his mouth.

When Yusef reached the bottom of the ladder he made a sound as if he was going to dry-heave, but he got his nausea under control. Suliedor used his burnoose as an odor filter, holding the fabric against his nose. Kane stepped forward, leading with his Sin Eater. Brigid and Grant followed him, alert and watchful. The three people stopped and stared. A neon light tube flickered overhead with a dim yellow illumination.

"What is it?" Yusef demanded in a strident whisper from behind them. "What's in there?"

Grant threw him an over-the-shoulder scowl, making a sharp gesture across his throat with a forefinger. Then he waved him forward. Stepping with almost exaggerated caution, Yusef and Suliedor crossed the threshold.

They stood in a large, low-ceilinged room with a dozen desks, most of them covered with computer terminals and keyboards. A control console ran the length of the right-hand wall, consisting primarily of plastic-encased readouts and gauges. The left wall was composed of panes of glass, beaded with condensation. Their eyes took in at a glance the heavy tables loaded down with a complicated network of glass tubes, beakers and retorts.

"What is this place?" Suliedor asked, eyes wide with wonder and fear.

"It's the place we were looking for," Brigid told him quietly.

She didn't add that Djebel Kif was probably honey-combed with tunnels and passages under the monastery ruins. The lights and the air-conditioning indicated a power source, probably provided by one of the mini-nuclear reactors that kept most of the systems running in the Totality Concept–related redoubts.

A large color-coded map bolted to the wall showed three passages forking off in different directions. One of them, marked with a downward-pointing arrow, was labeled "Environmental" and bore the traditional yellow-and-black radiation warning symbol.

Kane pointed toward an open door on the far side of the big room and stepped toward it. His companions followed him. A corridor stretched into darkness. All the neon lights were broken, and the glass fragments carpeted the floor like a patina of frost. Shining his flashlight ahead of him, Kane took the point again, walking silently heel to toe.

All the doors on either side of the passageway were open and Kane peered into each one. Nothing moved among the shapes of tables and medical equipment. One room held only Plexiglas confinement cages, big transparent squares perforated with holes for ventilation. All of them appeared to be empty, and several showed deep gouges in the plastic. Water bottles were clamped to the inner walls.

One room was divided by a thick partition of glass. Brigid, Kane and Grant stepped to it, peering through into a darkened niche. Beyond the glass was a transparent vat filled with a semiliquid amber gel. A very small figure, curled in a fetal position, floated within its gelid contents. The misshapen, inhumanly large cranium was a pinkish gray in color, spotted here and there with wispy strands of hair. The huge eyes were dull and fathomless. The hind limbs were disproportionate, far too long for the torso. The claw-tipped hands were pressed to its chest, almost in an attitude of praying.

Suliedor moved to Grant's side, stared and whirled away, covering his eyes with one hand as he gasped out "Jinn-spawn!"

Kane knew they looked at a corpse, but the sight still made him feel physically ill, his belly turning cold flip-flops, mouth filling with sour saliva. He forced himself to keep staring at the monstrosity.

"What kind of place is this?" Yusef stammered. His voice was pitched low to disguise the terror-stricken quaver in it.

"A genetics lab," Brigid intoned. "Biological experiments—the principal objective of which is the creation of a hybrid species."

"Hybrid species?" Yusef repeated faintly. "Hybrid of what?"

"That," said Brigid, a steel edge entering her voice, "remains to be seen."

They walked out of the room and back into the corridor. The next door was closed and Kane carefully turned the knob. It turned without resistance and he pushed it open, shining his light ahead of him. It took his brain a shocked moment to identify what his eyes were seeing. When it did, he instinctively recoiled, his finger nearly depressing the trigger stud of his Sin Eater. The five people stared blankly into a large room on the other side of the door.

Judging by the long tables, chairs, two upright refrigerators, coffeemakers and a large microwave oven, the room was a dining hall. Whatever had dined there last hadn't bothered to clean up after themselves.

Bodies lay everywhere, strewed over the floor and draped over the tables in a bizarrely ordered formation. Men and women, over a dozen of them, lay on their backs. Except for scraps of tattered clothing they were naked. They had been eviscerated and the uniform blue-tinted pallor of their flesh showed they were drained of all blood. Thoraxes were peeled open, the skin covering the chest and abdominal cavities slit and double-flapped aside.

The people had been dead for at least a week. Their flesh was covered by damp blotches edged with scarlet. The stench of decomposing flesh was horrendous, like an intangible hook reaching down the throat to yank up the contents of their stomachs. Yusef's shoulders shook in racking shudders and he hugged himself, muttering a fervent prayer in Arabic.

In a surprisingly steady voice, Brigid declared, "I imagine if we could check a personnel record for this place, we'd find that most, if not all of these people were recruited from Snakefish, from the various divisions."

"Why Snakefish?" Grant inquired.

"Utu is—was—Baron Snakefish, remember?"

Kane said nothing, but nausea leaped and rolled in

his belly and bile slid up his throat in an acidy column. He tried not to breathe through his nose. He swung away, pulling the door shut. He met Grant's grim gaze and nodded. Only one room remained in the corridor and Kane went to the door. It was partially ajar, but blocked by the body of a man.

"Here we go," he stated flatly.

Peering around Kane, Brigid said, "That's one of the Nephilim."

The man's nose was short, his lips a thin slash above a blunt chin. High cheekbones and craggy brow ridges framed his most disturbing feature, his eyes. They were deep set, the irises as white as pearls. They stared upward, unseeing. He was hairless and his dark skin bore a pebbled pattern of scales.

As the barons had reached their final stage of evolution as the overlords, so too had the rank-and-file servant class of hybrids been transformed. According to ancient legend, the hybrid offspring of the cursed fornications between fallen angels and human women were called the Nephilim. They were believed to be soldiers in the armies of darkness.

Like a soldier, the Nephilim wore form-fitting body armor of a magenta tint. From inch-thick reinforcing epaulets on his shoulders extended flexible conduits that stretched down over his arms to sheathe his forearms and hands in gauntlets.

From raised humps on both wrists rose three small flanges shaped like the letter S cut in half. The metal curves were tipped by the stylized heads of adders in postures of rearing back for a strike. They were ASP emitters, accelerated streams of protons, but Kane received the distinct impression they were inactive. The Nephilim's armor itself, like that worn by all the overlords, was composed of a smart metal, a liquid alloy that responded to a sequence of commands programmed into an extruder. A miniature cohesive binding field metallicized it from liquid to solid.

Brigid knelt, swiftly examining the man's body. His face was covered in dark purple patches that shone with little poisonous beads of moisture. She found three puncture wounds on the right side of the corpse's neck right at the carotid artery. They were tiny, pinhole perfect, the flesh around them febrile and scabrous. She saw no evidence of tearing in the flesh.

Kane could smell the odor of putrefaction. To Grant and Brigid he said, "Pretty obvious what happened here. After the fall of the baronies, the people who worked in the ville divisions were desperate for some kind of purpose, some sort of leader. Utu played on that and brought them here to nursemaid these biological nightmares, with one of his personal Nephilim acting as straw boss. But the nightmares escaped and turned on their keepers. It's possible the jinn were supposed to be disposed of."

Grant grunted. "At least we got here while there were some pieces to pick up. Won't last long, though."

Yusef dry-washed his face with his hands. "None of this makes sense!"

As Brigid stood up from the corpse, she replied, "It makes perfect sense, according to the paradigm we're forced to live by."

Shining his Nighthawk all around the room, Grant muttered, "Did he die without a fight? We know those ASP emitters are bad-ass weapons."

Tilting his head back, Kane examined the upper walls and ceiling. With the beam of his Nighthawk, he pointed to several black scorch marks in the tiles and the scars of superheated energy on the metal cross braces.

"The Nephilim must have drained his ASPs before he was drained himself," he commented dryly.

"Why was he shooting at the ceiling?" Suliedor demanded.

Grant shushed him into silence. A faint scuttle came from above. The five people froze, not moving or even breathing hard. A ceiling panel shifted and a little shower of dust sifted down. None of the people moved. Then, with a mushy crack, the panel split in half. A pale shape plummeted down, falling directly onto Suliedor's shoulders.

Screaming, whirling around like a dog trying to catch its tail, the man performed a dervish dance of pure panic. Grant lunged forward, closing his hands around the creature on the sheikh's back. He caught a blurred glimpse of a slime-coated tongue whipping out and retracting in the space of half a heartbeat.

Grant snarled in pain as spinelike quills lacerated the palms of his hands. It required all of his upper-body strength to wrench the creature away. When it came loose, scraps of Suliedor's burnoose and bits of flesh were hooked in its claws.

Grant hurled it down the corridor. The creature

landed on his hind legs with a scrabbling of talons. Crouching, it uttered a prolonged hiss, like steam escaping from a faulty valve. Although the jinn was no more than three feet tall, ropy muscles slid beneath the waxy, pallid flesh of its arms and legs. The head resembled an inverted teardrop in shape, terminating in a long, pointed chin. Huge, back-slanting eyes as big in proportion to its face as those of a cat's, gleamed with the color of fresh-spilled blood.

The nose consisted of a pair of slitted nares. The mouth gaped open, and behind double rows of pointed teeth stirred a long black tongue. It uncoiled like a striking serpent, extending at least eighteen inches toward Grant's face. He recoiled. Sprouting from the damp tip were three small curved spurs, either of bone or gristle. As the creature shuffle-footed forward, a series of sharp quills, like those of a porcupine, unfolded vertically along the center of its spine.

The pistols of Brigid, Kane and Grant roared simultaneously, the bores spitting flame and thunder. Steel-jacketed rounds drove into the jinn's head, and punched through its torso, pile-driving it backward in a flail of limbs, a flap of leathery membranes and a misting of blood.

Eyes wide and wild, Yusef exclaimed panted, "The damn thing ran from us before."

"I don't think it was the same one," Brigid bit out, double-fisting her TP-9. "We can't assume the others are as shy."

She sidled toward the creature's corpse, pistol trained on it, shifting her feet to avoid treading in the blood spreading out around its body. Kneeling down beside it, she cast the beam of her Nighthawk on its head.

"What the hell are you doing?" Kane demanded.

Brigid didn't answer for a long moment, her emerald gaze intense and penetrating. "Come over here and take a look at this."

Grant and Kane did as she said, approaching cautiously. They played their Nighthawks over the creature's skull, punched out of shape by multiple bullet wounds. Metallic, shiny objects glinted just beneath the flesh.

"Implants?" Kane inquired. "These things are remote controlled?"

Brigid shook her head. "Not exactly. The jinn are synthetic entities, made out of a mixture of inorganic and organic materials. They're probably cybernetic from birth. Look."

As she pushed the jinn's head to one side, her microlight cast an amber halo on a large exit wound at the rear of its skull. A mélange of brain matter and bone chips oozed out. A delicate webwork of circuitry glittered in the slurry of viscera.

Wryly, Brigid said, "Our old friend, the SQUID network."

A brilliant predark cyberneticist named Erica van Sloan had developed and perfected the SQUID implants, the superconducting quantum interface devices. Although she had not actually invented the SQUIDs, she refined them to a new level of sophistication and used them as the foundation of the first fully functioning, large-scale mind-machine interface.

"Do you think Erica has something to do with this?" Grant asked, his voice harsh.

"I couldn't say," Brigid replied as she stood up. "She didn't seem to want to have much to do with the overlords, judging by her attitude the last time we saw her."

"Yeah," Kane drawled sarcastically. "All of us know what a paragon of moral virtue she is."

Standing up, Brigid declared confidently, "This place is less an Overproject Excalibur genetic-engineering facility than a mechanic's workshop. Utu tried to jump-start the program to grow cyborgs without messy implant surgery."

Hand cupping the left side of his neck, blood streaming from claw-inflicted furrows on his cheeks, Suliedor asked fearfully, "How many do you think there are of these things?"

The door behind which the Nephilim lay suddenly swung inward. In the shadows beyond, they glimpsed a hint of stealthy movement. Pinpoints of red fire glowed, moving points of flame that seemed to dance and shift in weird rhythm. Faintly, they heard the soft pattering rustle of many feet and the castanet clicking of claws.

"If we decide to hang around," said Kane grimly, finger hovering over the trigger-stud of the Sin Eater, "I guess you can do a head count."

Chapter 7

Brigid's TP-9 made a door-slamming bang and a round caught one of the jinn directly in its bulbous head. The impact flung it back against its brethren, the back of its skull vanishing in a haze of red. Brain tissue, bone and blood flew from the wound, draping the wall with red liquid ribbons. Several of the little monstrosities turned on the dead creature, long tongues flicking out, barbed tips plunging into the entrance and exit wounds.

"Now we know why we didn't find any jinn bodies," Grant commented. "They eat their dead."

"Tidy," Brigid said, eyes darting back and forth from shadow to shadow.

Half the creatures continued to advance on them through the gloom, their eerie eyes glowing like distant candle flames. A sudden thought occurred to Kane. The things were being a little too obvious about coming out and holding their attention.

"I think we'd better move before they get the idea of surrounding us," Kane grated. "They may be vicious, but they're not stupid. Particularly if they're remote controlled."

"I don't think they are," declared Brigid. "They're running wild."

"Once we turn our backs on them," Suliedor said, hand still cupped over the side of his throat, "they'll be on us like jackals."

His words sounded slurred and his eyes had acquired a glassy sheen, but no one had the time to examine him.

Grant lifted his Sin Eater as if he were going to fire again and the jinn advance wavered, then halted. As one, the five people turned and ran. They raced down the corridor with all the speed of which they were capable. The jinn loped after them, lithe and surprisingly swift, like white leopards. They made wet, hissing noises as they ran.

They entered the big room filled with the confinement cubes. A jinn came squalling from a dark corner, tongue lashing out at Brigid. She dodged the barbed tip and Grant fired a triburst from his Sin Eater. The 9 mm rounds hit the creature in the chest and neck, the multiple impacts smashing it off its feet despite its overdeveloped hindquarters. It flailed backward, kicking over one of the transparent cages.

"I think we were herded back in here deliberately," Kane murmured. "It's dark and big with plenty of cover."

"If we could find the reactor," Grant rumbled, "we might be able to blow this place up. Or down."

Yusef suddenly drew in a sharp, raw breath. Kane turned to see him examining his father. Casting the beam of the Nighthawk on Suliedor's throat, he saw where the jinn's tongue barbs had pierced the flesh. The flesh surrounding three tiny punctures was beginning to mottle and turn dark.

"The kiss of the jinn is poison," Suliedor half gasped, seizing Yusef's shoulder. "Help me, lad—"

Suliedor Entwhistle's legs folded beneath him and he went down, hitting his head hard on the floor before anyone could catch him. Yusef bent down, cradling the man's head in his arms. Even by the poor light provided by the Nighthawks they could see how swollen the man's face had become. A purple pattern of discoloration crept up from his neck.

"Can't move," he rasped. "Feels like acid in my blood, eating away at my muscles."

Kneeling down beside him, Brigid laid a hand against his forehead. "You're burning up. The poison must be some sort of neurotoxin that breaks down internal organs to make them easier for the jinn to ingest."

Suliedor managed to force a feeble grin. "Is that supposed to make me feel better, woman?"

Brigid shook her head sadly. "I wish there was something we could do for you."

"I realize that. I hope you will accept an apology for treating you so disrespectfully—"

"Heads up," Grant interrupted, stiffening.

Yusef and Brigid rose to their feet as misshapen bodies suddenly rushed from all sides, toe claws clicking on the floor, leathery membranes rustling. The amber glow of the microlights cast a sickly illumination on the demonic faces of the jinn appearing out of the murk like distortions from a nightmare.

Kane's belly slipped sideways with loathing. Unclipping the Copperhead from his combat harness, he shoved it into Yusef's hands. "Point and shoot," he snapped.

The jinn moved like wraiths, affording the people only glimpses of them. Scarlet threads stretched from the laser autotargeters in the hands of Brigid and Yusef, casting bloodred pinpoints on the oversize skulls of the creatures.

Standing in a tight, back-to-back knot around the fallen Suliedor, Kane, Grant, Brigid and Yusef raised their weapons and opened fire. Flame wreathed the bores, smearing the gloom, casting an unearthly strobing effect on the inhuman faces snarling at them. The room became a Babel of hissing howls and high-pitched shrieks, punctuated by stuttering roars of guns on full auto.

The blistering barrage hammered into the front line of attacking jinn, lifting them from their feet and bowling them backward. Kane and Grant swung the flaming bores of their Sin Eaters in short left-to-right arcs, spent shell casings arcing out and tinkling on the floor. Even over the drumming roars, they heard rising-and-falling wails, like banshees riding the wind.

A barbed tongue lashed out at Kane's face, leaving a wet smear on the right lens of his night-vision glasses, the sharp tips scoring the polymer.

Cursing, Kane kept the trigger stud of his Sin Eater mashed down. He knew that sustained full-auto bursts only wasted ammunition, but his focus was on driving the jinn back, not scoring lethal strikes. Although he cycled through the entire magazine, he achieved his objective.

Hissing and shrieking, the creatures scattered, running with a scrambling, scampering gait into the murk, ducking down behind the cube-shaped cages. They left over a dozen of their brethren dead, leaking viscous fluids onto the floor.

The four people ceased firing, and swiftly Kane ejected his pistol's spent clip and toggled home a fresh one taken from his war bag.

"Anybody hurt?" Grant asked hoarsely.

He received negative replies and a panting Brigid said, "We can't stay here. For all we know there are enough of them to keep coming until we're out of ammunition."

Reloading his own Sin Eater, Grant said curtly, "We're all wide open for suggestions."

Brigid reached into her war bag and brought out two cylindrical concussion grenades of the Alsatex series, flash-bangs developed by the military two centuries ago for crowd control. Hefting them, she said, "Judging by the size of their eyes and the fact the overhead lights were broken out, the jinn have very sensitive optic nerves. Their hearing may be equally acute."

Kane nodded uncertainly. "Those grens might buy us some time, but—"

He felt a tug on his pant leg and glanced down at Suliedor, his stomach slipping sideways. The flesh around the wound on the sheikh's neck was puffed and swollen, streaked with ugly strands of red, parts of it so purple as to be almost black. A yellow pus oozed out of the three punctures.

"Kane, give me a weapon," Suliedor croaked.

Yusef knelt beside him. "Dad, we'll get you out of here." His voice was thick with the effort of controlling his emotions.

"I would only slow you down," Suliedor half gasped, glassy eyes darting from Yusef to Kane. "Give me a weapon and at least let my death serve a purpose."

Blinking back tears, Yusef gazed up beseechingly at Brigid. "Don't you have any medicines that can help him?"

She shook her head sadly. "Without knowing the properties of the toxin, anything I could give him would either have no effect or make matters worse."

Yusef swallowed hard and clutched Suliedor's wrist. "I won't leave you, Dad."

Suliedor lifted a trembling hand toward his son's face. Instead of a caress, the hand impacted sharply against this cheek. "Yes, you will, you lazy git. You have a responsibility to our clan. I'm dead anyway."

Fixing his eyes on Kane's face, he grated, "Cold-cock him if you have to, Kane. You spared his life when you could've taken it, so now he owes you."

Not responding, Kane reached into his own war bag and brought out a TH3 incendiary grenade. He shoved it into Suliedor's right hand, folding his fingers around it and saying tersely, "You hold it tight in one hand and pull the spoon with the other. Squeeze the safety lever to keep the striker in place. When you think the time is right, let go."

"What will happen?" the sheikh asked faintly.

"It has a thermite-and-phosphorus filler," Kane answered dispassionately. "If the explosion doesn't kill you instantly, the incendiary will."

"I'm not interested in what will happen to me," Suliedor snapped impatiently. "What about the jinn?"

"If we're lucky," Kane replied, "you'll take out at least four of the things and maybe blind twice that many. If we're lucky."

Suliedor nodded, glanced from Kane's face to those of Brigid and Grant and said, "I wish we had met at some other time."

Fixing his gaze on Yusef's face, he intoned. "Go, my lad. Lead well. *Allah akabar.*"

Shapes shifted in the murk and a sibilant hissing arose, like a score of teakettles building rapidly to a full boil. Kane tapped Yusef's shoulder. "We've got no more time. I'm sorry."

Slowly, Yusef rose, eyes on his father. He whispered, *"Allah akabar."*

Chapter 8

Brigid tweaked out the pin of the flash-bang. "Everybody look away. Once this thing goes, we need to start running and not stop."

She lobbed the metal-shelled grenade underhanded toward the pallid figures emerging from the gloom. It struck the floor and bounced. The four people turned their faces away just as the Alsatex detonated with an eardrum piercing bang. The eruption of white light turned the shadows into high noon.

Without a word, Kane, Grant, Brigid and Yusef kicked themselves into headlong sprints.

Kane leaped over two whimpering jinn as they writhed on the floor, paws over their eyes. The other creatures blocking the way to the door were stunned and dazzled, stumbling and staggering half-deaf and half-blind.

Voicing a warbling cry, Yusef charged forward, his Copperhead's killdot dancing from oversize head to underdeveloped torso. The subgun beat out a drumroll, the rounds punching dark periods in pale flesh. The jinn lurched away, not knowing what hit them, wild with pain, dazed from the shock of the multiple impacts, tendrils of blood squirting from their bodies.

The sounds uttered by the jinn were a mad babble, mingled cries of outrage and terror. Claw-tipped fingers and skinny arms hauled at them from all sides. Kane applied the frame of his Sin Eater like a bludgeon, trying to fend them off. Grant kicked and stamped and Brigid beat away the clawed hands with the butt of her TP-9.

Just as they reached the door, the entire room shuddered with a brutal thunderclap. A roaring white flash lit their way, casting their elongated shadows on the floor and wall ahead of them. They felt a scorching wave of heat and heard little yipping screams. As they piled through the doorway, a cloud of smoke billowed after them, bringing with it a scent like scorched pork.

"Your father is—was—a brave man," Grant managed to husk out to Yusef as they sprinted through the office suite.

Yusef didn't reply.

As the five people made for the entrance hatch, more of the jinn swarmed out of doorways and wedges of shadow, a milling mass creeping to intercept them. Brigid shouted a warning to her companions and hurled her other flash-bang into the shadows ahead of them.

The grenade detonated with a bone-jarring crack, like the breaking a of giant tree limb. Although they shielded their eyes, amid the blaze of light and the eardrum-slamming concussion, they caught fleeting glimpses of hideously misshapen bodies.

They fired their guns, clearing a path with a scythe of lead. Maimed and blinded creatures staggered into their comrades and jostled them from their feet. The jinn turned on each other, squealing like crazed rats, talons sinking into flesh. The entire horde fell upon one another in a terror-fueled fury.

When they reached the hatchway and the entrance shaft, the four people paused to catch their breath. Yusef demanded hoarsely, "So we have escaped them—now what? Can the ugly little bastards breed and overrun this land?"

Brigid raked her hair away from her face. "I doubt they can procreate, but I wouldn't be surprised if they're practically immortal. Extreme longevity is the usual methodology of Overproject Excalibur experiments."

Glaring into the darkness behind them, Grant gulped air and asked. "If this place is powered by a minifission reactor like we have in Cerberus, there has to be a way to speed up the reaction, right?"

Both Kane and Brigid swiveled their heads toward him, eyes and faces registering alarm. Brigid said, "If the cooling system malfunctions, we can probably initiate an uncontrolled fission reaction."

"What would happen?" asked Yusef dubiously.

"Extreme high temperatures," she answered curtly. "Anything organic in the vicinity would be cooked in their tracks."

Kane shifted position uneasily. "Including us?"

"Maybe," she admitted. "It would depend on the speed of the fission reaction."

"What about an atomic explosion?" Grant inquired, grimacing as he put weight on his wounded leg.

"That's a little less likely," Brigid responded. "But not out of the realm of possibility, depending on the instability of the reactor core. And if an explosion is triggered, it would be relatively small. It might not bring down Djebel Kif but it'll never look the same again."

The Cerberus warriors eyed each other speculatively. After a moment, Kane said, "If we just seal this place up and go, Utu could come back at any time and make the place impregnable. I don't know what he wants with the jinn, except as a renewable source of cannon fodder, but I don't want them left to seed."

"Me, either," Yusef agreed fervently. "Tell me what I can do."

"You're not doing anything but getting out of here and returning to your people," Brigid said severely.

"We'll take care of this," Grant assured him, peering into his war bag. "I've got an ounce of C-4. What about you two?"

Kane and Brigid checked the contents of their own bags and found five incendiary grenades between them.

"This should be enough to knock out the reactor's cooling system and set off an explosive reaction," Brigid stated matter-of-factly.

A wry half smile creased Kane's face. "I can't say I'm wild about this plan, but we don't have many alternatives."

Grant nodded brusquely. "Let's get it the hell done."

Yusef hesitated at the hatch. "I feel like a coward—"

"Don't," Brigid broke in. "Your father, your chief, charged you with a duty and fulfilling it is your first obligation."

"Yeah," Kane said dryly. "And blowing things up is *our* first obligation."

"We don't intend to sacrifice ourselves to destroy

this place," Grant stated. He glanced toward Brigid with narrowed, quizzical eyes. "Right?"

She shrugged. "I wish I could say there's not much risk to us, but I don't want to lie to you."

Kane shook his head in weary exasperation. "Just once I wish you would." He waved Yusef toward the ladder rungs on the inner wall of the entrance shaft. "You should get moving."

Yusef inclined his head in a short, respectful nod, touching his lips and forehead with the fingers of his right hand. "Allah be with you. I hope we will be reunited soon. If not here, then in heaven."

"Let's all try to put that reunion off as long as possible," Grant rumbled.

Yusef stepped into the shaft and pulled the steel door closed behind him. Brigid, Grant and Kane walked stealthily down the corridor until they found a door marked with a sign reading Environmental Control.

The door opened onto a concrete stairwell that pitched downward at a steep angle. They descended the stairs, noting how arrows painted on the walls at each landing pointed downward. Each arrow was accompanied by the circular, black-and-yellow radiation warning symbol. The flight of steps wasn't long, but Kane noted how Grant winced as walked down the risers, favoring his injured leg.

"You'd think there'd be a gateway unit here if it's a Totality Concept–related installation," Grant remarked.

"There probably is," Brigid agreed, "but I don't think the jinn will give us the time to find it."

"Besides," Kane said, "even if there is and we used it to gate out of here, we'd be abandoning the Mantas."

In the decade preceding the nukecaust of 2001, the gateway system had been set up all over the globe. By then, even the Totality Concept itself had begun to schism along factional lines. Certain project personnel decided to hedge their bets, putting gateways in places other groups didn't know about to further their own partisan agendas.

The stairwell led to a narrow corridor that ended a hundred feet away at a vanadium-steel door recessed into the wall. Affixed to the wall beside it was a sec code keypad. Beneath it was a plastic sign bearing red lettering: Radiation Hazard Beyond This Point! Authorized HazMat Personnel Only!

Brigid punched in the entrance code on the keypad. No matter how different the layout of the many redoubts they had visited, the one constant in every Totality Concept installation was the numerical sequence to release a security door's lock—3-5-2.

A combination of gears and pneumatics rumbled and hissed, and the heavy metal panel rolled aside. As it did, a shimmering haze of blue light spilled out into the corridor. Carefully, the three people stepped through the doorway and onto a balcony overlooking a pool of clear water. A wall of light shimmered all around it, turning it into a beautiful shade of cerulean blue.

Heat so intense it was almost suffocating rose from the surface of the pool in waves, but the water wasn't boiling. A pair of half-ovoid, metal-shelled generators rested on an elevated platform above the pool. They filled the chamber with a penetrating subsonic hum of power.

Squinting her eyes against the eerie luminance, Brigid said, "Cerenkov radiation. It appears there's already a cooling-system malfunction. Maybe the Nephilim was responsible, removing the carbon control rods so radiation poisoning would kill the jinn over a period of time."

Kane peered down into the pool at the cube-shaped reactor core. From what he could see, it looked almost identical to the one buried beneath the Cerberus redoubt—a big lead-lined block submerged in about twenty feet of water with three control rods projecting from its flat top, extending up to the underside of the platform supporting the generators.

"So what do we do now?" Grant asked.

Brigid nibbled at her underlip then said in a guilty rush. "I don't know. This is a breeder reactor, which uses neutrons generated by a fission chain reaction to convert uranium-238 into plutonium-239. We could dump all our grens and the C-4 into the cooling pool, but whether we'll get the desired effect or a case of the cure being worse than the disease, I just don't know."

Kane and Grant gazed down at the reactor for a silent few seconds, then Kane withdrew two grenades from his pouch. "I'm setting the timers for forty seconds."

Grant removed the rectangular block of C-4 from his war-bag and handed it to Kane. He attached the grenades to it with a loop of black electrician's tape. As he worked, Brigid said worriedly, "The water might already be so hot it'll set off the grens prematurely."

Grant grunted. "Then that's why we'd better run like hell."

Kane stepped over to the edge of the balcony, flicking tiny timer switches on the grenades. Glancing over his shoulder at Brigid and Grant, he said, "Get to the stairs."

They did as he said, waiting for him at the foot. Balancing himself on the balls of his feet, half-turned toward the stairwell, he opened his hands. The taped together collection of explosives dropped lazily in the blue borealis. By the time they splashed into the pool, he had already whirled away and started running. Grant and Brigid were ahead of him, pounding up the steps, taking the risers two at a time. The three of them surged upward in a wild rush.

"Thirty-eight, thirty-seven—" Kane counted down aloud as he ran, relying on the recitation of decreasing numbers to lend wings to the heels of his friends. The three of them raced upward, clinging and hauling themselves along by the handrail.

They retraced their route but weren't molested by the jinn. By the time they were in sight of the hatchway, hanging open as Yusef had left it, Kane panted, "Three...two...*one!*"

As they stumbled into the bottom of the shaft, Grant snarled angrily, "The goddamn grens didn't go off! Something went wrong—"

Kane chuckled breathlessly. "I set them for sixty seconds. I didn't know how much you'd slow us up with your game leg."

Grant was too out of breath to swear at Kane, but he was the first one to the ladder. The Cerberus warriors swiftly clambered up the rungs, swarming hand over hand. They emerged through the trapdoor into the empty cell and loped across the rock-strewed courtyard of the monastery.

"Thanks for the consideration," Grant half gasped to Kane. "But I don't think it was necessary—"

The rest of his words were lost in the distant thunderclap of an explosion.

The summit of Djebel Kif heaved beneath them, knocking them off their feet, sending them sprawling. Black webwork patterns splintered the flagstones, bursting up through them from beneath. Smoke spurted out of the cracks.

The prolonged grating of stone grinding against stone underscored the muffled, subterranean cannonade. Fragments of the taller structures broke away. More cracks streaked through the basalt underneath them.

Kane, Brigid and Grant staggered to their feet, hanging on to one another, reeling like drunks. Kane glanced up into the sky and glimpsed a silver speck arcing overhead. For a distracted second, he wondered if it were a shooting star. Then the speck resolved itself into a disk. It braked to an abrupt stop directly overhead.

Its configuration and smooth, featureless hull reminded Kane of the throwing discus used by predark athletes—if the disks were twenty feet in diameter and coated with quicksilver. The craft hovered silently, the moonlight gleaming from its surface.

Gesturing to it, Kane snapped, "Looks like the landlord is pulling a surprise property inspection—it'd probably be best if he didn't find us anywhere around."

The three people began running for the mouth of the path as slabs of stone toppled from the monastery walls. Dust clouds rose, whirling, to coat their tongues and sting their eyes.

Lurching against a crumbling wall, Grant spit out grit and said to Brigid, "What was that you said about Djebel Kif not looking the same again?"

Brigid Baptiste didn't waste breath on a response. She felt certain Grant's question was rhetorical, anyway.

Chapter 9

Domi lay on her stomach, her small body tensing like a bowstring. She tried hard to blend into her surroundings. With the charcoal-gray tank top and the high-cut denim shorts she wore, she knew she was only one more pattern of light and dark among many in the tree line. Long shadows lanced from the peak of the mountain towering high behind her.

The blazing glory of fusing sunset colors filled the Montana sky. Sunsets were always spectacular in the Outlands, due to the pollutants and radiation still lingering in the upper atmosphere. The rich palette was a beautiful sight, but the girl didn't notice.

Moving carefully so as not to disturb the brush around her, she undid the catches to the straps of her backpack and shrugged out of it. Removing a compact set of binoculars from their carrying case, she fitted them to her eyes, gazing down the face of the slope. She tried to locate the movement that had caught her attention a moment earlier.

The sun slanting through the leaves of the brush around her cast a dappled pattern of contrasting shadow on her bare arms and legs. The complexion of her limbs was as pale as creamed milk. An albino by birth,

Domi's bone-white hair was cropped short and spiky, the eyes on either side of her thin-bridged nose the ruby color of fresh blood.

Every inch of five feet tall, Domi barely weighed one hundred pounds and at first glance, she gave the impression of being waiflike. But there was little of the waif about her body, lean and lithe, with small, pert breasts rising to sharp points and flaring hips. Born a feral child of the Outlands, there was a primeval vibrancy, an animal-like intensity about her.

She scanned the brush and the tree line below with the patience born of long experience hunting game. A deep, thickly wooded gully yawned below the crest on which she lay. The forest was a rich, verdant green, decorated here and there with the bright blue petals of alpine forget-me-knots. On her left, beyond the treeline, rocky ramparts plunged straight down to a tributary of the Clark Fork River a hundred feet below. The tall trees were fir, pine and aspen. The shadows between them looked dark and coolly inviting.

Breathing slowly and regularly, she inched the lenses of the binoculars across the terrain, beginning to wonder if she had glimpsed a rabbit or some other small animal. Even as the doubt registered, she dismissed the possibility. She was far too canny and experienced to mistake an animal that belonged in the wild for something else, something that had triggered a mental alarm.

Since early that morning, Domi had been fixated on alarms. It was her turn to walk the line, running checks on the security network of motion and thermal sensors planted all around the Cerberus installation. Under other circumstances, she would have enjoyed hiking through the forest, rich with the smell of spring growth. Even though she appreciated the comforts provided by Cerberus—like regular meals and soft beds—she was happy to get away from its cold vanadium-walled confines and crowded corridors.

The fortified redoubt was built deep within a peak of the Bitterroot Mountain Range. Construction had begun in the mid-1990s. By the time of its completion in 1998, no expense had been spared to make the redoubt, the seat of Project Cerberus, a masterpiece of concealment and impenetrability.

The trilevel, thirty-acre facility had housed the Cerberus process, a subdivision of Overproject Whisper, which in turn had been a primary component of the Totality Concept. The researches to which Project Cerberus and its personnel had been devoted were locating and traveling hyperdimensional pathways through the quantum stream.

Once that had been accomplished, the redoubt became, from the end of one millennium to the beginning of another, a manufacturing facility. The quantum interphase mat-trans inducers, known colloquially as "gateways," were built in modular form and shipped to other redoubts.

Most of the related overprojects had their own hidden bases. The official designations of the redoubts had been based on the old phonetic alphabet code used in military radio communications. On the few existing records, the Cerberus installation was listed as Redoubt Bravo, but the handful of people had who made the facility their home for the past few years never referred to it as such.

The huge facility had come through the nukecaust with its operating systems and radiation shielding in good condition. When Mohandas Lakesh Singh had reactivated the installation some thirty years before, the repairs he made had been primarily cosmetic in nature. Over a period of time, he had added an elaborate system of heat-sensing warning devices, night-vision vid cameras and motion-trigger alarms to the surrounding plateau. He had been forced to work in secret and completely alone, so the upgrades had taken several years to complete. However, the location of the redoubt in Montana's isolated Bitterroot Range had kept his work from being discovered by the baronial authorities.

In the generations since the nukecaust, a sinister mythology had been ascribed to the mountains, with their mysteriously shadowed forests and hell-deep, dangerous ravines. The range had become known as the Darks. The wilderness area was virtually unpopulated. The nearest settlement was located in the flatlands, and it consisted of a small band of Indians, Sioux and Cheyenne, led by a shaman named Sky Dog.

Planted within rocky clefts of the mountain peak and disguised by camouflage netting were the uplinks from an orbiting Vela-class reconnaissance satellite, and a Comsat. The road leading down from Cerberus to the foothills was little more than a cracked and twisted asphalt ribbon, skirting yawning chasms and cliffs. Acres of the mountainsides had collapsed during the nuke-triggered earthquakes nearly two centuries ago. It was almost impossible for anyone to reach the plateau by foot or by vehicle, and Lakesh had seen to it that the facility was listed as irretrievably unsalvageable on all ville records.

The line of new alarms had been installed fairly recently, expanding in a six-mile radius from the plateau, following an attack on the redoubt staged by Overlord Enlil.

Although a truce had been struck, a pact of noninterference agreed upon by Cerberus and the nine overlords, no one—least of all Domi—trusted Enlil's word, and so the security network had been upgraded over the past few months.

A fly lit on her leg and she distractedly brushed it away with her right hand. Reaching down, Domi made sure her knife with its nine-inch, wickedly serrated blade was securely sheathed to her right calf. It was her only memento of the six months she'd spent as Guana Teague's sex slave in the Tartarus Pits of Cobaltville.

Years before, Domi had sold herself into slavery in an effort to get a piece of the good life available to ville dwellers, but she had never risen any further than Cobaltville's Tartarus Pits. Since ville society was strictly class- and caste-based, the higher a citizen's standing, the higher he or she might live in one of the residential towers. At the bottom level of the villes was the servant class, who lived in abject squalor in consciously designed ghettos known as the Tartarus Pits, named after the abyss below Hell where Zeus confined the Titans. They swarmed with a heterogeneous population of serfs, cheap labor and slaves like her. She ended her term of slavery by cutting the monstrous Teague's throat with the blade and saved Grant's life in the same impulsive act.

Like so many others, Guana Teague had dismissed her as a semimindless outlander. The average life expectancy of an outlander was around forty, and the few who reached that age possessed both an animal cunning and vitality. Domi was nowhere near that age—in fact she had no true idea of how old she actually was—but she possessed more than her share of both cunning and vitality.

She didn't miss the short and often brutal life in the Outlands. She had quickly adapted to the comforts offered by the Cerberus redoubt—the soft bed, protection from the often toxic elements and food, which was always available without having to scavenge or kill for it.

Domi had enjoyed similar luxuries during her six months as Guana Teague's sex slave. The man-mountain of flab had been the boss of the Cobaltville Pits and he showered her with gifts. He didn't pamper her, though, since she was forced to satisfy his gross lusts. He was obsessed with her, and that had brought about not only his professional downfall, but his bloody death.

Domi rarely dwelled on the past, but she often replayed how she had cut Guana's throat and how the blood had literally rivered from the deep slash in his triple chins. She always smiled in recollection of kicking his monstrous body as it twitched in postmortem spasms, just as she smiled at the memory of Grant comforting her and thanking her for saving his life.

Thinking about Grant caused her lips to twitch unconsciously in a half frown, half smile. Whenever she thought about the big man with his lion's growl of a voice, she felt a mingling of love, anger and disappointment.

She loved the man for his courage and compassion, but she experienced anger and disappointment that he never allowed that compassion to turn into passion—at least not toward her. Domi was too practical, too pragmatic to expend much energy on girlish daydreams that had long ago proved to be lost causes, particularly since she had entered into a relationship with Lakesh and Grant had professed his love for Shizuka, the fierce captain of the Tigers of Heaven.

As angry as she had been when she learned about Shizuka, Domi also knew Grant had not become involved with the Japanese warrior-woman to hurt her. He had many character flaws, but being petty was not one of them.

Grant presented a dour, closed and private persona, rarely showing emotion. He was taciturn and slow to genuine anger, but when he was provoked, his destructive ruthlessness could be frightening. With him, slights were never forgotten and she knew he still stung from the whip of angry words she had lashed at him many months ago. "Big man, big chest, big shoulders, legs like trees. Guess they don't tell the story, huh?"

Domi regretted speaking those words almost as soon as they left her lips, but she had never apologized. When Grant rejected her love again on that day, she swore it was for the last time. Then, a month or so later when she came across Grant and Shizuka locked in a fierce embrace, she also swore she would never forgive him.

Shaking her head, Domi tried to drive the memories of that night from her mind. There were a lot of memories swimming around within the walls of her skull she would as soon have excised, and that brief glimpse of Grant showering the Japanese woman's face with passionate kisses topped the list.

A sudden movement in the undergrowth at the base of the hill commanded Domi's attention, and she swiveled the binoculars toward it, vectoring in on the disturbance at ground level. She watched intently as the high grasses stirred, shifted, then parted. She half expected to see a snake. What she saw caused her lungs to seize and her breath to freeze in her throat. It took her brain few seconds to properly interpret the image fed to it by her eyes.

A small machine moved smoothly up the hill. Its bulbous metal body was no more than two feet in diameter. Mounted atop it was a round turret head connected to a neck made of a flexible metal conduit. Four glassy lenses that looked very much like convex crystals covered all sides of it.

Separate mechanical appendages resembling hook-tipped tentacles extended from beneath the machine's body, aiding in its climb. Eight jointed rods ending in trifurcated steel claws propelled it forward in a swift, scuttling motion that put Domi in mind of a cybernetic spider. The machine didn't produce a clatter of moving parts or even the growl of an engine. All she heard was a faint throb overlaid by a series of metallic clicks.

Holding the binoculars in place with her left hand, she slowly drew the Detonics Combat Master .45 from the holster strapped to her right thigh. Fingers securing a tight hold on the checkered walnut grips, her thumb flicked off the safety. The stainless-steel automatic, which weighed only a pound and a half, was perfectly suited for a girl of her petite build.

She continued to watch the cyberspider's steady progress up the hill. Her skin prickled with a superstitious dread at the sight of the machine. For a moment, her instincts warred with her intellect about the correct course of action to take.

Obviously the cyberspider didn't belong anywhere in Montana and certainly not so close to Cerberus. She was fairly certain the overlords had something to do with its existence, let alone its presence in the Bitterroots. But even by accepting that as a fact, the device exuded a sinister aura of the alien and she felt a surge of irrational xenophobia. She managed to tamp down her first impulse to shoot it. She considered transcomming Cerberus and asking Lakesh for suggestions, but the range was too great for the little radiophone in the backpack.

The cyberspider crawled closer, the multieyed head rotating on its flexible metal neck. The rotation suddenly stopped. The neck extended farther and two of the glass lenses seemed to stare directly at Domi. They glowed red, as if candles burned behind them. She wondered if the machine could sense her by her body heat and transmit the data readings to a distant receiver.

For a moment, she imagined an enormous computer sitting somewhere far away, with Enlil or one of the other overlords scrutinizing and digesting the images the cyberspider sent to it. She shivered at the thought of it, then dropped the binoculars and rose gracefully to her knees. Holding the Combat Master in a double-fisted grip, she swiftly brought the cyberspider into target acquisition, framing the turret head before the pistol's blade sight.

Breathing in, she centered the fore and back sights on her target and exhaled half a breath as Grant had taught her. She squeezed the trigger and the pistol bucked in her hand, the booming report sounding obscenely loud in the wilderness. To her astonishment, the cyberspider sprang straight up and the bullet dug a divot of turf out the ground beneath it.

Instead of dropping back to earth, the machine sailed high into the air, emitting a sharp pop. Twin tongues of flame and smoke spurted from exhaust tubes extending from its underside. As Domi gaped in wide-eyed shock, the cyberspider flew up a score of feet at a thirty-degree angle, rotated, paused and hurtled down, a pair of metal-sheathed tentacles streaking out for her. Tiny but razor-keen hooks glinted at their tips.

Chapter 10

Domi threw herself sideways and back, somersaulting to avoid the striking tentacles. The hooks snicked past her, missing her eyes by inches. They plunged into the ground, anchoring the machine in place. She kept moving, rolling desperately into the underbrush. Thorns scratched her exposed arms and legs, but she bounced to her feet and lunged to the attack.

Her bare left foot struck the cyberspider on its turret head in a fast, vicious kick. Domi almost never wore shoes unless the ground was either icy or exceptionally rocky, since her feet were thickly callused on the soles.

The machine spun wildly around, then righted itself, retracting the tentacles into itself with a clattering rasp. Dropping to the ground, the eight legs spread wide, the cyberspider set itself and sprang directly at her. She ducked, but another tentacle shot out from its underside, the pointed tip grazing her bare right shoulder.

Domi heard a crackle and pain erupted through every nerve ending. Her heart pounded so violently she thought her ribs would break. She hit the ground gracelessly and rolled, her vision blurred by the severity of the electric shock.

She fought and cursed her way onto her back, blinking back the haze and the amoeba-shaped floaters swimming across her eyes. She glimpsed the cyberspider jumping straight up again and she knew its trajectory would bring it down right on top of her.

Lifting the pistol in her right hand, she tracked the machine, leading it, then she squeezed the trigger, holding it down. She fired six rounds in such rapid succession the shots sounded like a single prolonged report.

The cyberspider's body flew apart in fragments under the .45-caliber barrage. Two of the eight legs spun away, end over end. For a second, the machine was surrounded by an orange halo of flame. Spinning crazily, the automaton listed to the left, then dropped to the ground with a clatter of loose parts. The red glow faded from the glass lenses on the turret head.

Grimacing, Domi rose to her feet, massaging the starburst-shaped scar on her shoulder. Nearly three years before, a bullet had shattered the bone. Reba DeFore had replaced the joint with an artificial ball and socket. After long weeks of painful therapy, Domi had made a complete recovery, but trauma against the joint still caused pain.

Domi ejected the empty magazine, removed another one from her belt and slid it into place, jacking a round into the chamber. Cautiously, she circled the fallen machine, gun barrel trained upon it. During her years in Cerberus, she had learned that the barons enjoyed access to secret technology, most of it created before the nukecaust. She assumed that as overlords, they would have an even greater selection once they reopened the ancient Annunaki vaults. She wasn't mystified by the workings of the cyberspider, but she felt distinctly apprehensive about it.

Suddenly, the glassy lenses in the automaton's round head glowed bright red. She recoiled, biting back a startled cry, her finger tightening around the trigger of the Combat Master.

Without warning, flame and smoke spurted around the base of the turret like an orange collar. The head launched itself from the flexible neck, propelled by wavering streams of fire. Hastily, Domi raised the Combat Master and squeezed off the remaining rounds in the magazine, but she missed.

The head inscribed a high, arcing trajectory, driven swiftly upward by tiny rocket thrusters. Within a handful of seconds, the device was only a miniscule, dully gleaming speck against the limitless expanse of azure.

Gritting her teeth, Domi glared at the inert cyberspider on the ground, noting the tendril of smoke curling from the end of the conduit that had served as the turret's neck.

Domi struggled with the urge to stomp on the machine in a frustrated fury, but decided Lakesh, Bry, Philboyd and the other Cerberus tech-heads wouldn't sympathize with her vindictive impulses. With a profanity-seasoned sigh, she reached for her backpack.

THE ROAD WOUND and twisted, as if its builders had followed the trail made by a giant broken-backed snake, thrashing and whipping in its death throes. The ancient two-lane highway wended its way up toward the chain of mountain peaks that comprised the Continental Divide and formed the natural boundary between Idaho and Montana.

Curving through a tumble of chert outcroppings, the road climbed higher and higher toward a hogback ridge. Domi looked northward toward a parallel mountain range, the Beaverheads. Its highest peak, the Garfield, was still snowcapped.

She turned another bend, then topped the rise. The road widened as it entered a broad plateau. At one time, steel guardrails had bordered the lip overlooking a chasm, but only a few rusted metal stanchions remained. The rusted-out husks of several vehicles rested at the bottom. They had lain there since the time of the skydark, the nuclear winter, weathering all the seasons that came after.

On Domi's right, the plateau debouched into the higher slopes, and the setting sun gleamed off the white headstones marking over a dozen grave sites. The fabricated markers bore only last names: Cotta, Dylan, Adrian and many more. Ten of them were less than a year old, inscribed with the names of the Moon-base émigrés who had died defending Cerberus from the assault staged by Overlord Enlil. The plateau itself was still pockmarked by the craters inflicted by that attack.

One the headstones read simply Quavell, and every time Domi saw it, her throat constricted and her eyes stung with unshed tears.

A grim, gray peak of granite shouldered the sky on the opposite side of the plateau. At its base was the vanadium-alloy security door that led into the heart of the Cerberus redoubt. The multiton door was already folded aside accordion-fashion as Domi crossed the tarmac. Lakesh and Brewster Philboyd stepped out of it, both of their faces drawn in masks of concern. They were dressed identically in the form-fitting white bodysuits that served as the Cerberus duty uniform.

"Are you sure you're all right, darlingest one?" Lakesh asked anxiously. A lilting East Indian accent underscored his cultured voice. "You said you were shocked by the—what did you call it?—cyberspider."

Mohandas Lakesh Singh was a well-built man of medium height, with thick, glossy black hair, an unlined dark olive complexion and a long, aquiline nose. He looked no older than fifty, despite a few strands of gray streaking through his temples. In reality, he was just a year or so shy of celebrating his 250th birthday.

As a youthful genius, Lakesh had been drafted into the web of conspiracy the overseers of the Totality Concept had spun during the last couple of decades of the twentieth century. Immediately after the nukecaust, Lakesh had volunteered to go into stasis. The plan was for him to be resurrected many years later in order to help facilitate the Program of Unification, an effort designed solely to rule what was left of the world.

"I'm fine," Domi responded, holding out the backpack in both hands.

Philboyd eyed it speculatively. "You're sure it's inactive?"

"Like I told you over the transcomm," she answered waspishly, "the head of the thing flew off for parts unknown."

Brewster Philboyd was a little over six feet tall and

lanky of build, seeming to be all kneecaps, elbows and knuckles when he walked. Blond-white hair was swept back from a receding hairline. He wore old-fashioned black-rimmed eyeglasses. His cheeks were pitted with the sort of scars associated with chronic teenage acne.

Philboyd was one of a number of space scientists who had arrived in the Cerberus redoubt from a forgotten Moon base over the past year and a half. Like Lakesh, he was a "freezie," postnuke slang for someone who had been placed in stasis, although conventional cryonics was not the method applied.

"Maybe you could sort of put it down," he ventured mildly, as if he didn't want to offend Domi—which, taking into account her tempestuous nature, he didn't.

She slitted her ruby eyes in annoyance and Lakesh said in an amused tone, "Friend Brewster is quite right. We should examine it out here and make sure it presents no danger before carting it inside."

Sighing impatiently, Domi knelt, placed the backpack flat on the tarmac and unzipped it with a triumphant flourish. Straightening up, she declared pridefully, "It's shot to shit, so you can damn well bet it's inactive, just like I told you when I commed."

When she had gotten within the one-mile range of the little radiophone, she had informed the redoubt of her skirmish with the cyberspider.

Philboyd and Lakesh bent over the machine, hands on their knees, eyeing the metal carapace punctured by three bullet holes. "Some sort of surveillance drone," Philboyd said musingly. "Too small to register on our motion detectors and not producing a thermal signature, either."

"And with a detachable sensory apparatus," murmured Lakesh, pointing to the conduit that had served as support for the turret head. "Very damn advanced piece of gear."

Philboyd pursed his lips contemplatively. "You're sure none of the barons had anything like this?"

"Quite sure. I would have known. No, this probe was dispatched by an overlord to spy on us, to test our defenses and security perimeter."

Domi cocked her head at a quizzical angle. "Then that screws the truce, right? Spying on us?"

Zipping up the backpack and lifting it with both hands, Lakesh replied, "Not really, since we don't know which overlord is responsible. Actually, I expected some sort of feint from one of them long before now."

"Besides," Philboyd interposed, "we're violating the terms of the truce ourselves by planting DeFore in Africa. She's checking out the possibility of overlord activity in the Congo. That's the same as spying."

"It's no longer a possibility," Lakesh said darkly. "I received a communication from her not more than twenty minutes ago. She reported that Overlord Utu is terrorizing the Waziri people in the vicinity of the Usumbur Tract, so the telemetry conveyed by the Vela satellite is confirmed."

Although most satellites had been little more than free-floating scrap metal for well over a century, Cerberus had always possessed the proper electronic ears and eyes to receive the transmissions from at least two of them. One was of the Vela reconnaissance class, which carried narrow-band multispectral scanners. It could detect the electromagnetic radiation reflected by every object on Earth, including subsurface geomagnetic waves. The scanner was tied into an extremely high resolution photographic relay system.

A year's worth of hard work on the part of Lakesh's apprentice, Donald Bry, at long last allowed Cerberus to gain control of the Vela and the Comsat. Knowing that the Annunaki empire had been originally established on the African subcontinent, Bry had programmed the Vela to transmit any imagery from there that fit a preselected parameter.

Only ten days before, Cerberus downloaded a telemetric sequence that showed an object resembling a silver disc flitting over the Congo, hovering over the only settlement in the region, then shooting out of sight so rapidly it almost seemed to vanish. Computer enhancement of the image proved what Lakesh and Bry had suspected anyway—the disc was one of the small fleet of scout vessels carried by Tiamat, the inestimably ancient, gargantuan Annunaki starship in Earth orbit. Apparently the overlords had access to at least one each.

"What else did she say?" Philboyd asked.

"Both of you can listen to the full report yourselves," Lakesh replied. "I'm interested in your input."

"More interested in washing up first," Domi replied, stepping over the threshold into the redoubt, finger scubbing her sweat-damp hair. "Hot out there today."

Lakesh followed her into the installation, smiling as she kissed the forefinger of her right hand and then planted the finger on the illustration of Cerberus on the wall beneath the door control. Although the official designations of all Totality Concept–related redoubts were based on the phonetic alphabet, almost no one who had ever been stationed in the facility referred to it by its official code name of Bravo. The mixture of civilian scientists and military personnel simply called it Cerberus.

Corporal Mooney, one of the enlisted men with artistic aspirations, went so far as to illustrate the door next to the entrance with an image of the three-headed hound that had guarded the gateway to Hades. Rather than attempt even a vaguely realistic representation, he used indelible paints to create a slavering black hellhound with a trio of snarling heads sprouting out of an exaggeratedly muscled neck.

The neck was bound by a spiked collar, and the three jaws gaped wide open, blood and fire gushing between great fangs. In case anyone didn't grasp the meaning, he emblazoned beneath the image the single word Cerberus, wrought in overdone, ornate Gothic script.

Domi had drifted into the habit of giving the illustration, the totem of the redoubt, little greeting and farewell kisses when she passed by. Lakesh found the ritual silly but endearing.

He had found very little endearing in the past fifty years of his life. Five decades before, he had been revived from stasis and drafted to serve the nine godkings who assumed lordship over the Earth. It was only after his resurrection that he had realized the horrific magnitude of their plan to conquer humanity.

Lakesh had tried many times since his resurrection to arrest the tide of extinction inexorably engulfing the human race. First had been his attempts to manipulate the human genetic samples in storage, preserved in vitro since before the nukecaust, to provide the hybridization program with a supply of the best DNA. He had hoped to create an underground resistance movement of superior human beings to oppose the barons and their hidden masters, the Archon Directorate.

A revolutionary force needed a headquarters, and the Cerberus redoubt seemed the most serviceable. The installation contained a frightfully well-equipped armory and two dozen self-contained apartments, a cafeteria, a decontamination center, an infirmary, a swimming pool and even detention cells on the bottom level. The facility also had a limestone filtration system that continually recycled the complex's water supply.

Domi padded barefoot down the main corridor, a twenty-foot-wide passageway made of softly gleaming vanadium alloy and shaped like a square with an arch on top. Great curving ribs of metal and massive girders supported the high rock roof.

Lakesh walked beside her, noting the looks she received from some of the people they passed, but the glances were essentially respectful and even admiring from the men. Like Kane, Brigid and Grant, Domi was considered something special among the personnel, a hero. The actions performed by the four of them had quite literally saved the world.

Unlike her three friends, Domi didn't mind the attention from the Manitius immigrants. Although Cerberus had been constructed to provide a comfortable home for well over a hundred people, it had pretty much been deserted for nearly two centuries.

When Domi, as well as Grant, Kane and Brigid arrived at the installation over three years before, there had been only a dozen permanent residents. Like them, all of the personnel were exiles from the villes brought there by Lakesh because of their training and abilities. Still, for a long time, the Cerberus personnel were outnumbered by shadowed corridors, empty rooms and sepulchral silences.

Over the past year and a half, the corridors had bustled with life, the empty rooms filled and the silences replaced by conversation and laughter. The immigrants from the Manitius Moon base had arrived on a fairly regular basis ever since the destination-lock code to the Luna gateway unit had been discovered. Whether the émigrés intended to remain in the installation or try to make separate lives for themselves in the Outlands, was still an open question. With the fall of the baronies, anarchy had overtaken most of the baronial territories. As they reached a T junction in the passageway, Domi turned left toward the residential wing. She nearly collided with Donald Bry, striding swiftly from his quarters. He muttered an apology and the girl went on her way without a backward glance.

When Bry caught sight of the backpack in Lakesh's hands, his eyes widened. A slightly built, round-shouldered man with an unruly mass of copper-colored hair, he asked eagerly, "Is that the cyberspider gadget?"

Before Lakesh could answer, he reached for the pack and Philboyd stepped up, putting a proprietary hand on it. "Hold on, Donny," he said sternly. "Who said you'd get first crack at it?"

"You're an astrophysicist," Bry shot back, grabbing the other end. "I'm the hardware man hereabouts."

For a few seconds, the two men engaged in a tug-of-war for possession of the backpack, despite the fact that Lakesh held on to the straps.

"Neither one of you can have it unless you learn to share," he said, not releasing his grip.

"Oh, come on," Bry said sharply. "I've got seniority—"

"Lakesh!" Mariah Falk's agitated voice blared out over the public-address transcom system. All three men jumped.

Turning to the nearest voice-activated wall comm, Lakesh called out, "What is it?"

"I need you in the command center," the woman replied. "The latest satellite telemetry from Africa shows one of Tiamat's scout ships on a direct heading with the Sudan—and the biolink readings on Brigid, Grant and Kane are spiking into metabolic shutdown territory!"

Chapter 11

The command center of Cerberus was a long, vault-walled, high-ceilinged room filled with orderly rows of comp terminals and workstations. The central control complex held five dedicated and eight shared subprocessors, all linked to the mainframe behind the far wall. Two hundred years ago, the computer had been an advanced model, carrying experimental, error-correcting microchips of such a tiny size that they even reacted to quantum fluctuations. Biochip technology had been employed when it was built, protein molecules sandwiched between microscopic glass and metal circuits.

On the opposite side of the operations center, an anteroom held the eight-foot-tall mat-trans chamber, rising from an elevated platform. Upright slabs of translucent, brown-hued armaglass formed six walls around it. Armaglass was manufactured in the last decades of the twentieth century from a special compound that plasticized and combined the properties of steel and glass. It was used as walls in the jump chambers to confine quantum energy overspills.

Lakesh glanced over his shoulder at the indicator lights of the huge Mercator relief map of the world spanning one entire wall. Pinpoints of light shone steadily in almost every country, connected by a thin, glowing pattern of lines. They represented the Cerberus network, the locations of all functioning gateway units across the planet. None of the tiny lights blinked, so no indexed mat-trans was currently in use.

In the cool semidarkness the huge room hummed with the quietly efficient chatter of the system operators. Lakesh and Bry strode down the wide aisle formed by two facing rows of workstations.

The control center was surprisingly well manned, but inasmuch as the complex was the brain of the redoubt, it naturally drew personnel from all quarters. Almost all of the people sitting at the various stations were émigrés from the Manitius Moon base. The only long-term Cerberus staff members Lakesh saw were Farrell and Banks.

Monitor screens flashed incomprehensible images and streams of data in machine talk. Bry, who had reluctantly relinquished his grip on the cyberspider out of a sense of duty, took a seat beside Banks at the environ-ops console. Philboyd had carried the cyberspider to the workroom adjacent to the armory.

Coming to stand beside Mariah Falk, who was seated at the biolink medical station, Lakesh asked curtly, "Status?"

A slender, wiry woman in her midforties, Dr. Mariah Falk's short chestnut-brown hair was threaded with gray. Deep creases curved out from either side of her nose to the corners of her mouth. Her face showed lines of strain.

"We've been getting sporadic high-stress signals for

the last couple of hours, but nothing like this." She nodded to the monitor she sat before. On the screen he saw an aerial topographical map of the Sudan. Superimposed over it flashed three icons. The telemetry transmitted from Kane's, Grant's and Brigid's subdermal biolink transponders scrolled in a drop-down window across the top of the screen.

The Comsat kept track of Cerberus personnel by their subcutaneous transponders when they were out in the field. Everyone in the installation had been injected with the transponders, which transmitted heart rate, respiration, blood count and brain-wave patterns. Based on organic nanotechnology, the transponder was a non-harmful radioactive chemical that bound itself to an individual's glucose and the middle layers of the epidermis.

The computer systems recorded every byte of data sent to the Comsat and directed it down to the redoubt's hidden antenna array. Sophisticated scanning filters combed through the telemetric signals using special human biological encoding. The digital data stream was then routed to another console through the locational program, to precisely isolate the team's present position in time and space. The program considered and discarded thousands of possibilities within milliseconds.

All of the icons glowed a bright, angry red, an electronic phenomenon Lakesh had never seen before.

"Every one of their metabolic functions are highly accelerated," Mariah said worriedly. "I'm not a medical doctor, but I know that's not good."

"Neither is this," put in Farrell, seated at the main ops console. The shaven-headed, goateed man gazed fixedly at the VGA monitor, a flat LCD screen nearly four feet square. "We've got a bogey right on top of them."

Glancing toward him, Lakesh saw that the top half of the screen glowed with a CGI grid pattern. A drop-down window displayed scrolling numbers that Lakesh knew were measurements of changing coordinates. One of the grid squares enclosed a bright bead of light. "Has it taken any hostile action?" he asked.

Farrell shook his head. "I don't think it needs to."

Lakesh squinted over at the screen. "Why not?"

Touching a key on the board, Farrell announced, "Because of this."

Shades of bright color bloomed up from the central grid pattern like the petals of an unimaginably huge flower. Hues of red, white, yellow, green, cyan, blue and even violet spread out across the terrain.

"This is a thermal line-scan," Farrell said dolefully. "The spectroscopic analysis indicates exceptionally high levels of radiation."

Lakesh didn't allow the sudden surge of fear to register either in his bearing or voice. "Source?"

"I don't know," Farrell answered. "It's a pretty rocky area, and if they were checking out an alleged Totality Concept site…" His words trailed off and he lifted his shoulders in a shrug.

Mariah stated, "If they're being exposed to radiation, then that might interefere with the transponder signals. We may not be receiving a true read."

Banks turned in his chair toward them. "That's very possible," he said encouragingly. A young black man with a neatly trimmed beard and an easygoing manner, he had undergone training over the past couple of years in medical matters, particularly the operation and limitations of the transponders.

"The biolinks send out steady, regular signals," he went on. "We've known the signals to be disrupted in the past by everything from atmospheric conditions to sun-spots. Maybe even a radiation spike in the nonlethal range could interfere with them."

"Even so," said Lakesh flatly, "I find the timing suspicious. Assuming the scout ship is piloted by Overlord Utu and not a remote-controlled drone as DeFore postulated, then he could be the culprit behind the radiation surge."

Farrell's fingers tapped the keyboard. "I don't think so. I'll replay the telemetry and see what I get."

Lakesh nodded. "Thank you, friend Farrell."

He turned toward a pudgy Eurasian woman sitting at a computer station. "Miss Nguyen, have you had any luck with the database search?"

She swiveled her chair around, a pair of eyeglasses pushed up on her forehead. "Almost too much," she said wryly. "The first authentic mention of Prester John was found in the *Chronicle of Otto,* Bishop of Freising, in 1145. Otto gives as his authority Hugo, Bishop of Gabala. The latter, by order of the Christian prince Raymond of Antioch, went in 1144 to Pope Eugene II, to report the grievous position of Jerusalem, and to induce the West to send another crusade—"

Lakesh raised a peremptory hand. "I'm less interested in the possible reality of Prester John than I am about this so-called collar of his and why it's so important to both the Waziri and Overlord Utu."

A bit defensively, Nguyen said, "I'm still researching."

Lakesh smiled encouragingly. "Carry on."

He returned his attention to the blood-colored icons on the biolink monitor, trying to tamp down a rising sense of dread. He told himself if the erratic readings were due to a glitch, the Cerberus people would find that out.

Most of the people who lived in the Cerberus redoubt acted in the capacity of support personnel regardless of their specialized skills. They worked rotating shifts, eight hours a day, seven days a week. For the most part, their work was the routine maintenance and monitoring of the installation's environmental systems, the satellite data feed and the security network.

However, everyone was given at least a superficial understanding of all the redoubt's systems so they could pinch-hit in times of emergency. Fortunately, such a time had never arrived. Their small numbers had been a source of constant worry to Lakesh, but with the arrival of the Moon-base personnel, there was a larger pool of talent pool from which to draw.

Grant and Kane were exempt from cross-training inasmuch as they served as the enforcement arm of Cerberus and undertook far and away the lion's share of the risks. On their downtime between missions they made sure all the ordnance in the armory was in good condition and occasionally tuned up the vehicles in the depot.

Brigid Baptiste, due to her eidetic memory, was the most exemplary member of the redoubt's permanent staff since she could step into any vacancy. However, her gifts were a two-edged sword as those self-same polymath skills made her an indispensable addition to away missions. Lakesh had long ago given up trying to convince her she was too valuable to risk her life on away missions. He couldn't order her to stay behind, even if he had been so inclined.

Over two years before, Kane, Brigid and Grant had staged a mini-coup d'état. Lakesh hadn't been completely unseated from his position of authority, but he was now answerable to a more democratic process. At first he bitterly resented what he construed as the usurping of his power by ingrates, but over a period of time he accepted sharing his command with the other Cerberus exiles. It was the only fair tactic to take, since the majority of them were exiles due to his covert actions.

Before the arrival of the Moon colony émigrés, almost every person in the redoubt had arrived as a convicted criminal—after Lakesh had set them up, framing them for crimes against their respective villes. He admitted it was a cruel, heartless plan, with a barely acceptable risk factor, but it was the only way to spirit them out of their villes, turn them against the barons and make them feel indebted to him.

This bit of explosive and potentially fatal knowledge had not been shared with the other exiles. Only Kane, Grant and Brigid were aware of it.

But deception and misdirection had been part and

parcel of the war they had waged for the past three years against the tyranny of the nine barons.

The barons—the hybridized god-kings who had inherited the Earth from their human cousins whom they scorned as "apekin"—were by their way of thinking, representatives of the final phase of human development. They had referred to themselves as "new humans" and empowered themselves to control not only their immediate environment, but also the evolution of other species.

The barons considered themselves the pinnacle of evolutionary achievement, as high above ordinary hybrids who were bred as a servant class, as the hybrids were above mere humans.

Baron and hybrid alike had been products a long-range genetic engineering program, a blending of human DNA and that of a race known as Archons. This race had been involved with humanity for many millennia, once associated with angels, demons and finally aliens known as the Grays. In reality, the Archons were hybrids themselves, a mixture of three races—the extraterrestrial Annunaki and Tuatha de Danaan and the very terrestrial Homo sapiens.

After a long and destructive war between the Annunaki and the Tuatha de Danaan, the two races chose to unite and create one combined people, a hybrid custodial race initially known as the First Folk, then much later as the Archons.

The establishment of the Program of Unification came in the second century following the nukecaust. The stated goals of the nine barons were to carry out the edicts of the Archon Directorate, of unifying the world and reducing humanity to the level of an expendable minority, existing only to be exploited as slave labor and as providers of genetic material.

Despite how mad the entire tale of Archon-human hybrids seemed initially, the Cerberus exiles used it as a focus of their hatred toward the baronial oligarchy. Then they learned their hatred was not only pointless, but pretty much without basis. The Archon Directorate did not exist, except as a cover story created in the twentieth century and expanded with each succeeding generation. It was all a ruse, bits of truth mixed in with outrageous fiction. Only a single so-called Archon existed on Earth and that was Balam, who had been the Cerberus redoubt's resident prisoner for over three and a half years.

Balam claimed the Archon Directorate was an appellation created by the predark governments. Lakesh referred to it as the Oz Effect, wherein a single vulnerable entity created the illusion of being the representative of an all-powerful machine that controlled humanity.

Lakesh, Kane, Brigid, Grant and the Cerberus exiles declared war on the dark forces devoted to maintaining the yoke of slavery around the collective necks of humankind. It was a struggle not just for the physical survival of humanity, but for the human spirit, the soul of an entire race.

Over the past three years, they scored many victories, defeated many enemies and solved mysteries of the past that molded the present and affected the future.

More importantly, they began to rekindle of the spark of hope within the breasts of the disenfranchised fighting to survive in the Outlands.

Victory, if not within their grasp, at least had no longer seemed an unattainable dream. But with the transformation of the barons into the overlords, Lakesh wondered if the war was now over—or if it had ever actually been waged at all. He was beginning to fear that everything he and his friends had experienced and endured so far had only been minor skirmishes, a mere prologue to the true conflict yet to come.

Farrell pushed his chair back and said matter-of-factly, "According to the Vela line-scan, the radiation readings began at least a minute before the arrival of the scout ship. The latest telemetry shows that it didn't hang around, either."

He indicated a grid square with a forefinger. The tiny bead of light shot through several squares and disappeared. Lakesh released his breath in a pent-up sigh. He didn't know why he suddenly felt so relieved. As far as he knew, his three best friends were even now dead or dying of radiation exposure.

Cerberus didn't receive real-time telemetry. There was a five-minute lag between transmission, reception and download. All the activity displayed on the screen had occurred minutes before. If Brigid, Grant and Kane were suffering, there was nothing anyone could do to rescue them, at least in anything approximating a timely manner and he found that thought surprisingly painful.

Lakesh had tried desperately, despite his often deceptive machinations, to remain loyal to his friends, people he now felt to be his family, regardless of the personal problems that had occurred among them over the years.

In spite of, or perhaps even because of their frequent disagreements and arguments, they always looked out for one another, and genuinely cared for each other's well-being. In some ways, the emotional bond he felt for the Cerberus exiles was stronger than that of blood kin. Of course, anyone to whom he was directly related was two centuries dead.

As far as Lakesh was concerned, the three people in the Sudan redoubt were his best friends, his colleagues, even his children, and the thought of losing them with nothing to mark their passing but computer-generated icons on a monitor screen nearly paralyzed him with dread.

"Hey!" exclaimed Mariah so suddenly that Lakesh jumped, startled. "The readings aren't spiking so high now. They're still at the extreme far end of the normal range, though."

Lakesh squinted at the screen, noting how the icons no longer glowed bright red, but the heart and pulse rates were still elevated. He guessed Kane, Grant and Brigid had been exerting themselves while in a high state of emotional agitation.

"Judging by their positions," he observed, "they've moved away from the epicenter of the radiation. That's something."

"True," Mariah agreed bleakly. "I just wish I knew if it was a good or bad something."

Lakesh suddenly realized how weak his knees felt. He turned toward the exit. "If they're still moving," he replied, "then I'll assume it's a good something…at least until we hear otherwise. Keep me posted, Dr. Falk."

Chapter 12

Lakesh and Domi walked through the armory together. He winced at the sudden stab of pain in his right knee as he bumped it against the corner of a misplaced crate filled with disassembled CAR-15 carbines. Even though he was primarily responsible for moving most of the ordnance into the redoubt over a period of many years, he was still surprised at the sheer magnitude of weapons of destruction that were housed in the Cerberus arsenal.

The big square room was quite likely the best stocked and outfitted armory in postnuke America. Glass-fronted cases held racks of automatic assault rifles. There were many makes and models of subguns, as well as dozens of semiautomatic pistols and revolvers, complete with holsters and belts.

There was also heavy assault weaponry like bazookas, tripod-mounted 20 mm cannons, mortars and rocket launchers. All the ordnance had been laid down in hermetically sealed Continuity of Government installations before the nukecaust. Protected from the ravages of the outraged environment, nearly every piece of munitions and hardware was as pristine as the day it was first manufactured.

Lakesh himself had put the arsenal together over several decades, envisioning it as the major supply depot for a rebel army. The army never materialized, at least not in the fashion Lakesh hoped it would. Therefore, Cerberus was blessed with a surplus of death-dealing equipment that would have turned the most militaristic overlord green with envy, or give the most pacifistic of them heart failure—if they indeed possessed hearts.

As he and Domi walked past the stands and racks, he favored his right leg. Domi noticed him doing so and asked, "Knee again?"

Lakesh nodded, knowing better than to lie to her about his physical condition. When he had first met Domi, his eyes had been covered by thick lenses, a hearing aid inserted in one ear, and physically he most resembled a hunched-over spindly old scarecrow who appeared to be fighting the grave for every hour he remained on the planet.

And then, not quite two years ago, Sam the Imperator had laid his hands on Lakesh and miraculously restored his youth. At the time, Sam claimed he had increased Lakesh's production of two antioxidant enzymes, catalase and superoxide dismutase, and boosted his alkyglycerol level to the point where the aging process was for all intents and purposes reversed.

Sam had indeed accomplished all of that, but only in the past year or so did Lakesh learn the precise methodology—when he laid his hands on Lakesh, Sam had injected nanomachines into his body. The nanites were programmed to recognize and destroy dangerous organisms, whether they were bacteria, cancer cells or viruses. Sam's nanites performed selective destruction on the genes of DNA cells, removing the part that caused aging.

For a time, he had felt he was living in the dream world of all old men—restored youth, vitality and enhanced sex drive, as Domi could attest.

However, the nanites in his body became inert after a time. He and DeFore feared that without the influence of the nanomachines, he would begin to age, but at an accelerated rate. But so far, that gloomy diagnosis had not come to pass. True, he was sporting new gray hairs and he noticed the return of old aches and pains, but so far, the aging process seemed normal. He was cautiously optimistic that he would not reprise the fate of the title character in *The Picture of Dorian Gray* and he hoped Domi shared that optimism.

It had been a great source of joy to Lakesh when he learned Domi reciprocated his feelings and had no inhibitions about expressing them, regardless of the bitterness she still harbored over her unrequited love for Grant. In any event, he had broken a fifty-year streak of celibacy with her and they repeated the actions of that first delirious night whenever the opportunity arose.

In the beginning, he had felt compelled to keep his relationship with Domi a secret, and he wasn't sure why. At first he tried to convince himself it was concern over raising Grant's ire, but he knew that was simply a feeble excuse. With Grant's heart more or less pledged to Shizuka, the big man was too preoccupied with his attempts to make a new life with her to give the more covert—and intimate—activities among the redoubt personnel more than cursory attention.

When Domi accused him of being ashamed of their relationship, he had suddenly realized the true reasons he had kept their affair a secret—he feared she would be swept up in the same karmic backlash that he had long feared would shatter him. When the punishment had been averted, due he felt to Domi's devotion to him, he had made a rather noisy fanfare of announcing their relationship to one and all. Much to his chagrin, most of the people in the redoubt already knew about it. Or if they hadn't, they could not have cared less—Grant included, or so it seemed.

The two people passed through the armory and into the adjacent workroom. Rows of drafting tables with T-squares hanging from them lined one wall. Only a few lights were on, but they saw Brewster Philboyd perched on a stool at a long, low trestle table at the far end of the room. He was bent over a gooseneck magnifying lamp, and they heard the muted click and clack of metal against metal. The cyberspider lay on its back, the underside of its thorax peeled open. Mechanical parts and tools were scattered all around it.

Resting atop a pedestal next to him, enclosed within a locked transparent Lucite box, was an object resembling a very squat, broad-based pyramid made of smooth, dully gleaming metal. Barely one foot in width, the height of the interphaser did not exceed twelve inches.

The interphaser had evolved from Project Cerberus.

Three years before, Lakesh had constructed a small device on the same scientific principle as the mat-trans gateways, a portable quantum interphase inducer designed to interact with naturally occurring hyperdimensional vortices.

The interphaser opened dimensional rifts much like the gateways, but instead of the rifts being pathways through linear space, Lakesh had envisioned them as a method to travel through the gaps in normal space-time.

The first version of the interphaser had not functioned according to its design, and was lost on its first mission. Much later, a situation arose that necessitated the construction of a second, improved model.

During the investigation of the Operation Chronos installation on Thunder Isle, a special encoded computer program named Parallax Points was discovered. Lakesh learned that the Parallax Points program was actually a map, a geodetic index, of all the vortex points on the planet. This discovery inspired Lakesh to rebuild the interphaser, even though decrypting the program was laborious and time-consuming. Each newly discovered set of coordinates was fed into the interphaser's targeting computer.

With the new data, the interphaser became more than a miniaturized version of a gateway unit, even though it employed much of the same hardware and operating principles. The mat-trans gateways functioned by tapping into the quantum stream, the invisible pathways that crisscrossed outside of perceived physical space and terminated in wormholes.

The interphaser interacted with the energy within a
naturally occurring vortex and caused a temporary
overlapping of two dimensions. The vortex then became an intersection point, a discontinuous quantum
jump, beyond relativistic space-time. Evidence indicated there were many vortex nodes, centers of intense
energy, located in the same proximity on each of the
planets of the solar system, and those points correlated
to vortex centers on Earth. The power points of the
planet, places that naturally generated specific types of
energy, possessed both positive and projective frequen-
cies, and others were negative and receptive.

Once the interphaser was put into use, the Cerberus
redoubt reverted to its original purpose—not a sanctuary for exiles, or the headquarters of a resistance movement against the tyranny of the barons, but a facility
dedicated to unfathoming the eternal mysteries of space
and time. Interphaser Version 2.0 had been lost during
a mission to Mars to unlock a few of those eternal mysteries and Version 2.5 had been completed less than a
year before, due mainly to the efforts of Philboyd and
Brigid Baptiste.

However, no Parallax Points or mat-trans gateways
could be located in the vicinity of the Usumbur Tract
or even the Sudan, so Brigid, Kane, DeFore and Grant
had flown to their destinations in the Transatmospheric
Vehicles known as Mantas.

Reaching the trestle table, Domi inserted her head
between the lamp's magnifying lens and the scattering
of electronic components and machine parts. "Learned
anything?"

Philboyd jerked upright at the sight of her enlarged red eyes. A startled curse sprang to his lips, then he smiled, unable to resist Domi's impish grin. "It's only been an hour," he said, "but in fact I have."

He turned toward Lakesh. "Any news from our people in Africa?"

Lakesh shook his head. "Not so far. The transponders are showing high-normal metabolic signatures of our away team but they haven't checked in yet. What've you got going here?"

Philboyd declared, "This little bug is a cybernetic work unit, basically a self-propelled tool, not remote controlled. It apparently had sensors that caused it to react. I'd say the head that detached itself was an observation and analysis system that sent images back to some control center. Now look at this."

With a pair of forceps, Philboyd reached into the thoracic cavity of the machine. The lamplight gleamed from a confusing mass of circuitry and microprocessors within. He withdrew a small cylinder that looked to be made of steel mesh, about the length and thickness of grown man's index finger.

Lakesh stared at it, unimpressed. "So?"

Philboyd picked up a set of needle-nosed pliers and probed one end of the little cylinder, pulling out a glittering object. Domi's and Lakesh's eyes widened at the sight of the sculpted yellow crystal, at first glance a flawless diamond. Philboyd placed it beneath the light and Lakesh studied it, seeing a tiny constellation of stars glowing deep within its facets.

"I think this is our bug's power source," Philboyd announced. "What used to be known as a CEM—a chargeable energy module."

"A rock?" Domi inquired dubiously.

Lakesh leaned closer, scrutinizing the stone closely. "Before the nukecaust, there was a field of study devoted to developing crystals as a solid-state energy source."

"I'm aware," Philboyd said stiffly. "The thesis was that crystals could be used as advanced energy-storage systems. In my work with NASA I experimented with crystals for electron imaging and convergent beam diffraction. But none of the researches went as far as this."

Glancing at Domi, he said, "If one of your bullets hadn't cut a power transmission coupling, I think the thing would still be running."

She lifted a shoulder in a negligent shrug. "Lucky shot."

Philboyd angled a questioning eyebrow, first at her then at Lakesh. "Yeah, luck is the word for it, all right."

Tapping the cyberspider's body with the tips of the pliers, he declared, "This thing was built with triple redundancies. You hit it in the right place at the right time."

Lakesh regarded him gravely. "What do you mean?"

"I mean Domi could have shot it literally to pieces and if she hadn't disconnected the CEM, it would be zipping around right now."

"How do you figure that?" demanded Domi.

"There are at least three pretty damn advanced microprocessors inside our little bug. If we could access just one, we'd be able to refer to all sorts of useful data about where this thing came from, how it's built, who built it—"

"Wouldn't doing that require a special interface?" Lakesh broke in.

Philboyd waved the pliers around dismissively. "With some of the techs we have here, it wouldn't be too much of problem to put one together."

Pursing his lips contemplatively, Lakesh fingered a bullet hole on the cyberspider's carapace. "What makes you think our two technologies are compatible? As damaged as this gadget is, how do you know if can be made functional again?"

"I don't," Philboyd retorted bluntly. "But there's a way to find out."

He brandished the yellow crystal gripped by the forceps. "I can hook the power feed conduit back up to this and see if can reboot the whole operational system."

Lakesh stared at him in disbelief for a long moment, then his eyebrows knitted together at the bridge of his nose. "I might have expected such a reckless suggestion from Kane, but not from you."

Philboyd chuckled self-consciously. "It's not as reckless a suggestion as you might think. As Domi said, this little bug is shot to shit. Most of its moving parts are wrecked, some are even missing and I gutted it of all its electronics. It's essentially a husk, a shell. All I want is to give it a taste of power to find out if it's worth the time and effort to build a processor interface."

Lakesh tugged at his long nose, gazing at the cyberspider speculatively.

"It would be like hooking up a battery to a junker car that's up on blocks," Philboyd continued earnestly.

"Just so we could test the electrical system, see if the radio and the lights still worked."

Lakesh sighed heavily. "You're sure the bug is dysfunctional? You have no doubt?"

Philboyd gestured to it, then to the litter of parts strewed over the tabletop. He arched his eyebrows meaningfully. "What do you think?"

"I think *you* think you're smarter than you really are," Domi stated flatly. "If that little monster was made by the snake faces, it's got to be tricky. You can't trust it."

Philboyd regarded the albino with a patronizing smile. "It's not magic, Domi. The overlords aren't gods and they didn't make a monster. This is just a machine they built, and machines have limitations."

Domi slitted her eyes. "Don't talk to me like I'm a jolt brain. I know damn well it's a machine. I'm the one who carried it uphill for six miles, remember? But I also know a machine made by a snake face might have a whole different set of limitations than what you expect."

"I'm sure friend Brewster will take all appropriate precautions," Lakesh said reassuringly. He speared the man with a frosty, challenging glare. "Right, friend Brewster?"

Philboyd smiled sourly. "I'd say doing everything but skinning and burying it is taking all appropriate precautions."

He bent over the cyberspider again, peering through the magnifying lens, inserting the crystal back into the steel-mesh container and then into the thorax. He manipulated the pliers and forceps swiftly and deftly. Lakesh gazed over the astrophysicist's shoulder at the operation as he reconnected the crystal.

"It's really not a very complicated piece of machinery," Philboyd murmured as he worked. "Those flying disks Enlil used against us were light-years beyond this clockwork doohickey."

Within three minutes, a soft, pale yellow glow suddenly washed within the thorax of the cyberspider. At the same time, the machine emitted a faint drone. "Here we go," Philboyd said confidently. "Nothing to it. My faith in electronics is restored."

Lakesh looked toward Domi to gauge her reaction and realized she wasn't present. He frowned slightly in annoyance, miffed that she was so distrustful of Philboyd's expertise that she would take herself out of the vicinity on the off chance anything went wrong.

Reaching for an amperage meter, Philboyd commented, "I'll just run a quick check on the power output and we can get a notion about what kind of interface—"

He broke off when the hum from the cyberspider changed in pitch to a buzzing whine. Both he and Lakesh stared at it. As they gaped at the machine in wide- and wild-eyed wonder, the bullet holes perforating the cyberspider's skin swirled and closed up. Within seconds, the two edges of the slit cut into its thorax stretched out over the cavity, joined and sealed with a barely perceptible seam.

All at once, memories rushed over Lakesh, his thoughts flying back to the night of the aerial assault on the redoubt and how bullets that struck the scout ships seemed to be absorbed into the hull. He recollected what Brigid had told him of the body armor worn by the overlords and the Nephilim—that it was composed of a smart metal, a malleable alloy that responded to a sequence of commands programmed into its extruder. A miniature cohesive binding field changed it from liquid to solid and back again.

An image of how the hull of one the scout ships, sent into a tailspin by a mortar shell, had morphed and extended glider wings leaped to the forefront of his mind.

Even as the memory registered, the underside of the cyberspider began bulging in places, as if fingers were poking at the underside of a malleable membrane. Then a section of the alloy formed a cone and stretched out a pseudopod, the blunt tip questing blindly like the head of slug. Lakesh glimpsed the glint of a tiny crystal, like a diamond chip at very end of it.

"What the hell?" Philboyd blurted, jumping up so suddenly the stool crashed loudly to the floor.

The realization surged through Lakesh in a shaved sliver of a second—as Philboyd said, one of Domi's shots had indeed been lucky, penetrating the cyberspider's body, knocking askew its power source and impairing the smart metal from employing its ability to morph.

The pseudopod suddenly shot straight out like a striking serpent. Constrictor fashion, it lashed around Brewster Philboyd's neck, dragging from his lips a choked cry of terror. The electronic whine turned into a metallic rasp, and the tentacle contracted into a tight knot.

Philboyd clawed at it, trying to fit his fingers between the enwrapping tentacle and his throat. "Lakesh—!"

As if sensing the man's efforts to free himself, the alloy-sheathed tentacle tightened its grip, cutting off Philboyd's voice and respiration. He uttered a single gagging cough, eyes bulging with fright and pain.

Shouting in alarm, Lakesh picked up a screwdriver from the table and lunged to help. He barely noticed a targeting pipper blooming on the side of the machine, shining like a perfect drop of blood.

The boom of the single shot was painfully loud, sending out a wave of eardrum-compressing sound. A wad of 20-gauge buckshot center-punched the cyberspider. Fragments of metal and glittering circuitry flew outward. It spun like a crazed carousel on the tabletop.

The tentacle around Philboyd's neck slithered loose. He and Lakesh stumbled out of Domi's line of fire as she marched in from the armory, a Remington Autoloader USAS-12 shotgun in her arms. She trained the front-mounted laser targeter onto the cyberspider's bulbous body.

"Get down!" she shouted.

As Lakesh and Philboyd frantically complied, she fired again at the cyberspider, and a blizzard of shot blew it off the table, scooping a ragged, splintery furrow in the wood. The machine clattered to the floor in several pieces.

Stepping around the two men crouched down on the floor, Domi swept the red light thread over the fragments of cyberspider scattered over the floor. It writhed along the tiles with groping, disjointed movements. Tiny shards of shattered alloy glinted in its wake. Domi brought the autotargeter to rest on the largest piece, a cup-shaped shard about the size of her fist.

It shivered violently and several smaller pieces of the device suddenly skittered across the floor tiles toward it, as if it exerted a powerful magnetic attraction. The tentacle reared up for an instant like a wounded snake, blindly seeking prey to strike.

Domi squeezed the trigger again, easily handling the shotgun's recoil despite her small stature. The boom of 20-gauge buckshot exploding from the bore was deafening. The tentacle of the cyberspider vanished in a billow of smoke and a spray of broken tiles.

In the sudden silence that followed, Domi announced matter-of-factly in her little-girl voice, "A man has got to know a machine's limitations…right, Brewster?"

Lakesh straightened up and exchanged a long look with Philboyd, who massaged his neck. He said darkly, "Now that darlingest Domi has pointed them out, the bug—or what's left of it—might be safe for further study."

Philboyd continued rubbing his neck and he regarded the shattered fragments of the cyberspider with loathing. In a faint, hoarse whisper he said, "I think I've lost my faith in electronics."

Chapter 13

Reba DeFore lay in the sling bed, naked arms and legs dangling, her face tilted to the rafters. Sweat gleamed on her brown face and limbs, pooling in the hollow between her breasts, plastering her ash-blond hair to her cheeks and forehead. It was only six o' clock in the morning, but the heat was already suffocating.

She had spent a fitful night in the guest quarters of Princess Pakari's dwelling, but her restlessness had little to do with the heat and oppressive humidity. Consumed with worry about her three friends in the Sudan, DeFore had kept listening for a signal from the satcomm. A call to Cerberus around two o'clock in the morning hadn't provided her with any information except the biolink transponders had registered exceptionally high stress indicators among them.

Lakesh had made a cryptic reference to a mechanical-spider problem the redoubt had experienced a few minutes earlier, but he hadn't gone into detail. He had informed her that data about Prester John was ready for satellite download into the laptop she had brought along, but she wasn't inclined to go through the setup process.

Concern for Brigid, Grant and Kane kept her awake,

but DeFore also worried about being bitten by the poisonous snakes and toxic bugs she was sure crawled all over the floor beneath her. She disliked in the extreme leaving the cool, sheltering walls of Cerberus and going out into the field. The few times she had joined away missions had resulted in situations that gave her nightmares for months. Over six years ago she had been recruited by Lakesh because of her medical background, not because she wanted to be either an explorer or an adventurer.

Nor had DeFore volunteered to join Cerberus. She had been forced to flee from her barony when her lover, tortured by Magistrates, had named her as a seditionist, as an agent of the Preservationists. Their existence was mentioned only in fearful whispers among the ville-bred, as a sinister underground resistance movement pledged to deliver the hidden history of the world to a humanity held in baronial bondage.

DeFore still retained vivid memories of her first days in the cavernous and uninhabited Cerberus redoubt, with its echoing corridors and empty rooms. The installation was like a vast city to her then, accustomed as she was to living in a tiny two-room flat in the residential Enclaves. The place felt haunted by the ghosts of a despairing past. The sleek vanadium walls seemed to exude the desperate terror, the utter despondency of the souls trapped there when the first mushroom cloud erupted over Washington, D.C., nearly two centuries before.

She had assumed the redoubt was the headquarters of the mysterious Preservationists. When Lakesh revealed to her that such an organization existed only as a myth for the purpose of presenting a false trail for the barons to pursue and fear, her first reaction was anger.

Lakesh explained how he had created the Preservationists to be straw adversaries, a nonexistent enemy for the Magistrate Divisions to focus their attention upon while the real insurrectionist work went on elsewhere.

However, DeFore had learned in the interim there actually were post-skydark precedents for groups like the Preservationists. A century or more before, a loosely knit organization called the Heimdall Foundation had been formed to keep alive the science of astronomy and astrophysics, not to mention Ireland's Priory of Awen, whose origins could be traced back over a thousand years, to its reputed founding by Saint Patrick himself.

Although she admired Lakesh's cunning, DeFore still felt a bit of lingering resentment over his deceptive actions. She had studied a bit of psychology and realized the man's motivations derived primarily from guilt, but it wasn't neurotic or misplaced.

Lakesh and other twentieth-century scientists had willingly traded in their human heritage for a shock-scape of planet-wide ruins. After all, they had been selected to survive in order to reshape not only earth, but also humankind in a nonhuman image.

He had used his position as an adviser to Baron Cobalt to select likely prospects to join Cerberus, but he always knew his tiny enclave of exiles could never overthrow the barons by staging a guerrilla war.

Humankind, at least those who were ville-bred, had been beaten into docility long ago. In the Outlands, a fragile, disorganized freedom remained, with pockets of Roamers, half-feral bioengineered mutants who had survived the purges, and tribes of Amerindians who had returned to their traditional way of life.

But even taken together, they represented only a fraction of a fraction of free humans. The population of hybrids swelled as the few truly human beings on Earth diminished, killed and bred and co-opted out of existence. Lakesh had been involved in the initial stages of that co-option and was desperate to find some way to balance out his sin.

Lakesh rifled Scenario Joshua's genetic records to find the qualifications he deemed the most desirable to breed into potential warriors in his cause. A few years before, Lakesh had arranged for Beth-Li Rouch to be brought into the redoubt to mate with Kane, to ensure that his superior abilities were passed on to offspring.

From a clinical point of view, Lakesh's plan to turn Cerberus from a sanctuary into a colony made sense. To ensure that Kane's superior qualities were passed on, mating him with a woman who met the standards of Purity Control was the most logical course of action. Without access to the ectogenesis techniques of fetal development outside the womb, the conventional means of procreation was the only option. And that meant sex and passion and ultimately, the fury of a woman scorned.

Kane had refused to cooperate for a variety of reasons, primarily because he felt the plan was a continuation of sinister elements that had brought about the nukecaust and the tyranny of the villes. His refusal had tragic consequences. Only a thirst for revenge and a conspiracy to murder had been birthed within the walls of the redoubt, not children.

DeFore shook her head to drive out the memories. Many changes had occurred in the six years since she had arrived at Cerberus, not only Lakesh's tactics but even her attitudes. Initially, she had resented the presences of Brigid, Grant and especially Kane. Now she considered them her closest friends, members of an extended family, the siblings she never had. And like siblings, they often exasperated her and worried her.

When she heard the bawl of cattle, the trumpeting of an elephant and the voices of people busy at their early-morning labors, DeFore decided to get up—not that it was easy to struggle out of the sling. She glanced down in annoyance at the mesh pattern imprinted into the damp flesh of her thighs.

She walked across the big room for her clothes, which consisted only of a thin, almost gauzy linen shift and a turban. It was like walking through warm molasses. The polished wooden floor, bare of vermin, nevertheless felt slippery under her feet. The room itself was shaped like the inside of a drum, the conical ceiling upheld by heavy beams. The walls were decorated by an arras of highly detailed fabric. A small table near the window held a decanter of water and she poured herself a cup. It tasted old, the temperature tepid.

Pakari's house was less a palace than a big rambling structure that had grown over the years, yet the new additions had blended with the old, adding to instead of detracting from the original conception of a tribal assembly hall.

It was a building that had expanded to embrace generations of Waziri as it had stretched to contain the accumulation of centuries of their rich culture. It was a place of dust and dreams, myths, folklore and ancient legends, but exerting a power over the tribespeople just the same.

As DeFore dressed, she looked out the window toward the Usumbur tract and the giant eucalyptus trees that bordered it. The early-morning sun was still low on the horizon, but its smoky red glow showed her several of Princess Pakari's personal guards standing sentry, either to protect the village from an incursion from the swampland, or to prevent an incursion into it. She wasn't sure which. She knew the Waziri held the tract in some sort of superstitious regard.

Despite gripping the hafts of long spears and holding their elephant-hide shields across their chests, the eyes of the soldiers were frightened and they didn't seem to know what to do.

DeFore didn't blame them for their fear or indecision. The night before they had witnessed two of their own struck down by what seemed like a supernatural power, wielded by an equally supernatural entity. All of the Waziri soldiers probably wondered if they would be next to suffer Utu's wrath if they didn't turn against their princess.

She looked to her left, gazing at the limitless tableland of the veldt, a fertile savannah that was the habitat of rhinos, antelope and elephants. Beyond rose the rolling swell of a distant mountain range. She knew one of the far peaks held great importance among the Waziri, too. The high priest Inkula had referred to it cryptically as the "rim of the world."

At the sound of a knock on the door frame, she turned. "Yes?"

Princess Pakari brushed aside the beaded curtain. "My apologies if I disturbed you, but I heard you stirring."

The young woman wore a traditional Waziri shift, dyed in bright native patterns, and a kind of cotton shawl over her shoulders. A band of golden beads held her hair back from her forehead. She was nearly a head taller than DeFore, her innate pride and royal bearing evident even in the most simple of movements. But out of the royal raiment, she looked young and vulnerable.

"I couldn't sleep," DeFore said.

"Nor could I," Pakari replied in her throaty voice. "I am worried about the arrival of Laputara and you, I imagine, are worried about your friends."

DeFore nodded. "That's about the size of it, Your Highness."

Pakari's full lips creased in a wry smile. "There is no need to address me as such. I am not your princess… nor am I officially the princess of the Waziri. But I am resigned to that tenuous position until the spirits of my ancestors decide otherwise."

The calm acceptance of her role impressed DeFore. Princess Pakari had impressed all of the visitors from Cerberus upon first meeting her three days before. Not only did she speak excellent English, touched with a faint British accent, but she also admirably concealed her astonishment when the four of them strolled into the village from where they had landed the Mantas.

"But your friends seemed very capable," Pakari continued. "Particularly the big grumpy one…the one you called Grant. He reminds me of my father in some ways."

DeFore smiled at the girl's description. "He pretends he's grumpy but in reality he's just bad-tempered."

Pakari acknowledged the comment with a short nod. "I want to thank you for the medicines and healing arts you have applied to my people. Many would have died if not for your skills."

DeFore shrugged, uncomfortable with the compliment. "Serendipity. I recognized the symptoms of cholera and had the proper vaccines with me."

The medic and the Cerberus warriors had arrived in the Waziri village a few days after the outbreak of cholera among several of the tribe. DeFore's swift diagnosis and treatment prevented the outbreak from becoming a full-blown epidemic.

"You have earned their trust," Pakari continued, "and Laputara will despise you for it."

"With all due respect, Princess," DeFore said, "your half brother doesn't seem to be thought of very highly here. Why would your people follow him over you?"

Stiffly and formally, Pakari said, "He believes he is the heir to the titles of Elephant Emperor, Lord of the Moon, Stars and Sun, Master of the Great Snake, hereditary king of all the Waziri tribal chiefs. It is not important what the people think of him, but what he thinks of himself."

"And with whom he is allied," DeFore pointed out.

Pakari nodded. "That, too. Fear is a very powerful tool by which to bend wills."

"Dammit, I've explained to you about Utu," DeFore said, worry and the heat fraying her temper. "He's not a god. He and others like him are fakes."

"I believe you," the princess replied. "But I am bound by the rules and customs of my people. Our society cannot survive without a firm basis in them, in the observance of ritual and tradition. As heirs to the throne, both Laputara and I must maintain our pride and position. We must abide by our places in the scheme of things. Perhaps you and your friends have met similar cultures in your travels?"

"Similar," said DeFore, thinking of several static societies doomed to fall apart beneath the influence and impact of changing ways. "But Laputara doesn't seem to be playing by your traditions."

Pakari sighed. "He was always willful, with a wild streak in him which made him disobey and rebel against discipline. Our father, Emperor N'gatawana, had many sons and daughters with five women. It is customary for the eldest of whatever sex to succeed to the throne by undergoing the pilgrimage to the rim of the world."

Her lips creased in a sad smile. "Of course, our brothers and sisters from different mothers have disappeared, most of them under suspicious circumstances. So that's leaves only Laputara and myself."

DeFore shook her head in frustration. "That doesn't seem to bother you."

"It bothers me a great deal, Doctor." Pakari's sad smile turned into a tremble-lipped frown, as if she were about to burst into tears. DeFore realized that despite the girl's self-possessed and dignified demeanor, she was still not much more than a child. "My youngest sister was only five years old when she vanished."

Before DeFore could even formulate a response, the distant roar of many engines penetrated the hazy heat and reached through the window. The sound was underscored by a number of gunshots, including the staccato hammering of subguns.

Without a word, Pakari whirled and ran through the house, DeFore following closely behind her. The two women stood on the verandah, gazing beyond the village beneath shading hands.

"Who is it?" DeFore demanded. "Are they coming this way?"

"I'm sure it is Laputara and his followers," Pakari said calmly. "And they are definitely coming this way."

She pointed and DeFore followed her hand. She saw the first of a convoy of six vehicles topping a rise, a plume of dust behind them. The open-bed trucks were old, dating back to well before the skydark, but they looked to be in good condition.

"What will Laputara do?" asked DeFore.

"Force me to give him the Collar of Prester John and then kill me." Although her voice was uninflected, her tone held a steel edge. "If Utu has given him the courage...and the means."

As the trucks drew closer, they could see they were filled with a ragtag platoon of troopers armed with an eclectic collection of weapons—guns, long-bladed *tonga* knives and intricately carved war clubs known as knobkerries. They looked as if they had just swarmed out of the jungles and jumped onto the trucks as they jounced by, many of them half-naked with bandoliers over their ritually scarred chests. Swirls of white-and-red paint distorted their features.

Stomach muscles spasming in fear, Reba DeFore asked sharply, "Are you just going to wait for him? Won't your soldiers fight for you?"

Pakari shook his head. "He is as legal an heir to the throne as I. The Collar of Prester John will make the final decision between us, who is best suited to rule."

DeFore watched the trucks roll closer. The troopers fired their weapons into the air, but the villagers fled from them just the same. An old bull elephant, the symbol of the Waziri crown, lumbered agitatedly around a kraal at the far edge of the settlement. He extended his trunk and trumpeted a challenge.

"I don't think Laputara will go through any ritual," DeFore said in a rush. "I think he'll just take this collar of yours and go...after killing you."

"He will never find it," Pakari stated confidently. "Only Inkula knows where it is, and the oath of his priesthood is such that he will die before violating the investiture ritual."

The first truck rocked to a halt just outside the square, the brakes squealing. Four troopers jumped over the tailgate and began shouting threats at the people in the vicinity. They caught sight of Pakari and DeFore on the verandah and pointed their rifles in their direction. DeFore, due to her years in Cerberus, recognized the weapons as old Kalashnikovs and the film of sweat on her face turned cold.

"They're telling us to not to move," Pakari translated. "I'm sorry, Doctor. There is very little I or anyone else can do now, not with all those hands raised against me."

DeFore opened her mouth to respond, then shut it. At the far edge of audibility, she heard a faint, keening whine. Pakari didn't react to the noise, so she wondered if, in her fear, she was experiencing an aural hallucination. Then she saw the half-naked troopers glancing around in wonder and tilting their heads back toward the sky, squinting against the sun, their mouths gaping open in astonishment.

Following their gaze, DeFore saw, far in the distance, a pair of tiny specks, looking like new-born tadpoles swimming through a pool. She paid them no attention at first, but she absently noted how the specks appeared to grow larger between one eye blink and another.

The two specks resolved themselves into definite shapes and when DeFore recognized the delta-winged configuration, she felt her knees go weak with relief. She couldn't help but laugh, softly and shortly but with a great deal of satisfaction.

Princess Pakari whipped her head toward her, golden eyes wide with bewilderment. "Doctor—"

"It's all right," DeFore told her quietly, repressing another laugh. "Maybe you can't do anything to save us, but the three heads of Cerberus will soon be biting the bloody hell out of all those hands raised against you."

Chapter 14

The blazing glory of dawn lit up the sky with cloud mountains of flame. The navigational computers of the Mantas brought them on a direct trajectory across the sunbaked terrain of the Sudan, then over the forbidding peaks of the Jur range and within half an hour, the two craft, flying wing to wing, crossed the border into equatorial Africa.

Grant dropped the Manta's altitude to a thousand feet and cruised above a panorama of open veldt and jungled valleys. Colored by the rising sun, the valleys looked peaceful, almost bucolic. But he, Kane and Brigid knew from painful experience that jungles invariably held nasty surprises.

"Not long now," Kane's voice said in Grant's helmet. "We should be in range of DeFore's transceiver in a few minutes."

Lifting his gaze, Grant looked out beyond the prow of the Manta at the tableland spreading out beyond the tangled swamps of the Usumbur Tract. A herd of gazelles bounded in graceful unison toward a water hole. The coordinates scrolled across the inner curve of his helmet's visor and he cut back on the Manta's airspeed, reducing it to under one thousand knots.

The maximum atmospheric cruising speed for the little transatmospheric vehicle was Mach 25, but neither he nor Kane had seen the necessity to boom through the sky from the Nubian Desert to the Congo at such an air-scorching velocity.

Grant wore a bronze-colored helmet with a full-face visor. The helmet itself attached to the headrest of the pilot's chair. A pair of tubes stretched from the rear to an oxygen tank at the back of the seat. The helmet and chair were a one-piece, self-contained unit.

The two TAVs he and Kane piloted held the general shape and configuration of sea-going manta-rays, and as such they were little more than flattened wedges with wings. Sheathed in bronze-hued metal, intricate geometric designs covered almost the entire exterior surface. Deeply inscribed into the hull were interlocking swirling glyphs, cup and spiral symbols and even elaborate cuneiform markings. The composition of the hull, although it appeared to be of a burnished bronze alloy, was a material far tougher and more resilient.

The craft had no any external apparatus at all, no ailerons, no fins, and no air foils. The cockpits were almost invisible, little more than elongated symmetrical oval humps in the exact center of the sleek topside fuselages. The Manta's wingspans measured out to twenty yards from tip to tip and the fuselage was around fifteen feet long.

Inside the cockpits, the instrument panels were almost comical in their simplicity. The controls consisted primarily of a handgrip, altimeter and fuel gauges. All the labeling was in English, squares of paper taped to the appropriate controls. But the interior curve of the helmet's visor swarmed with CGI icons of sensor scopes, range-finders and various indicators.

Of Annunaki manufacture, the Mantas were in pristine condition, despite their great age. Powered by two different kinds of engines, a ramjet and solid fuel pulse detonation air spikes, the transatmospheric vehicles could fly in both a vacuum and in an atmosphere. The Mantas were not experimental craft, but an example of a technology that was mastered by a race when humanity still cowered in trees from saber-tooth tigers. Metallurgical analysis had suggested that the ships were a minimum of ten thousand years old.

Grant and Kane had easily learned to pilot the craft in the atmosphere, since they handled superficially like the Deathbird gunships the two men had flown when they were Cobaltville Magistrates. But when they first flew two of the TAVs down from the Manitius Moon colony where they had been found, there came the unsettling realization that the ships could not be piloted like winged aircraft while in space.

A pilot could select velocity, angle, attitude and other complex factors dictated by standard avionics, but space flight relied on a completely different set of principles. It called for the maximum manipulation of gravity, trajectory, relative velocities and plain old luck. Despite all the computer-calculated course programming, both men learned quickly that successfully piloting the TAV through space was more by God than by grace. But so far, the Mantas had proved to be trustworthy in all maneuvers.

"How's your leg, Grant?" Brigid asked from the small jump seat in Kane's Manta.

"You know, it still kind of hurts," Grant retorted. "Like I'd been shot in it or something. Thanks for asking."

"At least your hair isn't falling out due to rad exposure," Brigid replied unsympathetically. "We were all very lucky."

"Yeah," conceded Grant gruffly. "Again."

Neither Brigid nor Kane responded to his rejoinder. In truth, the three of them had been more than fortunate to make it down from the summit of Djebel Kif with only a few abrasions—they were blessed.

The top half of the megalith had collapsed in on itself, imploding, burying the womb of the jinn under inestimable tons of rock. The scout ship hovering overhead hadn't lingered long after the explosion, lancing off into the darkness.

Yusef and his bedouin treated them like members of their clan, forcing nearly unpalatable food and drink on them. After resting a couple of hours, they had insisted on escorting the Cerberus warriors to the landing site of the Mantas. All in all, the night's events had turned out well, despite the deaths and injuries—Cerberus now had a new set of allies in a new part of the world upon which they could call.

The sun climbed higher above the horizon and the two Mantas glided wing to wing over the Usumbur Tract, following the muddy brown ribbon of the Julaba River.

"That's odd," Brigid remarked suddenly.

"What is?" Kane asked.

"Railroad tracks down there, coming out of the swamp. I didn't notice it before, but then we didn't approach the village from this direction."

Glancing down, Kane saw how a row of thorn trees overhung a narrow strip of rusty railroad track that ran along the river's edge, effectively blocking it from view unless, like the Mantas, an observer was directly atop of them.

"So?" Kane asked. "Before skydark, I thought the main way to get around Africa was by train."

"That was over two hundred years ago," stated Brigid impatiently. "Look closer. The tracks have been maintained, the ties repaired and replaced."

"That doesn't make much sense," Kane muttered distractedly, following the twin railed path. They stretched out of sight toward the horizon. Beyond it rose a mountain.

"No response from Reba," Grant said suddenly. "Maybe she's still asleep."

Kane removed his gaze from the railroad tracks and looked in the direction of the Waziri village. Seeming to float in the air between his eyes and the visor, a column of numbers appeared, glowing red against the pale bronze. When he focused on a distant object, the visor magnified it and provided readout as to distance and dimension.

He saw cattle being herded from the settlement toward the tract and a big elephant pacing in agitation around his corral, trunk swinging wildly between the long curved tusks. Looking beyond the animals, he focused on the vehicles and running figures cordoning off the village.

"I don't think sleeping is the problem," Kane declared.

After a few seconds, Grant said, "Me neither. How do you want to handle this?"

Kane studied the guns in the hands of the troopers and noted how a quartet of them ran toward Princess Pakari's bungalow. He glimpsed both Pakari and Reba DeFore standing on the verandah.

Judging by the way the men brandished the AK-47s and from the fierce expressions on their faces, he doubted they were there to express their devotion to the princess. He saw no sign of Waziri soldiers, but their spears and elephant-hide shields would be poor defenses against automatic weapons.

"Let's try to scare these guys off first," he suggested. "If that doesn't work, we'll discourage them in a more forthright way."

"By blowing them up?" inquired Grant hopefully.

"I guess that depends on how quickly they discourage," Kane replied.

"Very diplomatic," Brigid said wryly.

Grant snorted. "We've learned from the best."

The armed, face-painted men reminded both Kane and Grant of Roamers, the outlaw nomads of the Outlands. They possessed the same semisavage, barbaric appearances but not the discipline.

As the Mantas came rushing in from the direction of the Usumbur tract, the men invading the village stopped and gaped up at the aircraft in shock. Then they bolted in all directions. A few even threw aside their rifles in wild panic.

The troopers posted on the old trucks apparently had received more stringent training. Using the high sides of the vehicles as breastworks, they set up an effective triangulated crossfire with their Kalishnikovs. The rounds couldn't penetrate the hulls of the Mantas, but the jackhammering racket of multiple impacts and the keen of ricochets quickly annoyed Grant. A flyover showed both men that all the trucks contained PRB 424 mortar launchers.

"Time to ramp up the discouragement process," Grant announced, adjusting the controls of the TAV. "Before they start shelling the village."

His Manta came screaming around in a fast, flat, crescent curve. His fingers squeezed the triggers on the handgrip and a pair of mini-Sidewinder rockets burst from the pod-sheaths under the aircraft's wings.

The missiles struck a truck dead on target. The cab and bed vanished in a double eruption of billowing orange-yellow flame. The detonations hurled bodies and pieces of metal in all directions.

Kane changed his Manta's course toward the trucks. His fingers hovered over the nose-mounted cannon's trigger on the handgrip and his helmet's HUD automatically adjusted the CGI crosshairs, superimposing them over the image of the nearest vehicle.

"This isn't exactly a fair fight, you know," Brigid pointed out sourly.

"Men with automatic rifles and mortars invading a village guarded by guys with spears doesn't meet my definition of an even playing field, either," Kane countered.

Even as he spoke the AK-47s in the hands of troopers roared in a stuttering rhythm and bullets struck the wings of his Manta with semimusical clangs. Kane achieved target acquisition and squeezed the trigger switch. A stream of the armor-piercing shells punched a cross-stitch pattern in the dirt in front of the truck. The lines of impact scampered across the ground, flinging dirt divots and fountains of dust skyward. They intersected with the rear of the truck and penetrated the fuel tank.

The vehicle was swallowed by a mushrooming yellow fireball. The other four vehicles inscribed sharp U-turns, two of them almost colliding as they went bouncing and jouncing away from the village and the burning trucks. Troopers on foot raced after them, but one man stood his ground within the swirls of smoke, glaring defiantly up at the circling Mantas.

"Where have you been?" Reba DeFore's strident question filtered into the helmets of Grant and Kane and through Brigid's Commtact. "Why didn't you call?"

"It's been a busy night," Grant replied laconically. "Besides, we thought we'd let you sleep in."

The transcomm DeFore spoke over accurately conveyed her snort of derision. "Little chance of that. If it's not the heat, it's the bugs and if it's not the bugs, it's Pakari's crazy half brother, Prince Laputara. That's him standing out there, by the way."

Kane asked, "Does she want us to sever their familial connection?"

In agitation, DeFore exclaimed, "That's the last thing she wants! If you did, you'd only make things worse."

"What things?" demanded Brigid.

"We'll explain as soon you land."

"That would be nice," Grant growled. "Some breakfast would be, too."

"We'll see," DeFore retorted.

Engaging the vectored-thrust ramjets, Kane and Grant dropped their Mantas straight down and gracefully brought them to rest on the extended tripod landing gear. Fine clouds of dust puffed up all around.

The two men opened the seals of their helmets and unlatched the cockpit canopies. Sliding them back, they made wordless utterances of dismay at the stifling heat and cloying humidity. After first shedding their field jackets, Grant, Kane and Brigid climbed out of the TAVs, sliding down the wings to the ground. They stood shoulder to shoulder between the two ships as a big man strode fearlessly through the smoke and the sifting dust clouds.

Prince Laputara stood six feet five inches tall, naked to the waist except for crisscrossing cartridge bandoliers across his broad, scarred chest. He looked enormous, stripped down to bare muscle and sinew, exuding an aura of physical power that struck all three people like a blow and as a challenge.

He wore green fatigue military pants and high-laced combat boots. A headband bearing the gilded tip of an elephant's tusk encircled his head. The accessory looked almost ridiculously out of place. He carried an AK-47 in one hand and a double-edged *tonga* short sword in the other. The weapons fit perfectly with the rest of his ensemble. His features were regal, haughty and cruel.

Pointing the *tonga* at them one at a time, Laputara intoned grimly in English, "Kane. Baptiste. Grant. Enemies of my god and enemies of me...and therefore enemies of the Waziri people. You intervened in matters that concern only the Waziri royal family, an offense that cannot be forgiven. I command the three of you to bow and offer me your necks for immediate execution."

Chapter 15

"I'd say that bit dates back to the very first spoiled-brat god-king," Kane speculated aloud to Grant and Brigid.

"The 'bow-yield-kneel-let-me-kill-you' bit?" Grant inquired. "Yeah, it has some mold on it, all right."

"Maybe he's got a nice little twist to it," Brigid suggested.

Kane eyed Prince Laputara critically, as if he were examining a malfunctioning machine. Then he said, "Nope, I don't think so."

"Oh, nuts," Brigid muttered in mock disappointment, sliding a pair of sunglasses onto her face.

Laputara's dark eyes flicked back and forth between their faces, his nostrils flaring like those of a maddened bull. He took half a step forward, raising his *tonga.* Grant stiffened his wrist tendons and the Sin Eater slapped solidly into his palm, his index finger depressing the trigger stud.

The single shot struck the blade of the short sword at midpoint, shattering it with a sharp chime. Half of the length of steel fell to the dust at his feet. Laputara staggered back, eyes wide, blood starting from a shallow laceration on his right cheek where a sliver of metal had nicked him.

He stared in wonder at the broken sword in his hand, then rage distorted his face. He hurled the useless hilt to the ground. Lips peeling back from his teeth, he snarled, "You dare—"

"We *all* dare," Kane broke in coldly, his own Sin Eater sliding into his hand. "And if you're a follower of Utu, that makes you our enemy. So you'd better get real busy convincing us why we should keep you alive."

Laputara's eyes seethed with hatred and his body trembled violently in the grip of a homicidal impulse. Slowly he began to bring his AK-47 to bear, swinging it around.

"That's not how to convince us to do much of anything," Grant warned, training the bore of his pistol on the center of the young man's broad chest. "Except to drop your ass dead."

Laputara continued to raise the rifle.

"Impulse control," Kane commented. "That's your problem. But if you don't stop moving, we'll cure you of it—permanently."

"Akifu!" cried a strident female voice. "Stop!"

Laputara's swiveled his head to the right and though he didn't drop the automatic rifle, he lowered it. The Cerberus warriors turned to see Princess Pakari and Reba DeFore approaching through the wisps of smoke. They were followed by a trio of spear-brandishing soldiers.

Laputara and Pakari exchanged a rapid-fire flurry of angry Swahili, then Pakari held up a peremptory hand. *"Basi!* Enough!"

Laputara glowered at her. "Only I have the right make that decision, little half sister."

"You have no more rights than I."

Tapping the elephant tusk with a forefinger, the big man snapped, "This gives me the right."

Pakari uttered a scoffing laugh. "I have a duplicate of the crown in my room. Just because you choose to wear yours when you act like a common thug doesn't make you a king—it makes you a common thug masquerading as a king. Why should I not treat you as a thug?"

"You don't dare." Laputara nodded toward the spear-brandishing soldiers. "They would not obey your orders to harm me. They are bound by tradition to serve the royal house of the Waziri."

"Maybe not," Grant remarked conversationally. "But we're not bound by tradition. As far as we're concerned, you're an ally of an enemy and that makes you a fair target."

Laputara didn't respond, but indecision, even fear flickered briefly in his eyes. Pakari stepped forward, the expression on her face softening. Beseechingly she said, "Brother, our people are one. To survive, they must remain as one and it is our duty to bind them together, not divide them. We cannot allow our individual ambitions or the machinations of a trickster to drive a wedge between the Waziri who follow you and those who follow me.

"You and I must join one another in common cause, or the Waziri nation will drown in the blood spilled in a struggle between son and father, mother and daughter, sister and brother."

Staring unblinkingly at Pakari, Laputara seemed as

if he seriously considered the girl's words. "And what of the Great Snake, the Collar of Prester John? Only one of us may wear it on the pilgrimage."

"The high priest Inkula will decide that," Pakari replied. "As has been our people's tradition for hundreds of years when there are two equal contenders to the Elephant Throne."

Laputara's dark features contorted in angry contempt. "That has never happened before now! It's a scheme, a conspiracy! Inkula has always favored you so how can he be an impartial judge?"

"But Lord Utu can be trusted?" Pakari countered. "An outsider, an alien—"

"A *god!*" Laputara roared. "Utu is the ancient god of our people, of all of Africa! He has shown me visions of how it was long ago, when the Waziri and the Zulu conquered all the tribes between here and the sea! With Utu's help, with me on the throne, we will again form a mighty army and will sweep forth upon the world like a pride of lions to restore our glory!"

An extended silence followed Laputara's furious pronouncement. Then Kane said mildly, "Princess, what would happen if I just put a bullet through that asshole's head?"

He extended his Sin Eater toward the young man. "Utu wouldn't have a pawn, you'd have the Waziri throne and the rest of us could go on back to the cool mountain breezes of Montana. What's the worst that could happen?"

Laputara gaped at him, astonished into speechlessness. Pakari said sadly, "Kane, I would have no choice but

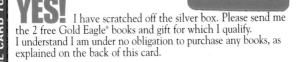

The Gold Eagle Reader Service™ — Here's how it works:

Accepting your 2 free books and mystery gift places you under no obligation to buy anything. You may keep the books and gift and return the shipping statement marked "cancel." If you do not cancel, about a month later we'll send you 6 additional books and bill you just $29.94* — that's a savings of over 10% off the cover price of all 6 books! And there's no extra charge for shipping! You may cancel at any time, but if you choose to continue, every other month we'll send you 6 more books, which you may either purchase at the discount price or return to us and cancel your subscription.

*Terms and prices subject to change without notice. Sales tax applicable in N.Y. Canadian residents will be charged applicable provincial taxes and GST. Credit or debit balances in a customer's account(s) may be offset by any other outstanding balance owed by or to the customer.

to order you to be put to death. Regardless of his plans, Laputara is a Waziri prince, as legitimate a royal heir as I. Custom forces me to avenge all wrongs inflicted on members of the royal family—despite how richly they may deserve them."

Laputara regarded the outlanders and Pakari from beneath lowered brows. An expression of paranoiac anger crossed his face. His massive chest rose and fell as he fought to control himself. Kane didn't lower the Sin Eater. He waited for the young man to make a violent move either against him or the princess.

Then all at once, Laputara began to laugh softly, almost to himself as he glared at Kane then at his half sister. "All right, you've got me now. We can settle up later. You'd better prepare for it. None of you have much time."

The big man turned smartly on his heel and marched away, back toward the veldt where his trucks had fled. Within moments, the smoke from the burning vehicles swallowed his form.

No one spoke for a long moment, then DeFore asked, "Didn't somebody say something about breakfast?"

Staring into the smoke, Brigid said softly, "I think I've lost my appetite."

INSIDE THE BUNGALOW, Princess Pakari ordered her soldiers to make sure Laputara and his troopers withdrew completely from the vicinity of the village. DeFore and her three friends quickly exchanged stories. The four of them sat cross-legged on the floor around a low table next to an open window.

DeFore insisted on examining Grant's leg wound. Pakari fetched DeFore's medical kit from her room and assisted her as she applied a fresh dressing. Grant affected not to notice the young woman's attention, although Brigid and Kane exchanged raised eyebrows.

When she was done, DeFore smiled at Brigid approvingly. "You did great."

"I had a good teacher," Brigid replied.

A servant entered, placing small dishes of sliced groundnut bread and *m'bazzi* peas on the table, as well as cups of cold fruit tea. The repast was intentionally light, due to the oppressive heat. Pakari handed Grant a cup of the tea, permitting the others to help themselves.

"Utu was there, in the Sudan?" DeFore asked, sipping at the sweet, slightly acidic beverage. "He really gets around."

Grant shrugged. "Those scout ships are pretty damn fast."

"I don't mean that," the medic said irritably. "What does he have going on here on African continent? Do we know anything about Utu?"

"He used to be Baron Snakefish, if that's any help," Kane interposed.

DeFore sighed. "I mean as an Annunaki overlord."

Chewing a piece of banana bread, Brigid said, "Utu was among the top pantheon of Sumerian gods, a member of the royal family. He was the twin brother and rival of Inanna, a civilizing goddess, also known as Ishtar. Utu was often confused with Shamash, the Akkadian sun god, but who as we know is also one of the nine overlords.

"According to myth, Utu visited the underworld

once a month during the waning of the new Moon where he judged the souls of mortals. He traveled through the sky in his silver chariot, drawn by four elemental forces. He was also something of the armorer of the Annunaki. That role corresponds roughly with Hephaestus in the Greek pantheon, who acted as the weapons forger for the gods of Olympus."

Kane nodded. "Even Enlil said Utu was a genius in all things mechanical."

DeFore frowned thoughtfully. "When I talked to Lakesh a few hours ago, he said something about Cerberus having an infestation of metal spiders."

Brigid angled a quizzical eyebrow at her. "What did he mean by that?"

DeFore shook her head. "He didn't elaborate and I was too hot and worried about you three to ask much about it. He told me the problem was solved, though. You can call him later and get the details."

"I wouldn't be surprised to find out that Utu was responsible," remarked Grant.

"Me, either," Kane agreed. "It's my guess he's going around digging up things here in his former estate that might be of use to him in the future. The overlords might not be at each other's throats right now, but territorial disputes are sure to start."

Princess Pakari spoke for the first time since entering the bungalow with them. Apologetically, she said, "Even though you told me about Utu when you arrived here days ago, I confess I don't understand. You say he is a fake, an imposter, yet now you speak of him as though he actually were a god. Which is it?"

The outlanders all exchanged questioning looks. Finally Grant rumbled, "It's a little of both, actually. I'm not even sure if I understand the whole deal. It's complicated."

"Why does he claim to be the god of Africa?" Pakari asked.

"More than likely," replied Brigid, "he was worshipped as Butu, a Zulu sky deity. But at this juncture, it's far more relevant to learn why Utu is fixated on an artifact that most historians assumed was completely legendary."

Pakari smiled wanly. "I can assure you the Collar of Prester John is anything but."

"You can show it to us?" Kane inquired.

Pakari hesitated. "High priest Inkula is its guardian. He might be persuaded to allow you to look upon it."

DeFore gestured toward the quarters she had been given. "We can always uplink to the satellite and download the data Cerberus sent about Prester John."

"Who the hell is this Prester John?" Grant demanded.

Pakari rose from the floor in one smooth motion. "High priest Inkula can tell you that, too. Let me find out if he will receive us."

Out of courtesy and respect for her title, the outlanders rose, too, but Kane asked, "Can't you just command him to do a little show and tell for our benefit?"

Princess Pakari stared at him wide-eyed, scandalized by the suggestion, then said quietly, but with a great deal of disapproval, "There is much you must learn about us, *wageni*."

Kane couldn't be sure, but he assumed Pakari used the native term for ignorant outlander.

Chapter 16

Inkula looked so ancient that he could have passed for one of the telekinetically animated mummies the Cerberus warriors had encountered in the city of Aten the year before. His bearded brown face was dry, weathered, deeply inscribed with wrinkles. His blind eyes were equally ancient in their wisdom.

"We may dispense with the formalities," he said in a reedy but forceful voice. "And get to the point."

"Dispensing with the formalities is always our first choice, too," Kane muttered inanely.

Inkula inclined his head in his direction. "Yes, I received that impression about you when we first met."

The high priest sat on a wicker stool, his thin body wrapped in a bright orange robe beneath a leopard-skin pelt resting on his downsloping shoulders. His gnarled hands held a long staff of black wood. It was crawling with engravings, topped by a carved elephant's head. The end resting on the floor tapered to a sharp point.

Behind Inkula stood three soldiers, as immobile as the life-size wooden sculptures of ebony and mahogany warriors positioned around the beehive-shaped hut. A number of relics were scattered about, from crossed elephant tusks to water buffalo horns. Mounted on a pedestal between the upright tusks was a gleaming, three-foot-long scale model of an old steam locomotive.

Decorated with yellow lightning stripes, the number 88 was emblazoned in scarlet on the side of the engine. All the brass parts from the drivers to the rods to the rivet heads shone with a bright polish. It seemed a very strange objet d'art to find in an African witch-doctor's hut.

A young girl turned the crank of a rope-and-pulley assembly connected to a ceiling fan directly above In-kula. The big flat blades turned sluggishly, only stirring the air, not cooling it off. The range of temperature they had encountered so far varied from very warm to very hot to sickeningly hot, so Kane felt justified in mopping his sweat-drenched face with a scrap of cloth he picked up from a table.

Princess Pakari knelt beside the old man, putting a hand on his arm. Softly, she said, "Your holiness, can you tell our friends about Prester John?"

Inkula's milky, sightless eyes blinked. "They do not know of him?"

"We know the legends," Brigid said. "That Prester John founded a great Christian empire here in Africa in the twelfth century. He was a European who became a great military leader and established a nation that en-compassed the frontiers of India and stretched to the headwaters of the White Nile. But in our land, Prester John is dismissed as only a myth."

Inkula waved his arms in an expansive gesture. "But not here. In Africa, the past has hardly stopped breath-ing. Sit, and we will speak."

The four people looked around and saw only cushions covered in zebra hide on the floor. Carefully they sank down onto them. Grant's knee joints popped and he uttered an embarrassed curse under his breath.

Inkula declared in a challenging tone, "Yes, you know part of the story, but like all Americans, knowing only a little has not stopped you from involving yourselves in the affairs of other cultures."

Kane scowled and a profanity leaped unbidden to the tip of his tongue. Before it could leave his mouth, Pakari leaned over and whispered urgently in the old man's ear.

With a sigh, Inkula said, "I have been informed that all of you have earned the respect of my princess and therefore the friendship of the Waziri nation. So I will tell you all that I know, a story handed down from priest to priest for nearly a thousand years.

"Prester John conquered the monarchs of Merdia, Persia and Samiardi, emerging victorious from a terrible battle that lasted three days, but ended with his conquest of Abyssinia. After that, he and his armies started for Jerusalem to rescue the Holy Land, but the swollen waters of the Tigris compelled him to return to Abyssinia. Or so our legends would have it."

Brigid said, "Most of the legends actually began in Europe. Around 1165, copies of a letter purporting to be written by Prester John to the Holy Roman Emperor Manuel began circulating through Italy, Spain and Portugal. This letter claimed that Prester John was the greatest monarch under heaven, as well as a devout Christian. That was a very odd combination for an African king."

Inkula nodded his bald head. "A European he was by birth, but Prester John belonged to the race of the three Magi who paid homage to the newborn Christ, their former kingdoms being subject to him. Prester John's enormous wealth was demonstrated by the fact that he carried a scepter of pure emeralds.

"His empire extended over the three Indias, including that of Fartherest India, where lay the body of Saint Thomas, and back again down to the ruins of Babylon and the tower of Babel. All the wild beasts and monstrous creatures commemorated in legend could be found in his dominions, as well as all the wild and eccentric races of men of whom strange stories were told, like the centaurs and Cyclops."

Kane only half listened, distracted by sweat stinging his eyes and the growing desire for an iced drink of some kind.

"Prester John's territories contained the monstrous ants that dug gold and the rivers that flowed into the Fountain of Youth," Inkula went on. "There were pebbles that gave light, restored sight and rendered the possessor invisible."

Kane and Grant repressed groans of impatience, not just with Inkula's long-windedness, but with the rapt expressions on the faces of Reba DeFore and Brigid Baptiste.

"There were no poor in his dominions," Inkula said proudly, "no thief or robber, no flatterer or miser, no dissensions, no lies and no vices. His palace was enormous, built after the plan of that which Saint Thomas erected for the Indian king Gondopharus. Before it was a marvelous mirror erected on a many-storied pedestal. It was called a *speculumin* and in it Prester John could discern everything that went on throughout his dominions and detect conspiracies.

"There was another, smaller palace, but still of wonderful character. In that, balanced on the rim of the world and guarded by an army of ferocious apes, Prester John pent up his treasures."

Kane asked, "What kind of treasures?"

Inkula smiled. "Instruments, devices. A devout Christian he was, but Prester John also had an interest in a new art known as science. He would not have been able to rule over his enormous dominions if he had not possessed certain instruments."

DeFore ventured, "Like the collar, the Great Snake?"

Inkula nodded. "And Prester John's Mirror. The collar and the mirror were important parts of the emperor's control of his country. When these were lost, his empire fell."

Grant frowned. "Lost? Or stolen?"

Inkula tugged at his beard. "Who can say, *wageni?* But many nations sprang up in the shadow of Prester John's empire. Six hundred years ago, the chief native power was in the hands of the Zulu tribe. Then the Mazimba and the Waziri came down from the Lake Nyassa quarter, and together all of them built a strong kingdom in Manicaland.

"The thing to remember is that all these little empires thought themselves the successors of Prester John. They all worshipped a great white king in the north, whom they called by twenty different names. They had forgotten about his Christianity, but they remembered that he was a conqueror. The Waziri and the Zulu revered the story of Prester John, but by this time it had ceased to be a historical memory, and had become a religious cult of zealots."

Kane swallowed a sigh, although he wasn't surprised to hear about a religion springing up around a legend. He hated dealing with people whose spirituality had turned down the path of fanaticism.

"They worshipped a great power," Inkula continued, "who had been their ancestor, and the favorite Zulu word for him was *umkulunkulu*. The belief was perverted into many different forms, but this was the central creed—that Umkulunkulu had been the father of the tribe, and was alive as a spirit to watch over them.

"But it was more than a creed with the Zulu and the Waziri. Somehow or another, a fetish had descended from Prester John by way of the Mazimba folk. Always it was in the hands of the tribe, which for the moment held the leadership, passing from the Zulu to the Waziri to Zambesi. The great tribal wars of the sixteenth century were not struggles for territory but for leadership, the possession of this fetish."

"I presume you mean the collar," DeFore said.

Inkula nodded. "When it fell into the hands of the Zulu, they called it Ndhlondhlo, which means the Great Snake, but of course it wasn't any kind of snake."

"Of course," murmured Brigid. "The snake was the Zulu tribal totem and so they would naturally name their most sacred possession after it."

"Have you have heard of Shaka?" Inkula asked.

"Yes," Brigid answered. "He was a sort of native Napoleon early in the nineteenth century. He made the Zulu the paramount power in South Africa, slaughtering about two million people to accomplish it."

"He had the Collar of Prester John," Inkula stated. "And it was believed that he owed his conquests to it. The Zambesi and the Cetewayo tried to steal it lest Shaka destroy their tribes. But upon Shaka's assassination, it disappeared. The collar was gone out of existence, and with it the chance of a single African empire."

"Except," Grant said quietly, "the Waziri had it all along."

A thin smile stretched the old man's lips. "My people did not use it as Shaka had. We hid it from those who wished to repeat Shaka's atrocities. The Waziri were scattered and divided, but we have long memories. Even in the nineteenth and twentieth centuries, when the influence of the British, the Europeans and the Americans reached across Africa, we told the story of Prester John and his miraculous collar and his mysterious mirror."

Inkula stopped speaking and an expectant silence fell over the hut. After waiting a moment, Kane cleared his throat and asked, "Okay, I'll be the straight man. What's so miraculous about the collar and so mysterious about the mirror?"

"No one really knows," Inkula stated matter-of-factly. "We have only folk-tales. Myths."

"I thought that was what we've been listening to for the past five minutes," rumbled Grant, shifting position on the cushion.

Inkula turned his face toward him. His milky eyes chilled Grant's blood and he almost looked away. In a soft tone barely above a whisper, the priest said, "There are myths that are so ancient that they spawn hundreds of other myths, like a flower spreads seeds. The truth is a mixture of reality and legend, fear and veneration."

"What's the real stuff?" Kane demanded tersely. "Where did the collar and the mirror come from?"

"I distinctly heard Utu take credit for making the collar," DeFore interposed.

Inkula's lips twisted as if he tasted something sour. "Perhaps he fashioned it, but he did not supply the materials."

"Which were what?" asked Brigid.

"Stones," Inkula answered. "Jewels. Flawless rubies to be exact, fifty-five of them. But I don't think they are really rubies."

"Why not?" Pakari asked, her golden eyes troubled. "You think the collar is a fake?"

"No, my child. But nor is it what it appears to be, either. Legend and even reality agree that several thousand years ago a meteor or perhaps even a comet exploded above central Africa. Pieces of it were found all over the land and it became known by many names—the Kala, the Shining Trapezohedron, the Chintamani Stone even the Messiah or Godstone."

Brigid, Grant, Kane and DeFore all stiffened as Inkula spoke, swiftly exchanging startled glances with one another. Pakari noticed their reaction but didn't interrupt the old man.

"The Christian Bible even makes reference to it," he continued. "The prophet Zechariah refers to a holy stone that will transform man into messiah. The ancient rabbis claimed a fragment of this stone occupied a place in the Ark of the Covenant. Even King Solomon was said to have had a piece of the stone set into a ring."

"What was so special about these pieces of meteorite?" asked Brigid.

Inkula sighed. "The stones are reputed to endow their bearer with extraordinary powers of influence over the minds of people. With them, perhaps in tandem with Prester John's mirror, which is also alleged to have been made from the meteor, a person develops the power to bend the will of others."

Brigid said noncommittally, "There have been other such objects throughout history with powers like those attributed to the stones. The rings of Solomon and Genghis Khan come to mind."

"Perhaps so," Inkula said. "But Pakari and Laputara's father and my good friend Emperor N'gatawana investigated the myths, the fables. He came to believe that a cult of Waziri wise men collected all the largest pieces of the meteor that had fallen in Africa. They hid them in a valley that became known as Ophir.

"At least three thousand years ago, the pieces were stolen and made into a collar, a necklace of sorts. Many men wore it, conquerors, god-kings, mighty men of old from Gilgamesh to Alexander to even a white barbarian named Arturus. Each one tried to exert control over the entire ancient world and each one, after achieving some success, met an ignoble end."

Inkula's lips stretched in a patronizing smile. "But I

don't expect *wageni,* Americans at that, to believe in the power of an object no one but a handful of superstitious witch doctors have seen in many hundreds of years. If you cannot see, feel, touch or taste an object, then you reject any other attributes of that object. You have been conditioned to be materialists."

Pakari squeezed the old man's wrist, saying reprovingly, "Hush! They are our honored guests."

"They are guests, perhaps," Inkula said coldly. "It remains to be proved if they should be honored."

Shaking her head in exasperation, Princess Pakari turned toward the Cerberus people and said, "I apologize for Inkula. He is a great man, but he tends to draw premature conclusions. He thinks you are just humoring an old man in his fantasies."

Brigid chuckled, not sounding the least bit offended. Casting a sideways glance toward Kane, she replied, "Inkula is not the only man here who suffers from that malady. But it might surprise him how much we *do* believe in the power of an object nobody has seen in hundreds of years."

Inkula's sparse gray eyebrows rose. "How so?"

Brigid jerked a thumb toward Kane. "Because Kane here not only handled some pieces of the so-called Messiah stone—"

"I chucked them over a cliff," Kane broke in loudly, proudly.

Inkula's mouth gaped open in astonishment. "Over a cliff?"

Kane grinned at the astounded expression on the priest's face. "And I'd do it again, you sour old bastard."

Inkula stared in his direction, and although his seamed, chocolate-brown face showed no emotion, he was obviously struggling to accept Kane's pronouncement as truth. At length, he said calmly, "Then we have much to discuss...honored guests."

Chapter 17

The atmosphere in the little hut became less formal as the antagonistic energy between Inkula and the four outlanders abated.

Feeling his way with his staff, the priest and the little servant girl fetched tea and sesame sweetbreads for their guests. While they were so occupied, Kane and Grant rose from the floor to stretch their legs and look around the interior of the hut.

"I think it's pretty obvious what Utu's connection is to the Collar and Mirror of Prester John," Brigid said.

"Same old routine, sounds like," stated Grant. "Giving humans some technological toys to go out and do the Annunaki's bidding so they don't have to get their own hands dirty—or bloody."

"Technological?" Pakari inquired. "I thought we were talking about rocks or jewels."

"If the rubies in the collar are fragments of the Shining Trapezohedron," Brigid replied, "then they're not exactly rocks, either."

Kane smiled crookedly. "We never did figure out what the trapezohedron actually was."

Brigid matched his smile with a rueful one of her own. "No, we didn't. And more is the pity."

A couple of years ago, the Cerberus warriors had become embroiled in a plot to use an ancient Archon artifact to alter the very fabric of reality. The artifact had been known by many names, by many peoples in civilizations both primitive and advanced—Lucifer's Stone, the Kala, the Kaa'ba, the Chintamani Stone, the Shining Trapezohedron.

During the course of the adventure, Brigid learned that many different cultures separated by time and distance venerated certain kinds of stones, particularly if they were of celestial origin. Apocryphal religious texts told of Lucifer falling from the sky bearing a black stone that was split into fragments and scattered among humanity.

Ancient Amazonian legends related that the god Tivra built an altar on an island in Lake Titicaca to hold three holy stones called the Kala. In Hungary, a black monolith was worshipped by the backward villagers, and stones with supernatural properties were written about in ancient manuscripts from the Arabic Kitab al-Azif to the Ponape Scriptures of the South Seas.

Buddhist and Taoists legends spoke of the Chintamani Stone, alleged to have fallen from the star system of Sirius. The texts claimed that "when the Son of the Sun descended upon Earth to teach mankind, there fell from heaven a shield that bore the power of the world."

Only a short time before they had come across the *tai-me,* which seemed to be the Native American equivalent of a fragment of the Chintamani Stone.

Always the stone had been associated with the concept of a key that unlocked either the door to enlightenment or madness. It had served as the spiritual centerpiece of the race they had known as the Archons, even after it had been fragmented and the facets scattered from one end of the Earth to the other.

According to Balam, the last of his ancient people, the trapezohedron allowed glimpses of all possible futures to which their activities might lead.

But the stone was far more than a calculating device that extrapolated outcomes from actions. Balam had said, "It brings into existence those outcomes."

He had referred to the stone as a channel to "sidereal space," where many tangential points of reality lay adjacent to each other, the parallel casements of the universe, a multitude of realities co-existing with their own.

The tests performed on the pieces of the stone in the possession of Cerberus yielded inconclusive results. Lakesh had suggested that the artifact was a probability-wave packet, a mathematical equation in physical form that formed an interface between their universe and others.

Pakari took a tray from the servant and offered slices of fruit to Grant. "You lead very interesting lives in America," she said.

Picking up a chunk of melon and eyeing it critically, he grunted dourly, "Yeah, that's one way of putting it. I don't think 'interesting' would be the word I'd choose."

Kane repressed a smile at Grant's tone. Unlike him, Grant had not freely chosen the life of an exile, an insurrectionist. He had sacrificed everything that gave his life a degree of purpose to help Kane and Brigid escape from Cobaltville. Even after all the time that had elapsed since that day, Kane still felt responsible for what the man had given up and what he had suffered since then in the war against the hybrid barons.

But old habits died very hard. Kane and Grant had been partners for nearly fifteen years, and it was part and parcel of Magistrate Division conditioning to always back a partner's play.

When Kane, Brigid, Grant and the Cerberus exiles declared war on the dark forces devoted to maintaining the yoke of slavery around the collective necks of humankind, it was a struggle not just for the physical survival of humanity, but for the human spirit, the soul of an entire race.

Over the past few years, they had scored many victories, defeated many enemies and solved mysteries of the past that molded the present and affected the future. More importantly, they began to rekindle of the spark of hope within the breasts of the disenfranchised fighting to survive in the Outlands.

Kane paused in his pacing to scrutinize the model of the locomotive resting on a shelf.

"What's with the choo-choo?" Kane asked, prodding the miniature bell with a forefinger. It gave forth a feeble chime.

Inkula's staff darted out, the carved elephant's head rapping Kane's knuckles. "Don't touch that! It was a gift from Emperor N'gatawana himself."

Kane recoiled, massaging his hand. "Sorry," he

snapped angrily. "I didn't know this was your favorite toy."

"Old 88 is not a toy," Inkula stated with equal heat. "It is a work of art built by Emperor N'gatawana's own hands."

"He was a train fancier?" Brigid asked, shooting Kane an icy glare that meant she expected him to be on his diplomatic best.

Pakari nodded, her full lips creasing in a reverential smile. "My father was a fancier of many things, particularly mechanical marvels made in the predark. He had the gift."

"Emperor N'gatawana was a brilliant man," Inkula said. "He was voracious in his curiosities. He sought to learn all about the world, before and after the skies grew dark. Science, engineering, politics and religion— all of them fascinated him. He was particularly fascinated by Americans, believing them to be heroic but foolish, well-meaning but deluded, magnificent in their dreams but flawed in their spirits."

None of the Cerberus people responded.

"It was the Americans who built Old 88, you see," Inkula continued as if by rote. "Back in 1888. Built by Pittsburgh and Western, consolidation type, a 4-4-4. The emperor thought Old 88 to be a masterpiece of engineering, a work of art. When he found her on a yard near Stanley Falls many years ago, restoring her became his life's work."

Kane flicked his gaze from the model to Inkula's face. Dubiously he asked, "He rebuilt a three-hundred-year-old steam locomotive?"

"He did indeed."

"Why? Occupational therapy?"

"Hardly," Inkula retorted. "It was the emperor's contribution to the ritual of choosing a ruler. He felt the pilgrimage to the rim of the world should not be one of suffering a long trek on foot, but should be a joyous procession, with whistles blowing and bells ringing."

"If my father had one regret in his life, it was that he did not live long enough to pilot the first pilgrimage of Old 88," Princess Pakari said.

Brigid's eyes widened. "Are you saying this train is functional?"

Inkula shrugged. "We have no idea. It has never been tested since the emperor joined his ancestors three years ago. But I think we should do so in the near future…certainly before the Moon wanes."

"And Utu returns," DeFore stated grimly.

"Can you show us Old 88?" Grant asked.

"I'd rather take a look at the Collar of Prester John," Brigid put in. "That seems a bit more relevant."

Inkula turned toward her, lips stretching in a patronizing smile. "The collar and Old 88 are now as one."

Brigid gazed at the old man, perplexed. "I don't understand."

Inkula beckoned to her with a forefinger. "Come."

THE JUNGLE ERUPTED in a cacophony of squawks and squalls. Birds and monkeys expressed noisy outrage at the invaders.

"I don't think they appreciate us being here," Pakari murmured, gazing up at the vine-draped trees.

"I know how they feel," Kane muttered, slapping at a winged bug that landed on the back of his neck.

The tangled forest of the Usumbur Tract closed in on them with every yard of the path they walked. Kane would not have been surprised to actually see the vines and branches growing, reaching out to engulf them. The trail they followed was almost completely swallowed by the mass of green growth, but no one complained, not even DeFore.

Inkula led the way unerringly through the foliage although Kane and Grant's senses were on full alert for any signs of poisonous snakes, spiders or scorpions. Neither man retained fond memories of the other jungles and swamps they had traipsed through. Deadly vermin always seemed to lie in wait for intruders.

When Grant cursed and struck at a stinging insect on his arm, Pakari turned toward him. "Are you all right?" she asked, her expression and tone very solicitous.

Grant shrugged. "I guess the bugs hereabout prefer dark meat. But they don't seem interested in you or Inkula."

"I'll show you why." She broke off the stem of a hanging plant and squeezed out a pale green fluid into the palm of her hand.

Vigorously she rubbed her hands together for a few seconds, then swept them both over Grant's face and neck. She kept her eyes fixed on his all the while, saying softly, "This should bring some relief."

DeFore fanned the air in front of her face and walked around them. "I wish I'd thought to bring insect repellant."

With slow, languorous motions, Pakari applied a film of the juice to Grant's arms. "There is a lot of you to cover," she commented with a sly smile. "You are very much like N'gatawana."

Too hot and bug bit to care if he seemed rude, Kane reached around the princess and snapped off a stem from the same plant. He imitated her actions, spreading the fluid onto his face.

In response to a questioning look from her, he said curtly, "Sorry, but the bugs here seem to have a liking for my blood, too, the color of the packaging notwithstanding."

As he handed the stems to Brigid, he caught the brief, embarrassed eye play between Grant and Pakari, but he wasn't sure who looked the most uncomfortable. The girl was very pretty, but she was probably no older than eighteen.

Brigid applied the juice to her arms and face as they continued walking. The terrain became marshy, the air beginning to smell of swamp gas. Every step squished under their feet and released more of the vile rotten-egg odor.

Inkula led them carefully, testing the ground ahead with the tapered tip of his elephant-head staff. The sun blazed yellowly in the sky as it inched toward its zenith. The tract steamed in the noonday heat, the bright light glimmering from the surface of a sluggishly flowing stream. Crocodiles basking on its muddy banks caught sight of them and skidded into the water.

The six people entered a tunnel of trees, walking a path beneath intertwined boughs and branches. The brilliant sunlight was reduced to a dim flicker between the leafy limbs high overhead. Monkeys chattered among them.

Then through the screen of underbrush, Kane spotted a metallic glint. Clearing his sweat-stung eyes with his fingers, he saw a long, tall structure made of corrugated tin, almost completely covered by vines and creepers. The building had no walls, only support beams and a slanting roof. Beneath it, a gigantic black object loomed.

Inkula cast a toothless grin over his shoulder at Kane and gestured with the elephant head. "Old 88."

Chapter 18

The ancient locomotive stood in the shadows of the cavernous hut, the giant wheels overgrown by weeds, black coachwork rust pitted but awesome in its size. From the tip of the cowcatcher to the rear wall of the cab housing, the machine measured twenty-five feet. The red-and-gold paint that had once inscribed lightning bolts on the boiler had long ago peeled away.

The high smokestack, shrouded by flowering vines, almost protruded through the slanted roof of the hut. The number 88 was inscribed on a brass plate below the headlight. The engine reminded the outlanders of a slumbering prehistoric beast, a behemoth of black cast-iron skin and heavy brass bones.

Kane and Grant looked into the cab, noting that the pilot wheel was in good condition as were the pressure gauges and the throttle, even though the glass covers were scratched and dirty. The interior smelled of hot metal and scorched oil, touching off memories in both men of their first encounter with Titano, the old mobile command post appropriated by their Lakota allies. But the locomotive looked in far better shape, even though it was at least a century older than the MCP.

"Quite the toy," Kane said.

Inkula's bony hands tightened in anger around the staff and Pakari glared at him, but neither of them objected to his casual label.

A passenger carriage was coupled to the fuel tender behind the engine, an open affair with twin rows of chairs, six to a side, and a surrey roof of tasseled canvas to keep off the sun and the rain.

Brigid examined the huge driver wheels, the pistons and the narrow-gauge tracks that stretched out from under the cowcatcher to disappear into the undergrowth. "Emperor N'gatawana went to a lot of trouble over this."

Pakari nodded. "He was very proud of how he restored Old 88. She has seventeen-by-twenty-inch cylinders and sixty-six-inch drivers, a wagon-top boiler and an extended front end. My father was a master mechanic. He completely overhauled her, put on a new stack and built all new water-injection valves."

"What about the rail line?" Grant asked, scraping away dried mud from one of the wooden ties with the toe of a boot. "Your old man didn't lay it down, did he?"

Pakari shook her head. "Most of it was already there, but my father cleared it, repaired the tracks and the ties."

DeFore dabbed at the perspiration beading on her upper lip. "What purpose did Old 88 serve before the skydark?"

"She used to make weekly runs from the copper mines in Jukiwati to Nairobi," Inkula stated. "The emperor often said she was a marvelous machine and would still be running, three hundred years later, if she hadn't been neglected for so long."

Favoring his injured leg, Grant pulled himself up

into the cab and experimentally tugged at the brake lever and the wheel. He inspected the firebox, the steam chest and the fuel tender. DeFore stood up on tiptoes, peering in. "What do you think?"

"About what?" he asked.

"Can this thing run?"

Grant shook his head. "I have no idea. It looks like it was built to last, but I don't know jack-shit about trains or steam engines." He glanced over at Brigid. "What about you?"

She shrugged. "The study of steam locomotives isn't really my area of expertise. They were obsolete by the mid-twentieth century. I'm not even up on the actual operational theory."

Pakari announced in a clear tone, "A Greek engineer of about the third century, Hero of Alexandria, developed the first form of a steam engine—a turbine called an aeolipile. It wasn't until the 1600s that a practical, although primitive, reciprocal steam engine was built. However, the first man to put a steam engine to industrial use was Thomas Newcomen of England, in the early eighteenth century."

All eyes turned toward her and the girl cast her gaze down at her feet, suddenly self-conscious. Kane and Brigid chuckled and DeFore asked Grant, "Does that answer your question?"

"The emperor was very meticulous in his attention to even the smallest detail," Inkula said. "Cosmetically Old 88 could use a once-over, but mechanically she is sound. A day or so of preparation and she will be ready to embark on her pilgrimage."

Kane impatiently brushed back a soggy strand of hair from his forehead. "A pilgrimage to where? And why?"

"I thought I explained that, *wageni*," replied Inkula impatiently. "So the rightful heir to the Waziri nation can be anointed."

"If Pakari and Laputara are equally entitled to the Waziri crown," Brigid said, "then wouldn't Laputara by necessity have to participate in the pilgrimage for the ceremony to be legitimate?"

"Laputara knows of our traditions and his father's wishes," Inkula stated grimly. "He scorns them. Therefore it is left to me to sponsor one or the other of Emperor N'gatawana's heirs. Since the emperor's death, Laputara has eliminated—murdered—all of the other contestants to the crown."

"We figured that out ourselves," Kane said dryly. "So what do you want of us?"

"To help Pakari reach the rim of the world," Inkula answered, "and achieve her destiny."

Kane raised his eyebrows at the old man and the girl. "And what do we get out of it?"

"Allies," Pakari stated stolidly, "to aid you in your opposition to overlord expansion. I thought that would be obvious."

"It is," Kane countered. "I just wanted to hear you say it."

"Isn't it a sufficient exchange, so the future of humanity won't be circumscribed by aliens reborn as ancient gods?"

Kane saw no need to reply. Not long ago the Cerberus warriors had been afforded a glimpse of their future, and it bore no relation to a world ruled by the overlords. According to the message conveyed to them from twenty-eight years hence, Sam the Imperator ruled in a preeminent position of global power following a long conflict called the Consolidation War, but there had been no mention of Annunaki involvement.

However, the actions undertaken by Kane, Grant and Brigid to make sure such a future never came to pass could have shifted probabilities sufficiently to set in motion an entirely new series of events, which in turn created a branching timeline.

Or, he reflected bleakly, the rebirth of the Annunaki was always predestined—the future of the Consolidation War was the aberration, the accident. Something he had done or had yet to do—or not do—brought that alternate timeline into existence.

"Where's this rim of the world supposed to be?" Kane asked.

Inkula saluted the jungle in a southern direction. "About a hundred miles that way. On the old, old maps it is known as Magebali Kwa Belewagi."

Double lines of consternation appeared at the bridge of Brigid Baptiste's nose. "That translates as 'Mountain of the Apes,' unless I'm very much mistaken."

"You are not," Pakari assured her. "It is there where the legends say Prester John has a hidden vault which holds the only surviving icons of his reign."

"I don't think I like the sound of that." Brigid eyed the girl distrustfully. "Icons like what?"

"No one knows," Pakari answered. "No one has ever

seen them since Prester John pent them up there almost a thousand years ago. Only the collar will allow the vault to open. Those are the legends, the traditions of my people."

"If that's the case," rumbled Grant, "why didn't Shaka open it?"

"It's possible he tried," Inkula said. "And failed."

"Or," interjected Kane, "there isn't actually a vault to open. It could all be nothing but a fairy tale."

Princess Pakari's lips compressed and she squared her shoulders, turning to face him. "My father would not have undertaken such a task as rebuilding this train because of a fairy tale, Mr. Kane. He envisioned the pilgrimage to the sacred mountain as a great pageant, one with much pomp and ceremony as Old 88 carried the heirs across the Waziri nation to claim the Waziri throne."

Thoughtfully, Grant said, "There's a hell of a lot more to this than fairy tales if an overlord is involved." He cut his eyes over to Brigid. "Are you thinking what I'm thinking?"

A faint smile touched her lips. "If you're thinking that the icons of Prester John's reign were of Annunaki manufacture, perhaps made by Utu himself, and that for some reason the pilgrimage to the Mountain of the Apes must take place so can he reclaim them once the vault is opened, yes, we *are* thinking the same thing."

"If you're right," DeFore commented nervously, "then there's no reason to assume Utu will return when the Moon wanes...two days from now. He could be waiting for us at the village right now."

Pakari's golden eyes flashed with sudden fright. She turned to Inkula. "Do you think so?"

"No," Inkula responded calmly.

"And why not?" Kane challenged.

"Because Overlord Utu needs the Collar of Prester John. And he needs Laputara to recover it for him. They won't take precipitous action against us before the collar is in their hands. Utu is acting as Laputara's sponsor, as I act as Pakari's."

DeFore cast him a narrow-eyed glance. "Isn't that a breach of the protocols of choosing the heir? As the keeper of the collar, it seems to me you would be expected to be as nonpartisan as possible."

Inkula sighed, leaning on his staff. "Times change and laws that were once immutable must change with them. This is not the Africa of Prester John or of Shaka...or even of Emperor N'gatawana. But the hearts of good women and good men do not change. Pakari's heart is good. She cares about her people—she is the true queen of the Waziri. Laputara is mad, and he will kill Pakari if he has the chance. But he will not dare to move against her once she wears the collar, even if he is in league with Utu."

Brigid declared, "Obviously Utu believes the collar is more than a fashion accessory...and it just as obviously serves as key to Prester John's vault. But why does he want Laputara to have it? Why can't he just take it and use it himself without an intermediary?"

Pakari nibbled at her underlip. "I don't understand."

Grant leaned out of the cab of the locomotive, saying, "Utu needs either you or Laputara to have possession of the collar. It's got nothing to do with the legal line of succession. Both you and your half brother are nothing but pawns in whatever game he's running. For all we know, he could have been forbidden to take direct, hands-on actions by the Supreme Council."

Kane nodded distractedly, turning toward Inkula. "You said Old 88 and the collar were as one. What did you mean by that?"

A smile stretched the corners of Laputara's lips. He called out, "Mr. Grant, would you open the grate to the firebox there?"

Grant's perspiration-filmed brow creased. Bending down, he saw a square hinged door made of thick, slotted metal a couple of feet above floor level. He fumbled with the catch and realized that it and the hinges were oiled. The grate opened easily without so much as a squeak.

"Now what?" he called.

"Reach in," Inkula responded, "and bring out what you find."

Grant hesitated. "What if it's a black mamba?"

Inkula's smile widened. "They prefer the wet places near water where the prey is plentiful. Such snakes would not nest up inside of a steam engine's boiler."

Under his breath, Grant muttered, "Says you," but he extended his arm, reaching into the opening.

At first he felt nothing but a layer of powdery ashes and the debris of long-ago fires, but after a few moments of groping, his fingers brushed a slick, pliable surface. He almost jerked his arm back, then recognized the material as oilcloth.

Carefully, Grant withdrew an enwrapped bundle and climbed down from the engine cab. "Hell of a safe, old man. What makes you so sure Laputara wouldn't think to look in there?"

Inkula took the bundle. "Would you?" he retorted.

Grant considered the query for a few seconds, then decided he didn't know Laputara well enough to offer an informed opinion.

Inkula jerked away the oilcloth and held in his arms a box of carved, yellowed ivory, about two feet long and one wide. He handed his staff to Pakari, who stood beside him, and said, "I am violating a custom by showing you this now, here, rather than when we stand upon the rim of the world. But I feel all of you must see this object in order to understand us and our beliefs."

The priest opened the box, dropping the lid to the ground. Carefully, he pulled out a long object that swung from his hand like a cascade of solidified blood, the sunlight flickering and flaring up and down its length.

"Behold the Collar of Prester John," the old man said quietly.

With both hands, Inkula slowly lifted the necklace till it shone above his head like a halo of frozen starfire. The rubies blazed with the iridescence of the noonday sun. Kane squinted against the reflections dancing along the gems, noting that the largest were as big as a pigeon's egg and the smallest the size a thumbnail.

Attached to double strands of intertwining gold-and-silver wire, the rubies were oval, beveled on both sides, and on the faces of each one indecipherable characters were engraved. The Cerberus warriors had seen similar markings inscribed on the fragments of the Chintamani Stone. None of them was a gemologist, but all four outlanders knew the Collar of Prester John represented wealth beyond estimation. Kane couldn't help but think that there, hanging from the parallel lengths of wire, were the jewels that Solomon might have fondled and placed around the Queen of Sheba's neck.

As Inkula held the collar aloft, Pakari rocked to and fro on the balls of her feet with a strange passion. As she hugged herself, her adoring eyes were fixed on the rubies and a kind of sobbing, crooning moan came from her lips. In that instant, the Cerberus warriors learned something of the ancient secrets of Africa, of Prester John's empire and Shaka's victories.

The collar exuded not just a sense of antiquity but a vibration of pulsing force that surrounded them all with a tingling, buoyant web. The vibration clung to them, caressing their nerve endings, sliding through their minds in tiny, rippling waves of excruciatingly pleasurable fire.

Kane understood suddenly that the stones were not rubies, but crystals radiating an intangible aura that overwhelmed mere tactile sense and enhanced the emotions and warrior instincts of humanity. They had the power to build nations or destroy them.

Just looking at the Collar of Prester John made them feel like gods.

Chapter 19

"Lakesh, are you there?"

Blinking, Lakesh raised himself to his elbows and looked around. Bry's transcommed query still echoed from the walls of his quarters. He glanced to his right and noted with a quiver of unease that Domi no longer lay in the bed beside him. The mattress still showed the imprint of her small body and the sheets were still tangled from their earlier lovemaking, but she was nowhere to be seen in his three-room suite.

By squinting, he made out the glowing numbers of the wall chron. It was eighteen minutes after midnight, which meant he had slept uninterrupted for nearly three hours.

"Lakesh—"

"I'm here, Mr. Bry," Lakesh called, turning toward the voice-activated wall comm. "What is it?"

"You asked to be notified if we were able to get through to our away team in Africa. Brigid is waiting to talk to you, but the carrier wave is iffy. You should hurry before we lose it."

"On my way. Is Domi there?"

"No, I haven't seen her since dinner. And if you happen to see Brewster on the way, bring him along. I commed him, but he's either not in his quarters or he's sleeping damn heavy."

For an instant, Lakesh experienced a surge of suspicion that both Philboyd and Domi were nowhere about. He recalled how Domi had been speculatively eyeballing the man in the cafeteria, but he had dismissed it as a subtle form of mockery, silently taunting him because of his under-assessment of the threat presented by the cyberspider. He wondered if something else hadn't been going on.

He dismissed his paranoid thoughts almost as soon as they occurred to him. True enough, Domi was tempestuous in her passions, but she had always proved to be loyal unless disloyalty was shown to her. Besides, Brewster Philboyd was afraid of Domi and he wouldn't be inclined to plan a post-midnight rendezvous with her.

Pushing himself off the bed, Lakesh crossed the room to the small mirror hanging above the built-in bureau. By the dim light he examined his reflection. For the two score years following his resurrection from stasis, he had always experienced a moment of disoriented shock when he saw a wizened, cadaverous face gazing back at him. For the first three years after his awakening, he was discomfited by the sight of blue eyes staring out at him from his own face.

The year before the nukecaust he had been diagnosed with incipient glaucoma, and although the advance of the disease had been halted during his century and a half in cryostasis, it had returned with a double vengeance upon his revival. The eye transplant was only the first of many reconstructive surgeries he underwent, first in the Anthill, then in the Dulce installation.

The vision in his blue eyes was still sharp. He glanced down with distaste at the pair of eyeglasses resting on top of the bureau. They were dark-framed, with thick lenses and a hearing aid attached to the right earpiece. For most of the last decade he had worn them, knowing he resembled a myopic cadaver. For the past year and a half, they hadn't been necessary, but the prospect that they might be again always made him nervous. He didn't so much fear losing his restored vitality, but losing Domi's love.

For a long time, Lakesh had not wanted to admit to himself the depth of his feelings for Domi, but he finally accepted he loved the girl, her upbringing in the Outlands notwithstanding—or he reflected, that upbringing was one of the reasons he loved her. Outlanders were the expendables, the free labor force, the cannon fodder, the convenient enemies of order, the useless eaters. Brigid, Grant, Kane and all of the exiles in Cerberus were outlanders. Only Domi was one by birth, so in the kingdom of the disenfranchised, she was the pretender to the throne.

Lakesh had been fond of her since the day they first met, and over the past couple of years that affection had grown to love. He had not been able to demonstrate his feelings for her until a few months before. It was still a source of joy to him that Domi reciprocated his feelings and had no inhibitions in responding to them, regardless of the bitterness she still harbored over her unrequited love for Grant. In any event, he was glad his fifty-year streak of celibacy was over.

Lakesh pulled on the white, one-piece bodysuit that served as the redoubt's duty uniform. Zipping it up, he left his quarters and emerged into the main corridor. Walking the passageways of Cerberus late at night often dredged up uncomfortable and embarrassing memories of his years laboring for the Totality Concept.

The operations center was sparsely populated, not surprising for so late an hour. Other than Bry at the master ops console, Lakesh saw only a couple of the Moon base émigrés seated at workstations. At least half of the immigrants from the lunar colony had been assigned to the Operation Chronos redoubt on Thunder Isle.

They studied and salvaged the technology, making a complete examination and investigation of the facility, in order to turn Thunder Isle into a viable alternative to the Cerberus redoubt in Montana.

As Lakesh approached Bry, he heard him saying into a microphone, "Rubies? They were rubies?"

Lakesh leaned over the slightly built man's shoulder. "I'm here, Brigid. I'm very glad to hear your voice. You have a report to make?"

"I do," Brigid Baptiste's crisp voice responded, shot through with static. "I don't know how long I can maintain this relay carrier wave, so save the questions until I'm done."

In her characteristic clear, concise way Brigid outlined all the events of the past twenty-four hours, starting from their arrival in the Sudan to the revelation about the Collar of Prester John and the steam locomotive.

"I'm not sure if the collar has been technologically

enhanced," she concluded, "but gauging by the temporary effect it had on our emotions, I'd guess it gener-
ates some kind of radiation that induces euphoria and
impairs the judgment centers of the brain."

Lakesh pursed his lips. "Extraordinary. My own
guess would be that Utu was involved in its manufacture, particularly if fragments of the Chintamani Stone
were employed."

"Could be." Brigid's tone sounded doubtful. "What
was that you told Reba about a cyberspider infestation?"

Lakesh quickly related the experience with the machine. Brigid's reaction surprised him. "So Brewster
wasn't hurt?"

"Only his pride, apparently."

"He didn't act strangely? Was he examined medi-
cally?" Brigid's questions came in sharp bursts.

"No and no," replied Lakesh, perplexed. "Why do
you ask?"

"You, more than anyone I've ever met, reject the
concept of coincidence," she answered brusquely. "The
cyberspider is part of a multipronged campaign either
from Utu or another overlord with whom he's struck an
alliance of convenience."

"Perhaps so," Lakesh agreed. "But why do you want
to know if friend Brewster was behaving in an odd
manner?"

The transmitter accurately conveyed Brigid's weary
sigh. "Maybe I've been hanging around Kane so long
that I tend to conclusion-jump myself. But in both the
installation in the Sudan and here in the Congo, we've

come across evidence of some kind of remote mind-control tech. Even you can't deny that a connection from cybernetic jinn to cybernetic spiders isn't that far off the mark. I think we've stumbled into a project of Lord Utu's."

Lakesh hesitated before stating, "It's possible, but since we've yet to go head-to-head directly with an overlord other than Enlil, we can only speculate as to their modus operandi."

"We can't assume an overlord's M.O. will be the same as a baron's," Brigid countered tersely. "As Baron Snakefish, Utu was accustomed to working exclusively through pawns like Magistrates. As an overlord, he apparently has no compunctions about going out into the field and taking a more hands-on approach."

Lakesh found himself reluctant to agree with Brigid Baptiste's assessment and he wondered why. He guessed bleakly that he didn't want to accept the new dynamic. The barons, as venal and as vicious as they had been, were at least fairly predictable. They had needed the complex support system of the villes, the Magistrate Divisions, the forced labor supplied by the Tartarus Pits to remain in power.

Once the barons evolved into overlords, they had turned their backs on the villes and all of their territories, discarding them with no more consideration than a child tossing away a cheap bauble he had suddenly realized served no useful purpose.

"Lakesh?" Brigid inquired impatiently.

"Yes, you're quite right, dearest one," Lakesh responded hastily. "What are your plans?"

"If Old 88 can be made operational—and Inkula insists it can be—then we'll escort Princess Pakari on her pilgrimage to the rim of the world, to the so-called Mountain of the Apes. Have you ever heard of anything like that?"

Absently, Lakesh tugged at his long nose, dredging through his mental storehouse of cultural myths, fables and legends. "I've heard of it only in a folkloric sense. Sindbad the sailor was alleged to have found a fortress on a mountainside in Africa, guarded by a band of hideous, ferocious and carnivorous apes. According the tale, they ate at least two of Sindbad's crew."

Only silence broken by the hisses and pops came over the transmitter. Lakesh wondered if the signal had been lost, and then Brigid said wryly, "Kane and Grant will love to hear about that."

"Like I said, it's folklore."

"That's what we thought about Prester John, right?" Brigid shot back. "With our luck, there won't be Prester John's vault of on the mountain, but we'll find all the carnivorous apes. I'll make another attempt to contact you before we set off down the track aboard Old 88. Over and out."

Lakesh straightened up, absently kneading the small of his back. Bry said casually, "You know, I'm surprised nobody, particularly Brewster, has made a connection between the so-called cyberspider and the little bugs Megaera and her Furies used."

Jerking slightly as if shocked, Lakesh stared down at Bry for a long moment, his memories flying back over a year to the incident that brought Brewster Philboyd and the other Moon colony personnel to Cerberus.

When the Cerberus network sensor link registered activity in the gateway unit in Redoubt Echo, Kane, Brigid, Grant, Domi and DeFore had traveled to Chicago to investigate. There, they encountered the bizarre group of Furies led by a fanatical woman named Megaera who meted out their own terrible form of justice with the Oubolos rods.

In ancient Greek mythology, Megaera was a Fury, one of three sisters charged by the gods to pursue sinners on Earth. They were inexorable and relentless in their dispensation of justice. A bit of old verse about them claimed that "Not even the sun will transgress his orbit lest the Furies, the ministers of justice, overtake him."

The Oubolus was the collective name for the payment given by souls on their way to the underworld, a form of coin given to Charon, the ferryman for passage across the River Acheron. According to myth, if payment was not made, a soul must wander the riverbank throughout eternity.

Megaera's version of the Oubolos was a little device that was fired from the hollow baton. It attached itself to a target, a sinner, and it delivered an incapacitating jolt of voltage. Once judgment was levied against the sinner, the wristband control mechanism initiated a horrifying process by which the skeletal structure and internal organs were dissolved, leaving only an empty, carbonized husk in the shape of the sinner.

A few months later, the Cerberus warriors had

learned that Megaera and her Furies, as well as the Oubolus rods, originated on the Moon. The devices were of Annunaki manufacture, found in the lunar catacombs that the Niburians had excavated to serve as royal tombs.

A sudden, frightening realization washed over him like a bucket of icy water. Without a word, he spun on his heel and strode swiftly from the operations center. The similarities between the cyberspider and the deadly little device Megaera called the Oubolus crowded into the forefront of his mind.

The shattering of the cyberspider's CEM and the ripping out of a single live connection had not seemed to have a terminal effect on the robot. Apparently, it depended on just how vital to the cyberspider's functionality the broken part happened to be. It was a colony robot, individual components designed to operate both interdependently and independently of the greater whole.

Lakesh didn't waste any time getting to the armory. He jogged through it toward the workroom, his mind racing ahead of his body like the most sensitive kind of alarm system, warning him that every second counted and what he had begun to dread in the operations center might very well be true.

What he saw when he reached the workroom doorway took him completely by surprise. Lakesh rocked to a halt, standing stock-still, distantly realizing he must look comic with his mouth gaping open and his eyes wide. But there was nothing humorous about what he saw.

Domi stood at the end of a trestle table, staring straight at him, an expression he had never seen before stamped on her face—one of sheer terror. She struggled furiously to wrest away the pair of hands savagely squeezing her neck.

The hands belonged to Brewster Philboyd.

Chapter 20

Lakesh's muscles felt as if they were filled with frozen mud. He couldn't move for what seemed like an eternity. Only when a convulsive trembling shook Domi's petite frame did he shout, "Brewster!"

The astrophysicist cast a glance over his shoulder, and the expression on his face chilled Lakesh to the marrow and turned his stomach sideways. Philboyd was beyond anger or even outrage—there was a ruthless cruelty, a homicidal single-mindedness in his eyes, impossible to misinterpret. Four red vertical scratches showed on the left side of his face where Domi had clawed away his glasses, probably seeking his eyes.

Lakesh met his stare, suddenly consumed with the fear that he would not be able to regain control of his limbs before Brewster Philboyd broke Domi's neck. Then the frozen mud in his muscles seeped away and Lakesh crossed the workroom in a running leap.

Grabbing the taller man by the shoulders, he swung him around, raining blows on him more or less at random. His only aim was to stun the man, and if possible, disable him long enough so Domi could tear herself free of his stranglehold.

Lakesh pounded both fists solidly into his kidneys

twice, but Brewster Philboyd's only reaction was to grunt softly. He chopped down on the inside of the astrophysicist's left elbow joint three times, not randomly now, but with a calculated precision. He struck the clump of nerve ganglia on his forearm, and Philboyd's fingers slipped from Domi's neck.

Twisting her body, Domi broke free of Philboyd's hands and staggered back against the far wall, her white flesh inflamed with the imprint of his stranglehold.

Philboyd turned toward Lakesh, blazing fury in the glare he trained on him. He reached for the scientist's throat, trying to secure the same kind of grip as he had on Domi. Lakesh backpedaled, not wanting the man's fingers to come anywhere near his windpipe.

Rather than trying to duck or dodge, Lakesh kicked the tall man in the groin. Brewster Philboyd clutched at his crotch and bent almost double. He went stumbling backward against the edge of the table. A gasping croak came from his lips.

Domi wrenched loose a foot-long piece of iron pipe from the serrated jaws of a vise on a tool bench. Face contorted in a mask of bare-toothed fury, she sidled around the table on the opposite side of Philboyd and flailed at him with it. Only her shorter reach and the fact he was bent over saved the man from a fractured skull.

"Domi, no!" Lakesh cried, gesturing at her. "Something's wrong with him."

"If there's not," she grated hoarsely, raising the pipe again, "there sure as hell will be!"

With a groaning grunt of exertion, Philboyd lurched upright, spittle flecking his lips. He lunged away from the table, reaching for Lakesh. He stepped inside his arms and drove his left fist into the Philboyd's stomach. The astrophysicist jackknifed at the waist, and Lakesh glimpsed the flash of metal at the nape of his neck, where his skull joined with his spinal column.

Lakesh felt a surge of disgust when he noted the object's resemblance to an alloy-sheathed tick. Its body was not much larger than the nail of his pinkie finger. Legs no thicker than eyelashes curved out from all around the body, embedded deep in Philboyd's flesh.

The astrophysicist snatched a double fistful of Lakesh's bodysuit and the two men grappled with one another, staggering to and fro on wide-braced legs. He wrestled Philboyd in Domi's direction, snaking out a foot and back-heeling him so he fell backward on top of the trestle table.

Releasing his grasp on Lakesh's bodysuit, Philboyd planted a right hand under Lakesh's chin to force his head up and with the other gripped him tightly around the throat.

"Hit him!" Lakesh cried, voice muffled by Philboyd's hand.

Domi's face registered confused surprise. "What? I thought you said—"

"I know what I said!" Lakesh shouted impatiently, Philboyd's chokehold turning his voice strained and guttural. "When I pull him up, hit him on the back on the neck!"

Domi eased forward as Lakesh manhandled Philboyd into a sitting position. Her crimson eyes widened, then narrowed when she saw the tiny metal object attached to the astrophysicist's neck. Sharply but economically, she snapped the pipe lengthwise against the base of the man's skull. The sound of metal colliding with metal echoed sharply in the workroom.

Brewster Philboyd's body instantly became as slack limbed as that of a dummy filled with straw. His hands slid away from Lakesh's face and neck, his arms flopping bonelessly onto the tabletop.

Panting, Lakesh clutched at the front of Philboyd's bodysuit. To Domi he said, "Help me turn him over."

As the girl helped him muscle the unconscious man onto his stomach, she spoke in little bursts. "Got bad feeling about him after I shot up spider. At dinner I saw him watching me. Gave me creeps. Bothered me all night. Finally got up and looked for him. Found him here."

Under stress, Domi always reverted to the abbreviated mode of Outland speech. "He fool around with pieces of machine. Instincts told me not a good idea to let him."

She nodded toward a tray at the far end of the table. Lakesh saw the CEM crystal glowing among the litter of metal fragments that was all that remained of the cyberspider.

Lakesh smiled at her fondly, impressed once more by Domi's animal wisdom, which often perceived more than a human possibly could. "Your instincts were sound again."

Once Philboyd lay on his stomach, folded over the table, Lakesh examined the tick attached to the man's neck. The alloy casing was cracked, but the object was so small he couldn't secure a grip on it with his fingers. With the needle-nosed pliers Philboyd had used to dissect the cyberspider, he pinched the tiny body between the two tapered tips and carefully worked the tick loose.

"Ideally," he said, "we should perform this extraction in the infirmary, but I don't want to take the chance of exposing the rest of the redoubt to this thing in case it's not really inactive."

Domi rubbed her reddened throat. "Why did you come here this time of night?"

"Fortunately, I was called to the ops center. While speaking with Mr. Bry, he put a bug in my ear about the similarity between the Oubolus and the cyberspider."

The girl frowned. "Put bug in your ear? Bry gone crazy, too?"

He flashed her a fleeting grin. "Never mind, darlingest one. I was making a very small pun. And speaking of small—"

The tick came free of Philboyd's neck, leaving a precise oval of tiny red pinpricks in the flesh. From the underside of the device trailed a hair-thin filament about four inches long, so delicate it was almost invisible. At its end glinted a tiny speck of crystal.

Domi eyed it suspiciously. "That little mite made him try to kill me?"

"More than likely, yes. Don't look so disbelieving, Domi. Think about all the miniaturized menaces we've come across over the years…the implant-delivery system incorporated into the ring of Genghis Khan, the Oubolous, the infrasound wands—"

"The nanites that made you young and horny," Domi

interjected with a crooked grin. "Those still seem to be working."

"Yes, don't they just," he conceded in a sardonic drawl, holding the object trapped between the plier points up to the light. "And almost all of those things have one thing in common...they originated with the Annunaki."

Domi did a poor job of repressing a shudder of loathing. "It all gets back to those damn snake-faces."

Lakesh's only response was a weary smile. Despite her oversimplification, he couldn't really dispute Domi's observation.

A low groan from Brewster Philboyd commanded their attention. Stirring feebly at first, he managed to prop himself up on his elbows after two faltering attempts. Domi stepped back half a pace, nervously patting the end of the pipe against her thigh. "Mebbe we should call a security detail just in case he gets all zombified again."

"What?" Philboyd croaked, his glazed eyes darting back and forth. "Zombi-what?"

Lakesh put a steadying hand under Philboyd's arm. "Try to stand up. Slowly now."

The lanky astrophysicist did so, blinking around dazedly. His legs wobbled and Lakesh eased him down on the edge of the table. Touching the back of his neck, Philboyd grimaced and then frowned at the little specks of fresh blood shining on his fingertips.

He glanced first at Lakesh, then at Domi. "What the hell happened?"

"I cold-cocked your ass," Domi chirped cheerfully,

waggling the end of the pipe under his nose. "With this."

He squinted at it, then at Lakesh. "What the hell for?" He sounded bewildered, not upset.

"You didn't give us much choice," Lakesh stated. "Apparently, when you reactivated the cyberspider and it latched on to you, it wasn't attempting to harm you, but to implant you with one of its component units. If the robot couldn't complete its mission on its own, then it was programmed to find a host to which it could attach itself."

He moved the little metal tick caught between the tips of pliers close enough for Philboyd to see. "It jammed this little neural trip switch into you so it could interface with your cerebral cortex. I'm sure if we put it under our electron microscope, we'd find the absolute pinnacle of biotechnology."

Philboyd's face paled by several shades. Tentatively he touched the scratches on his face, and horrified comprehension suddenly glinted in his eyes. "Oh, my God. I remember now."

He turned toward Domi, reaching for her, but she leaned cautiously away from his touch. "I'm so sorry. Can you forgive me?"

She shrugged negligently. "Sure, why not?" She tapped the pipe against the palm of her hand meaningfully. "But don't expect me to be so understanding the next time you try to break my neck."

Lakesh frowned at her and she subsided. "Do you have any recollection of the task you were instructed to perform, friend Brewster?"

Philboyd rubbed the back of his neck again. "Bits and pieces. I recall looking for certain components of the machine that I could expose to the CEM…which I think would kick in its self-repair program so it could continue with the mission."

Domi arched a challenging eyebrow. "It would still be able to fix itself after I blew it to scrap metal? How?"

Lakesh and Philboyd exchanged swift glances, then both uttered the same word at the same time in the same dark tone. "Nanites."

Chapter 21

The sound of the explosion rolled through the night and roused Grant from his labored sleep. His eyes snapped open just as the room shook and dust sifted down over the mosquito netting that draped his sling bed.

Moonlight shone through one of the two open windows, casting broad squares of silver on the floor. Lifting his arm, he squinted at the glowing LCD face of his wrist chron, but a weight at the crook of his elbow prevented him from bringing it before his face.

Grant turned his head and stared into a pair of wide-open eyes shining like golden coins, only inches from his. Only then did he become fully aware of the weight of a naked thigh across his belly and the sweat-slick smoothness of bare breasts on his chest.

"What the hell—!" he half snarled, struggling to sit up.

"Please, Mr. Grant," Pakari whispered, clutching at him. "I'm so frightened!"

She wrapped her arms tightly around his waist as the sling bed swayed back and forth. "It's Laputara, he's shelling the village!"

As Grant came to full wakefulness, he felt the pressure of hard nipples digging into his side, but even if he was so inclined to comfort the girl by taking her into his arms, it was simply too hot to do more than disengage from her and stumble to his feet. He tore through the mosquito net, reaching for his clothes. Outside he heard shouting in Waziri and screams from children.

A second explosion sounded much closer, sending a shock wave slapping against Pakari's bungalow, rattling the walls. She stood up, as naked as he, eyes wide with fright. It took Grant a moment to force his eyes away from her, dismayed by her aura of sensuality, even though she was trying to project a sense of sheer terror. For some reason, he didn't think she had been truly frightened of much of anything since she was three years old.

Grant desperately struggled into his underwear and then into his pants, wanting to be dressed before any of his friends burst in and saw the nude princess. "What the hell are you doing here anyway?" he snapped at her.

She replied with a question of her own. "What do you think we should do?"

"I think we should put some clothes on."

Pakari's eyes narrowed at his stern tone. Her brown body flowed silently across the room, through a square of moonlight and out the far door. He couldn't help but admire the firm rondure of the rear end she turned toward him.

Within seconds of her exit, he heard the thump of running feet. He turned just as Kane sprinted through the other door, struggling to tug his black T-shirt over his head. The power holster for his Sin Eater dangled from his right hand.

"Laputara is shelling the Mantas," he announced tersely.

"I figured as much," Grant retorted, strapping his own weapon to his forearm. He decided to dispense with a shirt. "I guess we'd better go see about putting a stop to it."

As the two men sprinted out of the bungalow, they heard more shouting in the Waziri language, and above the clamor came the dull crump of a mortar, followed a moment later by a third explosion. They met Brigid on the verandah, looking damnably clear-eyed and fresh. She inserted an extended 30-round magazine into the Copperhead she held and joined the run for the TAVs.

Kane saw small bursts of flame in the far distance as two mortars continued to launch explosive shells in the general direction of the grounded Mantas. Villagers stood outside their huts and although they milled about uncertainly, they didn't panic. They held crying children and stared at the fireballs blooming outside the village perimeter.

The lion-maned, spear-brandishing soldiers were in position at a wooden palisade like silent sentinels, taking no action, but not backing away, either. They didn't acknowledge the three outlanders who dashed past them onto the open veldt.

The angry trumpeting of the bull elephant in his enclosure echoed through the darkness. Grant said breathlessly, "Old N'gatawana isn't happy about having his sleep disturbed."

Kane's eyebrows quirked. "That elephant is named after the emperor?"

Brigid commented, "Pakari says he holds the essence of her father."

Uttering a short, panting laugh, Kane stated, "So when Pakari said Grant reminded her of her father, she wasn't necessarily referring to the king."

Although the face of the Moon was blotted out by small mushroom clouds of black smoke rising from craters in the ground, the Cerberus warriors saw by its illumination that the Manta ships were undamaged. A fountain of flame burst up from the ground within yards of the TAV Kane had piloted. Small rocks and clods of turf rattled noisily on the wings.

"Bastards are finding the range now," Grant panted between clenched teeth.

Kane wasn't overly concerned about mortar shells inflicting irreparable damage on the Manta ships since the hulls, although they looked like bronze, were composed of a substance far more dense and resilient. Still, the possibility existed that direct hits could wreak enough damage to disable them.

Earlier in the day, upon their return from the Usumbur Tract, the three of them had removed all the ordnance from the TAV's cargo compartments, which included extra ammunition, survival rations, weapons and additional equipment.

Princess Pakari had assigned a group of laborers to repair Old 88, following blueprints provided by Inkula. Another work crew was charged with the task of chopping enough logs for fuel. Kane had no idea of the progress of the crews or if they had stopped upon hearing the mortar attack. Both Inkula and Pakari had dismissed out of hand the likelihood of Laputara braving the dangers of the tract at night. Inkula claimed that despite his aggressive manner, he was superstitious in the extreme.

Kane, Brigid and Grant came to a halt, and crouched, eyes searching the shadow-shrouded savannah for the mortar emplacements. The expanse of rough, uneven grasslands, dotted here and there by clumps of thorn trees, didn't provide a great deal of cover, but it was sufficient for the wilderness-born like Laputara's troopers. They saw a small flare in the darkness to their north, followed by a mushy pop, like the bursting of a wet paper bag.

Less than three seconds later, a dazzling flare and ear-knocking concussion nearly bowled them off their feet. Dirt blown out of the crater rained down over them. Spitting out grit, Kane said grimly, "The bastards are *really* finding the range."

Fanning the acrid smoke away from her face, Brigid said, "The best tactic is for one of you to get airborne and knock out the emplacements from the air."

Knuckling his stinging eyes, Grant said, "Who gets the honor?"

A quick game of rock-paper-scissors determined that Grant would be the one to take flight. As he turned toward his Manta, nearly a dozen shadows detached themselves from the night.

They had been surprisingly stealthy in their approach, rising from declivities in the ground that were hidden by the waist-high grasses. They fanned out in a wedge. If Grant hadn't chosen that instant to turn around, Laputara's troopers would have gotten the drop on them. The men looked crazed, like a madman's dream of a military unit. Each of the men wore part of a uniform, old olive-green field jackets, battered combat boots without laces, but kept on their feet by multiple twistings of twine and vines, but other than that, they were naked but for brief loincloths.

Their bare chests shone darkly under the jackets as if oiled, their brown faces distorted by the heavy welted scars of warrior rituals. Strings of hacked-off human fingers, dried and turned to the consistency of leather, hung from their throats.

They wielded long knives, but the man in the lead carried a British Army revolver by a long lanyard around his neck. The ten troopers were like the epitome of the worst of two worlds blended and merged into a frightening whole. Even by the uncertain light shed by the Moon, the Cerberus warriors saw how the pupils of their eyes were inhumanly enlarged.

"It's a trap!" Kane bit out, his Sin Eater slapping into his hand. "They're fused out, flying high on something!"

When the troopers realized the three outlanders had seen them, they screamed like dying hyenas. A knife hissed through the air, barely missing Brigid's right shoulder and burying itself in the ground behind her. The knife thrower screamed again, this time in frustration.

Kane squeezed off a triburst, but he aimed at the troopers' knees, keeping in mind that Laputara's followers were still Waziri. One of the men fell howling and screeching headfirst, clawing at his right leg. Another pirouetted away and fell heavily, disappearing from view in the tall grass.

"Quick!" Grant snapped. "Back to the village!"

As they wheeled around, a solid wall of men dressed in the same savage half-uniforms rose from the high grasses. They all had the same long knives in their belts and different makes of firearms in their hands.

The men charged from both sides, shouting a wild medley of Waziri and wordless screams, tightening a cordon around them with stunning swiftness. They surged forward, blades flashing. Brigid lifted her Copperhead, finger curling around the trigger as she stroked a long burst from it. She didn't even think about shooting to incapacitate.

A trooper's war cry ended in a gargled grunt as a storm of 4.85 mm rounds tore blood-bursting gouges in his throat and knocked him backward. Miniature volcanoes erupted crimson sprays all over his torso. He fell heavily, but with sudden concert and fierce, terrifying animal cries his companions rushed among them in a wave.

One of the Africans fell, struck by a shot from Grant's Sin Eater, then the clarity of the situation changed. Instead of easy-to-see targets, the veldt became a blur of bodies and mad movement, separating the three outlanders from one another.

Laputara's troopers, barbarians and drugged though they might be, had an instinctive grasp of tactics. They spread out across the area, some trying to cut their quarry off from a retreat. Although their blasters were old, they knew how to use them, but fortunately not very accurately.

Shots cracked and boomed. A bullet thumped past Kane's ear, and another tugged at the longish hair at the nape of his neck. He dived into a depression in the plain, his finger pressing the trigger of his Sin Eater. Three bullets took a trooper's left ear off, bit into his neck and hammered him between the eyes, blowing out the back of his skull in a gouting slop of blood, bone chips and brain matter.

Brigid dropped to one knee and brought her Copperhead to her shoulder, and squeezed off short bursts, not wanting to hose the ammo around in a full-auto stream for fear of hitting Grant and Kane. The short staccato hammering of gunfire interwove among yells and screams.

A *tonga* short sword swiped at Brigid and with the sharp ring of steel against steel, the Copperhead was plucked from her hands. The tip of the blade slashed it from her grip as neatly as if it had been used as a scythe to cut off the head of a flower.

Brigid threw herself backward, somersaulting wildly through the grass, using one foot to kick upward into the man's groin. She felt the impact and heard a fierce grunt and curse exploding from her attacker's lips.

The trooper lunged after her, the *tonga* poised for a downward stroke to split her skull. A pair of 9 mm rounds fired from shadows hit the man with a 248-grain punch, knocking him backward, the *tonga* blade flying from his hand into the high grasses.

Brigid Baptiste didn't know who had fired the lifesaving shots, whether it was Grant or Kane or both, but she wasn't inclined to find out at the moment. She bounded for her fallen Copperhead and snatched it up from the ground as if it were a long-lost lover.

A keening Waziri raced directly for her position, swinging a curved sword over his head and working the trigger of the big black revolver hanging from his neck. Brigid felt and heard the thumping passage of bullets all around her, shearing through the grass. Shifting the barrel of her subgun, she let loose a burst. The trooper cried out, doubling over, bleeding from three wounds in his belly. He fell face down, writhing convulsively in shock and agony.

The thunder of the gunfire was deafening, echoing across the savannah, and to add to the confusion, the cacophony was underscored by the angry bawls of the bull elephant, sounding surprisingly close by. A moment later, Brigid saw the reason why.

The high grasses swished and rustled violently, the ground trembling underfoot. A huge gray mass loomed out of the murk, propelled by four massively muscled legs. Everyone heard the animal's lumbering progress through the undergrowth and its panting grunts of exertion.

The old bull elephant named N'gatawana came crashing into the middle of the melee. The long wrinkled trunk swung this way and that, and the huge ears flapped forward like leathery fans. Blood ran down his hide from several raw scrapes, inflicted when he had torn through the wooden stockade fence. Lifting his trunk from between the long, yellow tusks, the gigantic animal gave vent to a prolonged, eardrum-compressing roar.

Several of the troopers yelled in terror and ran in panic-stricken flight.

N'gatawana surged over the ground in a juggernautlike charge, his tiny eyes reddened with rage. The dull reverberations of the elephant's heavy footfalls against the ground set a repetitive, drumming rhythm that sent a shiver up Brigid's spine, despite the heat and humidity. She dived into a hollow between intertwining grasses and lay there, fisting her Copperhead.

The formation of Laputara's troopers wavered, and then began to break up. They ran across the savannah, retreating from the twin tusks of N'gatawana. A man shouted stridently and though Brigid didn't understand the words, she recognized Laputara's maddened voice. She knew it was an order for the soldiers to stand fast and close up ranks.

One of the troopers ran directly into the elephant's path, raising his AK-47. He squeezed off a single shot before the massively muscled trunk swung out from the ponderous head and slammed into him like weighted pendulum, cartwheeling him off his feet. The man had time for one scream before N'gatawana reared up and stamped down with both front feet. There was a sound like a multitude of branches breaking simultaneously.

Howling in terror, the surviving troopers turned on their heels and ran. Sounding bugle calls of anger and triumph, the bull elephant thundered past Brigid's hiding place, pursuing the fleeing men like a dog chasing rabbits.

The cries of fright and thudding footfalls receded.

Brigid, Kane and Grant crept out of various hiding places. As they gazed after the dim gray shape of N'gatawana, Kane remarked blandly, "I don't believe I've ever been saved by an elephant before."

Grant nodded absently, brushing off his arms. "That was one pissed-off old pachyderm."

Brigid released her pent-up breath in a sigh. "This was all a trap to draw us out into the open and butcher us. It might have worked if N'gatawana hadn't broken loose."

"Or was set free," Kane said.

The sudden glare flashing down from above blinded them. A column of white light illuminated the small area in which they stood with a dazzling halo as bright as the noonday sun.

Chapter 22

None of the three people needed to see the ship hovering overhead to know it was there. They knew it was a circular craft of dully gleaming "smart" metal, appearing to consist of two thick disks each at least twenty feet in diameter placed one above the other.

They looked for an avenue of escape, but their only option lay in the direction of the village. The Cerberus warriors retained very vivid memories of the plasma weapons Enlil's fleet of attack disks had unleashed against the redoubt. They assumed that if they sought shelter under the Mantas, the TAVs would be destroyed from on high. Firing on the disk would have little effect, since the semifluid composition of the hull absorbed projectiles.

As they took their first running steps toward the village, short pencils of light streaked from the half dome bulging out from the craft's undercarriage. Fist-sized craters opened up in the ground with little spurts of flame, and they felt the concussions of the explosive impacts.

The shaft of light swept around them, blocking them when they turned in the opposite direction. When they began to fan out, separating from one another, the halo of light expanded to capture them all. Kane, Brigid and Grant stopped moving and stood beneath the glare of the enormous eye floating less than fifty feet overhead.

Shielding his eyes, Kane snarled in angry frustration, "The son of a bitch said he wouldn't be back for two more days—"

"For the collar," Brigid broke in bitterly. "Not for us."

Grant growled deep in his chest. "It would've been nice if someone had thought to make that distinction earlier."

The silver disk ship dropped straight down, landing gear sprouting from beneath it. It settled silently and gracefully on the veldt less than thirty feet away from them.

A section of the hull split wide in a triangular shape, as if it were cloth slit open by an invisible blade. Kane resisted the urge to trigger his Sin Eater at the aperture. He had seen the phenomenon before and he knew gunplay wouldn't do him or his friends any good at this point.

A ramp extended outward, the smart metal of the ship forming a long walkway, as if the ship itself were sticking out its tongue. However, the humor of the overlords turned in a far darker direction than childish, impudent gestures.

From within the ship emerged a contingent of magenta-armored Nephilim, jogging down the ramp and enclosing Grant, Kane and Brigid in a crescent formation. All of the eight figures held their right arms straight out from the shoulder. Flanges shaped like the letter S cut in half sprang out from the pods mounted on their gauntlets with flares of sparks and crackling hisses of energy. Red energy pulsed in the gullets of the stylized adder heads that comprised the actual emitters of the accelerated stream of protons.

The deep-set white eyes of the Nephilim didn't blink, nor did their craggy faces register emotion and the outlanders knew why. A half-ovoid shell sprouted from the rear of their armor, sweeping up to enclose the back and upper portions of their hairless skulls. From its underside hair-thin filaments extended down to pierce both sides of their heads, turning the people into mind-controlled drones.

Then Overlord Utu came marching down the ramp, an ankle-length cloak of dark green attached to the shoulder epaulets of his elaborate armor belling out behind him. He looked much the same as when the Cerberus warriors had last seen him, on the bridge of Tiamat in the company of the entire Supreme Council, tall, slender, strong—and awesomely arrogant.

He stopped at the foot of the ramp and swept them all with cold, haughty eyes. Utu's face was human enough in shape—hollow cheeked with angular, arching bones. It was as perfect as if sculpted in marble, with no softness or irregularity anywhere about it. He had no hair, either on his face or head, only a finely wrought pattern of pale red scales and a crest of back-slanting spines running down the center of his cranium. The spines were of a deeper red than his flesh, the same shade as his elaborate body armor.

The eyes in Utu's face weren't even remotely human. They were like little pools of molten brass, bisected by black, vertical-slitted pupils—deep, impenetrable, without heart or soul or warmth.

As when they had first seen an overlord, the Cerberus warriors struggled to reconcile the sight of the tall, regal aristocrat coldly surveying them with memories of the small, fragile creatures who had ruled the baronies from the shadows of their high, isolated eyries.

Utu stared at them unblinkingly, a withering scorn evident in the tilt of his head and the posture of his body. Brigid, Grant and Kane stared back, keeping their expressions neutral.

At length Utu stated, "I cautioned the prince you were far too canny to be caught by such a clumsy trap." His voice was like smooth velvet wrapping hard-edged steel.

"They *were* caught," said Laputara, striding around the disk. He cast a sullen glance first at Utu then at the three outlanders. "That fucking elephant ruined everything. I'm sure Pakari set him free."

Laputara was garbed in an even more mismatched and bizarre outfit than his soldiers. He wore a field jacket far too small for him and a red beret sat at a jaunty angle on his head. Lion's teeth and the bright feathers of jungle birds formed a fringe around the brim. He carried a long, fur-bedecked assegai lance in his right hand.

Lips peeling back from his teeth in a ferocious grin of pure malice, he spit, "I told you we'd be settling up."

Laputara took a long menacing step toward the Cerberus warriors, lifting the spear for a cast. He rocked to an unsteady halt when three gun bores were suddenly trained on him. Blinking in childlike confusion, he turned toward Utu and cried out petulantly, "My lord, they haven't been disarmed!"

Utu allowed a lazy smile to play over his angular face. "You noticed that, did you? And if they were disarmed, what would you do?"

Laputara jabbed the blade of the lance forward, screeching, "*Kill* them!"

"And would killing us get you the Collar of Prester John?" Brigid inquired, as if she were only mildly interested in the matter.

Thrusting his head forward belligerently, Laputara snapped, "Why wouldn't it? What do you have to do with—"

His words trailed off and an expression of puzzlement crossed his face.

Grant snorted out a disdainful laugh. "That's a great candidate you're backing for king, Utu."

"He is a puppet, Grant," Utu replied quietly. "One does not choose a puppet because of their mental acuity. They are selected based on how they react to the pull of the strings."

Kane stared levelly at Laputara. "Is that what you are, Prince? The mindless puppet dancing on the end of an inhuman schemer's string?"

Laputara glowered at him from beneath a wrinkled brow, but he didn't answer.

"I am his god," Utu said casually. "He has freely chosen to be the instrument of my will."

Laputara turned toward Utu, bowing his head. "O mighty one, I beseech you to strike down the intruders before they further corrupt my country. They have already poisoned my half sister—"

"You managed to do that without any help from us," Brigid interpreted contemptuously.

Laputara whirled around as if stung. Shaking the spear at her, he bellowed, "*Askut!* Silence! *Askut!*"

"*Askut* yourself," Brigid countered. "We don't recognize your authority."

Kane favored Utu with a humorless smile. "Or yours, either, in case you were wondering."

Still wildly brandishing his spear, Laputara roared, "Kneel in the presence of the great god Utu!"

Grant rolled his eyes in weary exasperation. "Are you always this hyper, boy? You wear me out just looking at you."

Turning to Utu, Laputara said angrily, "Force them to kneel before you, my lord!"

Utu shook his head. "They would not do so."

"Then strike them dead or permit me the honor!" Spittle flew from Laputara's lips as he worked himself up into a rage.

A taunting smile crossed Kane's face, and he waggled his Sin Eater at Laputara. "Come ahead and try, O Prince."

Infuriated, Laputara whirled toward him. Utu reached out and dropped a gauntleted hand on the young man's shoulder. Metal-shod fingers dug in and Laputara's face twisted in surprised pain. His knees bent under the pressure.

"Enough of these childish theatrics, Laputara," he whispered, releasing his grip. "Calm yourself."

Regarding the Cerberus warriors with hooded eyes, Utu intoned, "You three continue to be vexations. Should I assume you destroyed the birthing ward in the Sudan, despite my precautions?"

"We only finished what one of your Nephilim started," Grant retorted. "On your orders, I imagine."

Utu nodded. "It was an old Overproject Excalibur facility dedicated to the development of transgenic cells. I've been aware of the place for quite some time, but only in the last year did I have the wherewithal to tour it personally."

None of the three people responded to Utu's oblique reference to the transformation undergone by the barons into the overlords. It was an event they still had difficulty accepting. Kane easily recalled the Magistrate conditioning that instilled in them the belief the barons were kings, demigods, their personal deities and thus deserving of their unquestioning obedience. Even learning the barons were products of synthetic wombs and recombinant DNA hadn't completely stripped them of their semidivine mystique.

To see one of the nine barons now, transformed and evolved into a creature of myth, an entity who had indeed behaved and long ago been worshipped as a god, still evoked emotions somewhere between awe and repulsion.

"The facility was in remarkably good condition, all things considered," Utu went on smoothly. "And since it lay in my ancient territory, I claimed it as a rightful possession."

"So you decided to jump-start the research," Brigid interjected flatly, "to synthesize your own monster army. You brought out-of-work personnel from Snakefish and put them to work, using one of your Nephilim as a straw boss. But the experiment got away from you."

Utu's lips stretched in a smirk. "As such experiments often do. My Nephilim was instructed to trigger a reactor overload during such an eventuality, but apparently he was unable to complete it. All things considered, I suppose it was fortunate you three came along before the subjects escaped."

Grant eyed the Nephilim standing on both sides of him and his friends, as motionless as statues with the ASP emitters positioned to catch them in a triangulated crossfire. He didn't like the odds at all, but his voice held no particular emotion when he asked, "Just like it was fortunate we came along to help the princess?"

Utu's smirk vanished and Laputara whirled around to glare at him with enraged eyes. "The three of you are taking a very, *very* big risk," Utu said in a low tone, heavy with menace. "Enlil could very well interpret this incursion of yours as breaking the truce."

"And like sending one of your mechanical toys to spy on Cerberus isn't?" Brigid shot back. "I don't think Enlil will be happy to hear about how you put his darling Ninlil in jeopardy with your own covert actions."

Utu glared at the outlanders and they glared back. They knew that the agreement observed by the Supreme Council and the Cerberus personnel had been made under duress and Enlil would use any excuse to consider it void. If not for Balam acting as mediator, a state of open war would have existed between the reborn Annunaki and Cerberus.

As it was, they were still trying to come to terms with the full implications of the maneuvers and countermaneuvers undertaken by Enlil as he had moved his chess pieces over a vast board of power plays that stretched across the world and millennia. Through the years, over the centuries, Enlil assumed many names and adopted many physical vessels in order to manipulate events and governments to best fit his agenda.

As far as Enlil was concerned, the nukecaust was a radical form of remodeling and fumigation. The extreme depopulation, as well as the subsequent atmospheric and geological changes approximated Niburian conditions. The reborn Annunaki set about reclaiming the nations and regions of Earth they had ruled millennia ago.

But with Tiamat in permanent orbit, hanging over the world like a dark angel of doom, the Cerberus warriors knew they had no chance of emerging victorious from a head-on confrontation with the overlords, even if they managed to kill all of them.

The giant ship was capable of dispatching remote probes, essentially smaller versions of herself, to blanket the planet with fusion bombs, biological and chemical weapons, and defoliants of all kinds.

As a result, the seas would be rendered toxic, the atmosphere contaminated, starvation and exposure to radiation would kill anyone who was unlucky enough to survive the initial onslaughts. Humanity as the dominant species on Earth would cease to exist.

Only the fact that Balam held an infant as a hostage prevented such a catastrophe from coming to pass. The baby, carried to term by the hybrid female Quavell, had been bred to carry the memories and personality of Enlil's mate, Ninlil.

In actuality, Quavell had given birth to a blank slate, a tabula rasa, an empty vessel waiting to be filled. Although the child carried the Annunaki genetic profile, she was born in an intermediate state of development. Certain segments of her DNA, strands of her genetic material, were inactive and needed to be encoded aboard Tiamat.

Once there, through a biotechnological interface, she would receive the full mental and biological imprint of Ninlil. Then the Supreme Council would be as complete as it had been thousands of years before and Tiamat could set into the motion the rebirth of the entire Annunaki pantheon. Enlil would not be pleased with any overlord who put at risk Ninlil and thus the long-range plan to remake Earth.

Utu forced an unctuous smile to his face. "Perhaps it would be best to leave Enlil out this situation altogether."

Kane nodded. "Sound decision, my lord Doo-doo."

The smile vanished from the overlord's scaled face in reaction to the mockery. "But that does not invalidate the fact you're trespassing and involving yourself in a matter than has no real meaning to you."

"But it does to me." Princess Pakari's strong voice cut through the murk. "As it does to the entire Waziri nation."

Although the Nephilim didn't move in reaction, both Laputara and Utu turned sharply to their right. Laputara's face contorted in rage and he bellowed, *"Mahawai!* Whore!"

Gripping the assegai shaft tightly at the midway point, Laputara cocked his arm back for a cast.

Chapter 23

Utu barked a single word in a language the Cerberus warriors had heard before but didn't understand. One of the Nephilim swung his extended arm toward Laputara. Triple streams of eyeball-searing yellow light spit from the serpent mouths of the ASP emitter, joining together to form a coruscating globule of plasma. It jetted toward the prince like a fireball launched from a catapult.

The kaleidoscopic bolt of colors and energy splashed against the iron spearhead and a sharp popping report echoed across the veldt. The shaft of the lance crackled within a cocoon of yellow flame. Laputara screamed in fright and pain, hurling the spear to the ground. The blade was gone, melted into little blobs of semiliquid steel glistening on the ground. A splatter of molten droplets gleamed on the sleeve of his jacket. Kane caught the sweetish whiff of burned human flesh mixed in with the odor of scorched wood.

Shrieking in agony, Laputara clutched the wrist of his injured hand and sank to his knees. Leaking blisters covered the palm of his hand and he craned his neck toward Utu, a look of pain and betrayal in his watering eyes.

"Why, Holy One?" he croaked. "Why?"

"Execrable idiot," Utu said, anger turning his voice into a sibilant whisper of spite. "Both of us want the collar. Killing your half sister before we have it will not avail either one of us anything."

Bracketted by four Waziri soldiers, Pakari marched fearlessly into the crescent formed by the Nephilim. She wore her royal finery, including the gilded elephant-tusk diadem. Gazing disdainfully at Utu, she said, "Without your tricks to make yourself seem larger than you really are, I can't understand how you tricked my half brother into following you."

The smile Utu turned on her was mocking and amused. "He is weak witted and addicted to a certain vice, an opiate that engenders a physical and psychological dependence."

Voice trembling with equal measures of disgust and hatred, Pakari snapped, "Which you have mercilessly exploited."

Utu nodded graciously in acknowledgment of her statement. "I explore opportunities when they present themselves. Still, I would much prefer to use you as the instrument of my will. It is not too late to accept my proposal."

Pakari's lips worked and she spit in the dust at Utu's feet. "*That* for you and your proposal."

Grant stiffened, finger lightly caressing the trigger stud of his Sin Eater. He knew the girl had to be careful—facing the Nephilim and the ruthless overlord, the life of the princess hung by the most delicate thread.

Utu's eyes flashed. "A silly little slut of a savage

should hold her tongue more carefully if she wishes to take her nation's throne."

Speaking loudly and clearly to draw Utu's attention away from Pakari, Brigid declared, "All you actually care about is regaining the Collar of Prester John, not who sits on the Waziri throne."

Utu shrugged, turning his reptilian face toward her. "To be accurate, it's a stool, not a throne. But you are right. My only priority is reclaiming my property. The collar is a talisman of great power, very dangerous in the wrong hands."

Kane raised his eyebrows in mock bewilderment. "Excuse me, but aren't those wrong hands *yours?*"

Utu drew himself up haughtily. "My hands created and crafted the collar. Therefore, I decide who wears it."

"Why do you care who does?" Grant asked.

"Because," Laputara half shouted in an unsteady voice, "he who wears the collar can seize control over all tribes, all peoples. Empires themselves cannot stand before the single man who wears the collar. Just like Shaka!"

"And Alexander," put in Brigid grimly. "And Solomon and Gilgamesh and perhaps even Ramses III."

"Perhaps," Utu said coolly. "Perhaps many more conquerors than those you mentioned wore the collar throughout your race's history. Princess, you should be appalled by the idea of a sot, a beast like your half brother wearing it."

Kane felt the shuddery touch of comprehension like an icy finger stroking the buttons of his spine. "It's not the Collar of Prester John at all, is it?" he challenged. "It's always been the Collar of *Utu*. Prester John was just one of the human pawns you allowed to wear it, as a symbol of your ownership and control over him. Now you want it back so you can put it around the neck of a new slave and set them marching to another war you've arranged."

Utu shook his head. "Not exactly, Kane. Yes, the collar needs to be around a human neck in order to gain my objective, but I'm not necessarily interested in waging a war of conquest." He paused and showed the edges of his teeth in a humorless grin. "And least not so early in my reign."

Pakari drew in a sharp, dismayed breath. With wide, shocked eyes she stared first at the kneeling Laputara, then at Utu. "You wish to enslave the ruler of the Waziri people so you can reclaim your territory in Africa. First you must open the vault of Prester John, but you need the collar around the neck of someone with Waziri royal blood to accomplish that!"

Kane said slowly, "I think I get this now, Utu. Just like the legends of the Shining Trapezohedron were always associated with keys, the Collar of Prester John is a key, too. Without it, you can't get into his vault and claim all the toys you tinkered together millennia ago."

Utu didn't reply for a long moment. He gazed at the Cerberus warriors stonily, then said in a surprisingly soft voice, "Hardly toys. They were my creations, but they were locked away in accordance with our pact with the Tuatha de Danaan. They were sealed in one of my ancient vaults and many decades later, Prester John occupied it. He was an adventurer, a thief, not my pawn. He stole the collar and used its power to carve an empire for himself here in Africa, making the native people tools for his ambition."

Brigid stared at Utu with green glints of suspicion shining in her eyes. "You expect us to believe you have don't have similar ambitions? If, as you say, Africa is your ancient territory, you'll need armies to reclaim it."

Utu's face registered scorn. "I am the god of the dark people of this land as I was thousands of years ago. But now, as in the old days of the Annunaki empire, I work for the good of the superior race, the ancient masters of humanity to reassert our rule over the Earth. When we mount our thrones, the only humans will be slaves, regardless of their skin color."

"Obviously you think the Collar of Prester John will help you achieve that end," Brigid said curtly, sounding not the least intimidated by the overlord's statement of policy. "So why shouldn't we take it out of Africa altogether?"

Pakari swiveled her head toward her, eyes widening with horror. "You can't—"

"Exactly," Utu said with a great deal of smug satisfaction. "The entire Waziri culture revolves around the collar, the inheritance of Prester John, the priest and king. When he ascended to Heaven, he left to his people the sacred collar, the ark of his valor, to be God's dower and pledge to the people whom he had chosen."

He turned toward Pakari and asked tauntingly, "Is that not right, Princess?"

When the girl refused to respond, Utu uttered a

laugh. "Without the collar, the soul of the Waziri people would wither. I don't think you want that on your consciences just to keep me from regaining it."

"It's not just the collar we need to keep from you," Kane said grimly, "it's what it will give you access to. What's in that vault you want so badly?"

Utu pursed his lips meditatively and he whispered, "Mine the glory, Kane. Mine the glory."

"That's no answer," Kane shot back angrily.

"It's all you'll receive," Utu replied quietly. "Fortune favored the sons of men for long enough. That time is over. Accept it."

"But you still need the sons of men to reach your goal," Brigid said contemptuously. "Just like when you and the Supreme Council threw your tantrums in your baronies."

Utu's lips writhed in a snarl, then he molded them into a smirk. "Even then the spirit of the proud Annunaki burned within us, sleeping but in anticipation of its awakening."

He gestured expansively to Laputara, to Pakari, to all of Africa. "They knew the legends of the day when Those-Who-from-Heaven-to-Earth-Came would arise and rule again. Through all the long centuries of savagery, they knew we would return to our ancient cities, our thrones, our vaults."

Pakari hugged herself as if a sudden chill breeze had come gusting over the veldt. Voice heavy with loathing, she said, "For some reason you can't enter the vault, even if you wore the collar yourself. What *are* you, really?"

"What I am," replied Utu in a low, deadly tone, "and

what I shall do, is of no moment to you, Princess. It is what *you* are and how I decide you will serve me that should concern you now."

Grant stepped forward and almost negligently raised his Sin Eater, ignoring the sparking serpent heads that turned in his direction. "Whether you'll be alive one minute from now should be your biggest concern."

Utu didn't react with either fear or resentment. "Expedience warrants the immediate removal of you and your friends, Grant. But you can be useful to me for a time."

Reaching down, he pulled Laputara to his feet and directed the whimpering man up the ramp into the skyship. "Go. I will heal your injury."

"You're not going anywhere, Utu," Grant declared in a flinty voice.

Turning, the overlord swept Grant, Kane, Brigid, and Pakari with a smile that was almost benign. Softly, he said, "None of you can stop me. The best you can hope for is to start a skirmish with my Nephilim, which will result in all of your deaths."

"And yours, too," Grant said flatly.

"How sure of that are you?" Utu's tone was smooth, oily and patronizing.

Grant didn't answer for a long moment and Brigid stepped up beside him, laying a hand on his arm. "Let him go, Grant. This isn't the time."

Slowly, reluctantly, by half inches, the big man lowered the Sin Eater. Utu inclined his head toward Brigid in a parody of a bow, and with a swirling flourish of his cloak, heeled around and marched up the ramp into the disk.

The Nephilim followed him, striding in single file like clockwork automatons through the triangular aperture. After the last one entered, the ramp withdrew into the bottom of the ship and the opening in the hull sealed, leaving not so much as a seam.

The silver disk silently rose vertically from the veldt. The landing gear folded into its underbelly and the craft shot straight up, as if drawn by a vast, celestial magnet. Within seconds, it was lost in the darkness, just one more star among the multitude glittering in the African sky.

Gusting out a sigh, Kane ran a hand through his sweat-damp hair and said peevishly, "That was about as pointless an encounter with Utu as the one we had last night with his hologram."

Brigid smiled, but it didn't reach her eyes. "I beg to differ. What Utu *didn't* tell us speaks volumes."

"It sounded like the same old humans-as-pawns crap the baronies practiced," Kane grated. "Which I guess is fitting, since the Annunaki originally came up with it."

Kane made an oblique reference to not just the god-king system created by the Annunaki many millennia before, but the influence of the illusory Archon Directorate. After the nukecaust, working through human and inhuman intermediaries, the so-called Archon Directorate intervened to prevent the rebuilding of a society analogous to the predark model. The Directorate interceded directly in the development of the most powerful baronies, and instituted the Program of Unification in order to prevent a resurgence of the inefficient preholocaust societal structure.

Grant turned toward Pakari, his eyes shadowed by his knitted brows. "What the hell were you thinking, charging in here like that?"

She regarded him with a dispassionate aureate gaze. "If I hadn't, you and your friends could very well be dead at this moment."

"It was reckless," he snapped.

"You're not my father, Mr. Grant," Pakari retorted crisply, turning her back on him so dismissively both Kane and Brigid instantly realized there was more to her attitude than offense at the questioning of royal authority.

In the distance came the trumpeting bellow of the bull elephant and Kane remarked, "He's not, but your old man's namesake sure saved our skins. Did you release him?"

Pakari nodded. "N'gatawana would have smashed his way out if I hadn't and probably would've seriously injured himself in the process."

Brigid gazed out across the veldt. "Shouldn't someone go fetch him?"

The princess shrugged. "When he gets hungry or bored, he'll come back. I have other matters on my mind."

Brigid eyed her questioningly. "Like what?"

Princess Pakari gestured toward the guardsmen indicating they should precede her back to the village. "Like preparing to embark on the pilgrimage to the rim of the world whereby I may be invested with the Collar of Prester John."

Grant and Kane stared at her, surprised into speechlessness for a long moment. Kane recovered his voice first, jabbing a thumb skyward. He demanded incredulously, "After what Utu just said, you still want to go through the ritual?"

Pakari cast him a grim, over-the-shoulder stare. "It's not a matter of wanting to, Mr. Kane...but Utu made it very clear that I must."

Chapter 24

Dawn arrived, filling the sky with a palette of blazing colors. Grant and Kane weren't looking at the sky—their eyes were fixed on the railway track at their feet.

The atmosphere of the Usumbur tract was like that within a greenhouse—rich with the overwhelming odor of flowering vegetation and heavy with humidity, even at such an early hour. The hot, moist air lay on the faces of the two men like the clasp of soft, moist hands. Their sweat-soaked T-shirts adhered to their torsos like a second layer of skin.

Palming away a film of sweat on his forehead, Grant rumbled, "When we get back to Montana, I'm going to climb the highest mountain peak I can find and lay naked in the snow for a couple of days. I've had my fill of equatorial Africa."

"Hell, this is golden autumn here in the Congo," Kane told him.

"Unbelievable," muttered Grant. "It's got be ninety degrees at daybreak…what will it be like at noon?"

Kane paused to kick at a steel tie. "Not too bad. According to Baptiste, it gets up to about one hundred at this time of year. In the real hot weather, you can count on highs of 115 for six weeks at a shot."

"No wonder everybody in this part of the world is so damn bad-tempered," Grant said dourly. "Heat rash is probably the number-one killer of anybody over the age of ten."

"I don't think we'll have to worry about dying of that," Kane pointed out wryly.

Grant removed the canteen from his web belt and uncapped it. "That's for sure. Not with the enemies we've made. Heat rash if we're lucky."

As Grant took a long swallow of water, Kane reflected gloomily that wherever he and the Cerberus team went, violence and death were only moments away. It was rarely planned that way, but terrible and bloody events always happened and the body count soared. In Moscow and Mongolia, England and Utah, Antarctica and Cambodia, it was always the same.

"We *do* seem to bring out the worst in people," Kane commented offhandedly.

Grant passed him the canteen. "Particularly the people who aren't completely human."

Kane upended the canteen, swallowing the tepid water in loud gulps. Grant eyed him critically and cautioned, "Don't drink so much or you'll founder. Then you'll really feel miserable."

Lowering the canteen, Kane unsuccessfully swallowed a belch and said flatly, "I already feel miserable."

Grant grunted and took the canteen from him. "I'm more miserable than you," he said unsympathetically.

Kane shook his head. "You're spoiled rotten and miserable. That's a hard combination to take."

Grant glared at him incredulously. "If I was spoiled,

I wouldn't be walking along a railroad track in the middle of the Congo at the crack of dawn—I can tell you that right now."

Although the two men were short-tempered due to the heat and lack of sleep, they did their best to keep the mission at the forefront of their minds.

Upon returning to the Waziri village after the departure of Utu, Princess Pakari had met privately with Inkula. When they emerged from his hut, both people agreed that the sooner she embarked on the pilgrimage to the rim of the world, the better.

Neither Brigid, Kane, Grant nor DeFore responded with much enthusiasm to the proposal, particularly since they weren't sure if the repairs had been made to the railroad tracks and to the train itself. By raising those issues with the princess, the four outlanders found themselves in the position of inspecting the work. So, for the past half an hour, Grant and Kane had walked along the tracks that penetrated the swampy undergrowth like a pair of giant petrified snakes lying side by side.

"I don't mind you being spoiled," Kane assured his friend as he nudged a cross timber with a foot. "I've always admired the way you're so up-front about your personality flaws. You just say to the world, 'I'm a spoiled, miserable bastard, take me or leave me.' That's very mature."

"Has it ever occurred to you," Grant demanded, "that the main reason I'm a miserable bastard is the fact we've been partners for fifteen years?"

Kane presented the image of seriously pondering

the query for a moment. At length, he admitted, "It's occurred to me."

They followed the tracks back to the work shed. Old 88 hadn't moved, but Waziri women were busy draping the gleaming body of the locomotive with garlands of bright flowers. Naked children polished all the brass fittings until they shone mirror bright. Others stacked logs into the fuel tender coupled behind the cab. The people's lively chatter and laughter seemed incongruous in the steamy swampland environment.

Brigid and DeFore stood at the passenger carriage, loading it with jugs of water and native foodstuffs, like small sweetbreads and diced pieces of fruit. The two women looked debilitated by the heat and humidity. DeFore had changed out of the native garb into khaki shorts and a gray T-shirt like Brigid's. Dark half moons of perspiration showed at their armpits and necklines.

At Kane and Grant's approach, Brigid looked up and asked, "What is the condition of the tracks?"

Grant shrugged. "Looks like some new rails and ties were laid down, but I don't know the standard to judge whether they're train worthy or not."

"They seemed secure," Kane said, "at least for the first mile."

DeFore brushed back a strand of ash-blond hair adhering to her damp cheek. "According to Pakari, every few months Inkula would send out crews to inspect and repair the tracks, as a way to honor Emperor N'gatawana. I still think this is a ridiculous tactic. Even if the old rattletrap 88 works fine, Utu can just blow it to scrap from the air."

"He can," Brigid said, "But he won't. It's in Utu's best interest for Pakari to complete the pilgrimage to the rim of the world…or at least one member of the royal Waziri family."

Kane said musingly, "I guess either Laputara or Pakari will serve his purposes. Utu prefers Laputara to wear the Collar of Prester John, but he'll make do with Pakari."

"She won't take his orders like Laputara," Grant stated positively.

Brigid leaned against the railway car. "Probably not. But whatever is hidden in the vault that Utu is so anxious to recover must be of paramount importance to him."

"He said he was working for the greater good of the superior snake-faces," Kane reminded her.

Brigid shook her head. "I don't think he is, not in this instance. If that were the case, the entire Supreme Council would be slithering around, or Enlil would be here at the very least. I think Utu wants to keep this little foray of his a secret from his council."

DeFore frowned. "What could be in the vault that he wants so badly?"

"Any number of things," Brigid answered. "Maybe this mysterious mirror, or items far more powerful. It's my theory Utu tinkered together a lot of nasty tech over the centuries and he liked to test them out on human subjects."

"That figures," Grant said dourly. "If we take Utu at his word that he was forced to lock his toys away as a condition of the pact with the Danaan, then it's possible the man known as Prester John stumbled onto the vault in historical times."

"I concur," Brigid stated. "Especially if he was a crusader, maybe one of the Knights Templar. He could've learned about Utu's vault through contact with the Priory of Awen. We know their influence was very widespread throughout Europe in the middle ages."

Kane ventured thoughtfully, "And so Prester John came to Africa, found the vault, the collar and the mirror and maybe a whole lot of other fancy trinkets that were passed around and stirred up legends in this part of the world—everything from magic rings to flying carpets."

"And now Utu wants it all back." DeFore cocked her head quizzically. "But why does he need a Waziri noble to wear the collar?"

Brigid smiled crookedly. "I haven't worked that one out yet, but I wouldn't be surprised to learn it has to do with a genetic marker of some sort. Utu can take possession of the collar, but it won't act as key unless the lock recognizes both it and a specific DNA signature."

She paused and added almost apologetically, "Of course, I'm just speculating."

"Most of the time your speculations are closer to reality than the actual truth," Kane responded. "I think you're right that Utu won't interfere with the princess until she opens the vault with the collar. He'll follow at a distance and strike when he feels he has the advantage."

"Maybe," Grant said skeptically. "Utu might not attack the train, but what's to stop Laputara? If Utu only cares about a royal heir completing the pilgrimage, then Laputara and his army of drug addicts could just hijack the train, take the collar and save Utu a lot of sneaking around."

DeFore nibbled at her full underlip, surveying the passenger car. "With the royal retinue on board, there won't be enough room to carry more than a handful of guardsmen. The four of us could defend her, but the risk factor would be high."

"Very high, I'd say," Kane said. "That's why we need the classic standby of the ace-on-the-line. A guardian angel."

The corner of Grant's mouth quirked upward. "An angel in the form of a Manta would pretty much fit the bill, wouldn't it?"

"I volunteer," Kane interposed quickly.

The corner of Grant's mouth turned downward. "Like hell. The score of the last rock-paper-scissors still stands. Brigid, you witnessed it."

He tapped his chest with a thumb. "*I'll* be the angel."

"In air-conditioned comfort," Kane snapped. "There's no reason why the princess can't have two aces flying on the line."

"Yes, there is," DeFore declared crossly. "You know I'm not very good with guns. Brigid is better but she's no expert." She glanced over at the green-eyed woman. "No offense."

"None taken," Brigid said with a wan smile.

"You can damn well bet Pakari's guardsmen aren't much with firearms, either," the medic continued doggedly. "It's not fair to rely only on Brigid's marksmanship if Laputara attacks."

Kane lifted conciliatory hands. "All right, all right. Why can't we just fly Pakari to the Mountain of the Apes? It would be a hell of a lot faster and easier than chugging across Africa in a three-hundred-year-old train."

"Actually, that's the entire point of the pilgrimage," Brigid said curtly. "To cross the length and breadth of the Waziri nation, for the princess to survey her holdings, to allow her subjects to see her, maybe for the only times in their lives."

She indicated the crocks of sweetmeats on the floor of the passenger carriage and the flower-festooned platform extending from the rear of it. "Princess Pakari will stand there, tossing treats and bestowing benedictions on the people who have gathered to cheer her. It's part of the investiture tradition of the tribe."

Grant shook his head in frustration. "It doesn't sound like one to me. It sounds like something her eccentric old man cooked up because he had too much time on his hands."

"No," said DeFore firmly. "I've spent a little more time with the princess than any of you. The traditional pilgrimage to the rim of the world was made on elephant back, with the royal retinue following on foot. It usually took a week, sometimes more, exposing the heirs to every kind of danger. N'gatawana didn't wish that on his children. He sounded like a good father to me."

Grant's face remained as immobile as if carved from teak. "He raised a psychotic son and spoiled little bitch of a daughter. I'd say his parenting skills needed some tweaking."

DeFore slitted in her eyes in annoyance. "I don't think you're in any position to judge, Grant. It's not like any of us know anything about raising children, right?"

Grant declined to respond. He knew to what she referred. In the baronies, children were a necessity for the continuation of ville society, but only those passing stringent tests were allowed to bear them. Genetics, moral values and social standing were the most important criteria. Generally, a man and a woman were bound together for a term of time stipulated in a contract. Once a child was produced, the contract was voided.

A number of years before, he and a woman named Olivia had submitted a formal mating application. Both of them had entertained high hopes of the application being approved and they managed to convince themselves that it would be. After all, babies still needed to be born, but only the right kind of babies. A faceless council determined that he and Olivia could not produce the type of offspring that made desirable ville citizens.

Once their application was rejected, he and Olivia had drawn attention to themselves. Their relationship became officially unsanctioned and couldn't continue lawfully. In the years since Olivia, he had never given much thought to fathering children. But since pledging himself to Shizuka, he'd started thinking about it a bit more seriously. He wondered if creating a new life might not be a way to balance out the ones he had taken over the years.

Certainly Lakesh had tried his hand at bringing new lives into the world as a way cleanse his soul of his guilt over his involvement in the Totality Concept conspiracies. Kane and Brigid might not have even existed if not for his efforts to clean his conscience by manipulating the in vitro human genetic samples in storage.

Grant scowled at DeFore. "That might be so. But how do we know for sure that Pakari is any more the rightful heir to the throne than Laputara?"

There was sudden clamor of a drum and the deep blaring of a horn in the foliage. The underbrush rustled and disgorged a line of enormously tall, ebony-skinned spearmen. Ostrich plumes floated above the lion-mane headpieces like white clouds. Their bodies were adorned with bracelets, anklets and armlets. The blades of the spears gleamed silver.

"They're wearing their Sunday best, looks like," Kane commented softly.

"It's an important day," Brigid murmured. "Maybe the most important day in their lives."

The eight guardsmen took up position on either side of the path. A moment later Inkula strode between them, feeling his way with the tapered tip of his staff. Fetishes of ivory, bone, hide and feathers hung from his wattled throat and were intertwined within his beard.

The priest was followed a heartbeat later by Princess Pakari, and at the sight of her, the women and children instantly prostrated themselves, pressing their foreheads against the ground.

The outlanders didn't follow suit, but there was no doubt in their minds that Princess Pakari was the rightful ruler of the Waziri nation.

Chapter 25

Princess Pakari swept up the aisle formed by her guardsman and paused, striking a pose with her right hand on her hip, sunlight gleaming in the satiny highlights of her slender body, sleek thighs and long legs.

A crown of aigrettes nodded above her head, and a jeweled coif in her hair sprouted feathers of many brilliant colors—rose, green and peach. Golden hoops shone in multiple strands around the graceful column of her neck. Bands of pure gold glittered on her wrists, arms and ankles. The gilded tip of the elephant tusk diadem shone with an aureate glow.

Her only garment was a white silken jerkin with a neckline that plunged down between her firm breasts and fell to her upper thighs, girded at the waist by a belt of leopard skin. Pakari gazed about her with a calm, regal dignity that dominated her surroundings. She stood straight and tall and no doubt showed in her lovely face.

The remainder of the royal retinue marched from the foliage, a half-dozen colorfully clad men and women who carried drums and giant horns made of elephant tusks. A teenage girl led a black goat by a leash and it bleated in protest.

The princess nodded to the outlanders, but made a very obvious point of not meeting Grant's gaze. She made an indifferent gesture toward the people bowing to her. "Rise."

As the people did so, Inkula shuffled toward the locomotive, tapping it here and there with the point of his staff, uttering soft grunts of approval or disapproval.

Pakari asked, "Is my conveyance prepared? Will it safely and speedily carry me and my party to the rim of the world?"

Kane arched a quizzical eyebrow. "Why ask us, Your Highness?"

"She is ready," Inkula stated confidently. "She has just told me."

Pakari's lips pursed in a moue that was either the ghost of a smile or the beginnings of a frown. "Will all of you accompany me on the pilgrimage?"

"No," said Grant and he brusquely outlined the plan agreed upon by he and his friends.

Pakari nodded. "Very wise tactics. However, my scouts reported that Laputara's men are moving in on the village. It might be wise, Mr. Grant, to leave now so your 'ace-on-the-line' can be reclaimed."

Brigid glanced toward the locomotive, confusion glinting in her eyes. "Who is going to be at the controls of Old 88?"

"I will be," Inkula replied, probing a swag of yellow blossoms with his staff.

"You?" demanded DeFore in disbelief.

Inkula turned toward her, regarding her with a toothless grin. "The emperor gave me years of instruction in the operation of Old 88. It is my vision that has gone dark, not my memory. However, I will rely on others to act as my eyes."

Grant and Kane exchanged worried glances but they said nothing. Gusting out a sigh, Grant said, "Just when I thought no situation could ever surprise me—"

In the distance came the faint but sharp crackle of automatic-rifle fire. Everyone's heads swiveled in the direction of the village. Inkula was the first to speak, shouting orders and gesticulating with his staff. People scurried to and fro with almost frantic haste. Several men began loading more logs onto the fuel tender.

"It will take about twenty minutes to build up a full head of steam," Pakari said calmly, but worry darkened her eyes. "We may not have that long before Laputara's men reach us here."

Grant moved toward the path, stepping around the princess. "I'll do what I can to buy you some time."

Reaching out, Pakari restrained him with a gentle hand on his arm. "Mr. Grant, do you know why I said you reminded me of N'gatawana?"

"Because of my resemblance to an elephant?"

"No," the girl replied in a voice barely above a whisper. "Because my father was a great warrior."

Grant locked eyes with her, then nodded tersely in appreciative acknowledgment. He set off down the path at a run, slapping brush out of his way. Kane called after him, "Don't forget not to get killed!"

Grant resisted the urge to respond with a shouted profanity. He decided to save his breath for the run. He sprinted through clouds of flying insects humming through the muggy air. Dappled sunlight filtered through the leafy, pungent eucalyptus trees. Scarlet beaked birds cawed at him from the branches. He glimpsed a huge snake slithering lethargically across the path into the brush.

Grant was careful to pace himself, not daring to run flat-out in the oppressive heat. As he neared the edge of the tract, he encountered three seven-foot-tall Waziri warriors dressed in formal tribal attire, with lion-mane headdresses and leopard-skin anklets. They were armed with very long spears tufted with red feathers and they pointed the sharp tips at him.

Grant's Sin Eater slid into his palm, but the guardsmen lowered their weapons. The tallest of the three said in English, "Her highness left us here to guard the path against the prince's soldiers."

"Any sign of them?"

Before they could answer, thunder rumbled in the distance, but Grant knew it wasn't thunder—it was heavy-caliber gunfire. Grant pushed past the guardsmen and sprinted across open ground, up the escarpment and into the village proper. He saw no one, the lanes empty of movement and life. Nothing stirred inside the huts. He guessed the people, the warriors included, had slipped away into the jungle and fields around the village.

Reaching the stockade fence, Grant made a swift visual survey of the veldt and saw figures creeping through the high grasses, moving cautiously and furtively. He clenched his teeth in frustration when he realized that Laputara's troopers were between him and the Mantas. At a quick count, he estimated there were perhaps twenty of them, maybe many more out of sight.

Given half a chance, the troopers would be delighted to capture him and take a very long time putting him to death. Grant knew that if the marauders as much as caught a glimpse of him, he faced either a lingering death or a swift one. He wasn't sure which he preferred.

Then suddenly dark heads rose from the sea of grass, like sharks. They swiftly formed a tightening circle around the contingent of creeping troopers. Grant stopped breathing as almost every point on the veldt disgorged a horde of dark-skinned figures. Their lean ebony bodies gleamed through beads and paint and scraps of animal skin. At first they ran silently, wielding *tonga* short swords and lances.

They struck the troopers from both flanks, pushing them toward the stockade fence. A resounding roar arose from the ranks of the Waziri guardsmen: *"Ulga uwa Pakari! Ulga!"*

The first troopers died quickly as the spears sank deep into their entrails and sword blades split their skulls like melons. Screams blended in with the clash of steel on steel. Two of Laputara's soldiers managed to get off shots before they were overwhelmed by a wave of the Waziri warriors.

The blades whirled, rose and fell. At each stroke the swords clove through skulls, sliced through flesh and severed limbs. Knobbed, hardwood kirri's smashed down on heads. Blood sprayed in a scarlet mist, hanging over the veldt like early-morning fog.

The Waziri ran through the grasses, their keen-bladed lances flying, war clubs crushing, short swords stabbing. Autofire crackled and two of the guardsmen went down, vanishing from view. Pakari's soldiers didn't run—they met the invaders with mad cries of *"Ulga uwa Pakari!"* exploding from their throats. It was the death fight of warriors who contemptuously courted death in order to mete out destruction, a blind, merciless struggle.

Back and forth the battle rolled, blades plunging into flesh, AK-47s hammering from the press of the combatants. More of the Waziri guardsmen crashed to the ground, their bodies stitched through by slugs.

Grant started breathing again and vaulted over the stockade fence, running at an oblique angle for his Manta. He tried to give the killzone a wide berth, not counting on the blood-maddened Waziri to recognize him as an ally. He skirted three corpses sprawled in puddles of gore, only one of them a Waziri.

Suddenly one of Laputara's troopers seemingly materialized out of the ground in front of him. His lips drew back from his teeth in a silent snarl, and he lunged, whipping a *tonga* in left and right vertical arcs, menacing Grant's head, throat and chest. Grant dodged, ducked, aimed his Sin Eater and squeezed off a single shot.

The man staggered to a halt. His eyes squinted, then widened as they looked at the small hole punched through his left pectoral. His mouth opened as if to ask a question, and a flood of vermilion spilled out.

The trooper fell to his knees then flopped onto his

face. Grant leaped over him and continued running but
he ran right into the middle of the screaming mass of
men locked in hand-to-hand combat surging out over
the savannah.

The veldt erupted with gunfire, screams and shouts.
Steel-jacketed bullets tore raw, ragged holes in naked
brown flesh. Grant was forced to evade, crouch and
drop to the ground instead of finding targets. The battle swirled around the outspread wings of the Manta and
he knelt, looking for an opening.

Grant was careful how he handled Sin Eater, not
hosing the ammo around indiscriminately. All of the
rounds he fired found targets, the well-timed and
-placed bullets knocking another AK-wielding
trooper's legs out from under him.

Impatience making him reckless, Grant kicked off
the ground in a run, dashing for the TAV. Suddenly a
rush of struggling bodies burst from the grass and
knocked him sprawling. A heavy weight dropped directly onto his back, driving him face first to the ground.
Knees pressed into his buttocks, and a pair of large
hands closed about his neck and squeezed.

Spitting and cursing, Grant heaved, bucked and
twisted. He managed to roll over onto his back and
look up into the hate-twisted, scar-distorted dark face
bobbing over him. The trooper was very strong and he
resisted each of Grant's efforts to throw him off. He
thrust a knife blade for his throat.

Grant wrenched himself aside and the edge of the
blade skimmed the side of his neck, drawing a thread
of blood. He fired his Sin Eater at the trooper, and a

crimson spray erupted from the bridge of the man's nose. His grip loosened and he slowly fell forward. Elbowing the dead weight from his body, Grant rolled to one side and got to his knees.

A bullet splashed hot hair on the left side of his face and he sighted a trooper leveling an old revolver at him. Grant squeezed off a single shot and sent a 9 mm wad of lead into his belly. The man folded over the wound and fell out of sight.

The area around the TAVs was screaming, bloody chaos. Guns blasted and spears lanced and skulls were split by tongas. Grant moved rapidly toward his ship in a half crawl. A trooper fell down in front of him, writhing around the spear-head lodged in his guts.

Another of Laputara's soldiers toppled, screaming wildly as he snatched convulsively at a spear embedded in his back. Grant caught a brief glimpse of the warrior who had hurled the lance spinning around, clutching at himself as a stream of autofire clawed open his chest, sending fragments of flesh and rib bones spinning off in all directions.

Reaching the wing of the Manta, Grant levered himself atop the sleek surface, fumbling for the hidden cockpit lock catch. His fingers found it, depressed it and the canopy slid open. As he slid inside, a storm of bullets struck the fuselage, sounding like a work gang of blacksmiths simultaneously pounding half a dozen anvils.

The cockpit cover hissed shut, substantially reducing the outside noise. Grant lifted the helmet from the back of the chair and placed it over his head. He felt a pressure shifting around the base of his neck as the helmet automatically extended a lining and a seal. He heard a hiss and the cool breath of oxygen pumped from the tanks mounted on the back of the chair touched his sweat-damp face. He sighed in relief. It felt wonderful.

Grasping the handgrip lever, he pulled it back slightly, then pushed it forward. It caught and clicked into position. The hull began to vibrate around him, in tandem with a whine that grew in pitch. On the inside of his helmet flashed the words: VTOL Launch System Enabled.

With a droning whine, the Manta slowly rose, a small and brief flurry of dust swirling beneath it. The landing gear retracted automatically into the TAV's belly. With a stomach-sinking swiftness the ship lifted upward. The humming drone changed in pitch as the aircraft rose as smoothly as if it were being raised on a giant hand made of compressed air.

The inventory of all the dials, switches, gauges and fire controls flashed across the helmet's visor. The helmet's HUD displays offered different vantage points of the ascent and Grant's eyes flicked from one to another. He couldn't help but smile grimly when he saw both the Waziri and the troopers fleeing madly in all directions. Both factions remembered the destruction wreaked by the aircraft the day before.

Grant stopped the ship's ascent at one hundred feet and he waggled its wings in a farewell to any of the Waziri warriors who might be watching. Then he en-

gaged the pulse detonation wave engines and with an
eardrum compressing boom the Manta raced across the
sky like a bullet hurtling from the barrel of a gun.

Chapter 26

Steam hissed and the boiler burbled and the cab was lit up by dancing flares from the open grate as Kane heaved two more logs into the fire. He kicked shut the iron door, interrupting a stream of spark-speckled smoke. Only the fact sweat rivered from his every pore and his T-shirt was soaking wet saved him from being burned. Eyes stinging with salt, he leaned out of the cab, desperately gulping breaths of fresh air.

"How much longer?" he asked hoarsely.

Inkula passed his hands lightly over the pilot wheel and the pressure valves, feeling the heat. "Five minutes, I'd judge."

Eyeing the blaze in the firebox, Kane commented, "Sure as hell hope you found another hiding place for the collar."

Inkula only smiled patronizingly.

Old 88 trembled and quivered like an elderly woman trying to rise from her rocking chair. Inkula adjusted valve wheels and nudged levers, going through the procedure strictly on memory and by feel.

Looking behind him over the fuel tender, Kane saw the royal retinue climbing aboard the passenger car, more than a few of them expressing apprehension, if not outright fear of the wheezing, hissing, smoke-belching machine. The goat bleated incessantly in either annoyance or anger.

Craning his neck, he tried to find Brigid Baptiste and Reba DeFore among the people, but didn't see them.

"Kane!" Brigid's voice blasted into his head through the Commtact, and he jumped, cursing, nearly falling into the stacked cordwood.

"Where the hell are you?" he demanded angrily to cover his embarrassment.

Brigid's response was amused. "Sorry. I tried yelling, but you couldn't hear me over the train's racket. Look to your left."

Brigid and DeFore approached the locomotive from behind the work shed, both women appearing to have been dipped in jet-black dye from the necks down. They were attired in midnight-colored shadow suits that absorbed light the way a sponge absorbed water. Although the black, skintight garments didn't appear as if they would offer protection from flea bites, they were impervious to most bladed weapons.

Ever since they had absconded with the suits from Redoubt Yankee on Thunder Isle, the bodysuits had proved their worth many times over. Manufactured with a technique known in predark days as electrospin lacing, the electrically charged polymer particles formed a dense web of formfitting fibers. Composed of a compiled weave of spider silk, Monocrys and Spectra fabrics, the garments were essentially a single-crystal, metallic microfiber with a very dense molecular structure.

The outer Monocrys sheathing went opaque when exposed to radiation, and the Kevlar and Spectra layers provided protection against blunt trauma. The spider silk allowed flexibility, but it traded protection from firearms for freedom of movement. The suits were climate controlled for environments up to highs of 150 degrees and lows as cold as minus ten degrees Fahrenheit.

Brigid extended a rolled-up shadow suit to him, saying loudly, "I thought you might want to put this on in case we have to run a gauntlet of Laputara's men. Besides, if you're going to be up there in the hot-box, the suit will keep you from succumbing to heat stroke."

Kane considered her words for a moment, then climbed down from the cab, taking the garment from her with a word of thanks.

"We have all the other ordnance from the Mantas aboard, too," DeFore declared, gesturing to several flat, oblong cases tucked under the benches of the passenger car. "If we're shot at, we can shoot back and lob grens at them."

Despite her uncharacteristically aggressive words, DeFore's brown eyes were clouded with worry. She had tied back her hair but hadn't attempted the intricate braiding technique she favored in Cerberus.

"Why don't you two get aboard," Kane suggested. "Inkula claims we'll be ready to roll in about five minutes."

"Any word from Grant?" asked DeFore.

Kane shook his head. "Not yet."

He walked into the nearest clump of underbrush and, screened by foliage, removed his sweat-soaked clothing, stripping out of the camo pants and jump boots. He tugged on the shadow suit by opening a magnetic seal on its right side. The garment had no zippers or buttons, and he donned it in one, continuous piece from the hard-soled boots to the gloves.

The fabric molded itself to his body, and he smoothed out the wrinkles and folds by running his hands over the arms and legs. After adjusting the high collar, he realized he felt about ten times better, particularly after the suit's internal thermostats cooled him off.

He strapped the Sin Eater's power holster to his right forearm and returned to the locomotive, climbing into the cab. Inkula sensed him and announced simply, "We are ready."

"Let's do it, then," Kane replied. Over his Commtact, he said to Brigid, "Have everybody take their seats, Baptiste. Old 88 is leaving the station."

Inkula twisted the valve handles, then slowly pulled back on the throttle. The cab vibrated around them and steam jetted out from a vent. A prolonged groaning came from deep within the locomotive, followed by a nerve-stinging squeal of steel grinding against steel.

The great wheels suddenly spun wildly, sparks spewing from the point where the rims met the rails. A clattering jolt shook the train from cowcatcher to the passenger car. Old 88 shuddered and trembled violently, and for an instant, Kane expected to see bolts, rivets and piston rods flying in all directions. Then the locomotive surged forward, wheezing and panting like a prehistoric beast roused from slumber. Black smoke boiled from the stack. The iron wheels turned slowly on the rails, finding traction as the locomotive strained to pull the fuel tender and the passenger car.

The train lugubriously lurched forward along the stretch of tracks built on an elevated causeway. Kane glanced up into the sky and beyond the treetops saw only a blue expanse with a couple of high cirrus clouds. He couldn't help but worry about Grant, wondering whether the man had managed to make it to the TAV or if he had disregarded Kane's reminder about not getting himself killed.

Almost as soon as the thought registered, a bullet ricocheted off the cab window frame with a keening whine. Above the chuff-chuffing, Kane heard a sporadic burst of gunfire. Crouching down, he searched the underbrush for the gunmen. He glimpsed five of Laputara's troopers running toward them from the front. Apparently they had come in from the direction of the river instead of through the village. A hail of bullets cracked and struck flares from the prow of the locomotive. Inkula didn't duck or flinch away.

"We're being shot at, old man," Kane told him, unleathering his Sin Eater.

"I made that connection," replied Inkula dryly. "I expect you'll let me know if the bullets come any closer."

The old man pushed the throttle lever forward. Old 88 gave forth with a groaning bellow, the drivers spinning madly before they caught, then the locomotive rolled ponderously along the stretch of tracks that followed the course of the Julaba River.

The train continued to gain momentum, gathering

speed with every foot it traveled. Trees, underbrush and patterns of light and darkness flitted past. Inkula twisted a valve wheel, feeding more heat to the boilers. Old 88 rattled and hissed as it struggled to pick up speed.

Glancing behind him at the passenger carriage, Kane saw the Waziri guardsmen clustered around Princess Pakari, their bodies and their elephant hide shields forming a protective bulwark.

Another bullet whipped through the cab, passing into one window and out the other, thumping the air between Kane and Inkula. Little tongues of flame spit from the underbrush, and several lengths of cordwood exploded into splinters. Kane heard the staccato chatter of a Copperhead from the passenger car as Brigid leaned out and strafed the overgrowth with a full-auto burst. A man tumbled out of the foliage, clutching at his face.

Kane hazarded a glance out of the window at the railway ahead. A trooper stood in the center of the tracks, trying to set up a mortar launcher. He was so engrossed in the task, he didn't jump aside fast enough and was struck a glancing blow by the cowcatcher. He flailed into the mud like a marionette with its strings cut. The mortar round burst from the launch tube, the shell exploding only a few yards to the left of the locomotive. Leaves burst up in a shower and shrapnel rattled briefly against Old 88's side. Kane felt a few pieces strike his left arm. The dense fabric of the shadow suit saved him from serious injury.

The track curved alongside a palisade of Borassus

palms that lined the riverbank. A quartet of troopers ran
across the tracks, plainly intending to wait until the locomotive passed and then climb aboard. Kane sent a
burst of fire in their direction. Two staggered away,
slapping at bullet wounds, and the other pair vanished
into the swamp.

"Can't you go any faster?" Kane demanded into Inkula's ear.

"Are you able to read the pressure gauge?" Inkula
said calmly.

Kane rubbed a gloved finger over the glass and saw
how the needle wavered at the outside edge of the red
band. "Just about redline."

The old man nodded in satisfaction. "Good."

He slammed the throttle lever full forward and Old
88 careened around the curve, rumbling and clicking
along the rails. Then the train burst out of the Usumbur Tract and roared out into the open savannah.

THE PLAINS SEEMED endless. The grasses bent beneath
errant breezes. In the cobalt-blue sky, the sun no longer
hid behind the interlaced branches of the jungle growth
and blazed fiercely. Here and there a solitary tree rose
to break the flat monotony of the veldt.

Old 88 averaged only a bit more than thirty miles per
hour. Far off in the hazy distance, violet mountains rose
from the horizon. Alert for any movement or shape out
of place, Kane kept constant watch on their surroundings, keeping his face turned toward the window partly
to overcome the nostril-clogging odors of smoke,
grease and heated metal.

He saw a waterhole, sunk deep into the surface of the ground. Zebra, antelope and even a rhinoceros clustered about it, drinking and wallowing in the mud. A herd of gazelles grazed nearby. An elephant, lumbering along like a giant boulder rolling down a slope, raised its trunk and acknowledged the train's passage with a long, loud trumpet.

Inkula pulled the whistle cord, sending out a high-pitched shriek of sound. The elephant responded with another bugle call. Inkula smiled. "Old N'gatawana gives this pilgrimage his blessing."

Kane squinted at the distant animal. "So that's him? How do you know?"

"I recognize his voice."

Kane cast him a penetrating glance, but the old man's wrinkled face was impassive.

Activating the Commtact, Kane asked, "How are things in first-class, Baptiste? Everybody all right?"

"Fine," she responded crisply. "The goat is in a pretty bad humor, though."

"Why the hell did they bring that damn thing along?"

Brigid's response was flat. "I have my suspicions."

Before Kane could request she elaborate, he glimpsed sunlight winking from metal high in the sky. Leaning out of the window, he peered up, past the cab's roof overhang. He released a long, gusting sigh of relief when he recognized the delta-winged configuration of a Manta. It skimmed toward them from the direction of the Waziri village.

The TAV inscribed a slow, circling flyover, tipping its port-side wing in a salute. Grant's voice filtered over the Commtact, "How are things aboard the little engine that could?"

"Hot and smelly," Kane retorted, ignoring the sour glance cast his way by Inkula. "You have any problems getting airborne?"

"None worth mentioning." Grant's tone was so studiedly casual, Kane instantly knew he was downplaying an incident of serious carnage.

"I'll be flying point," he continued, "checking the route ahead. Clear skies so far."

"Good," Brigid put in, "but don't exceed the comm range. We need to stay in contact. We've got about ninety miles before we reach Magebali Kwa Belewagi, and it won't be a sight-seeing safari along the way."

"I never thought it would it be," Grant retorted.

The Manta climbed high and followed a course paralleling the railroad tracks at a distance of a half mile.

The train continued chugging along, Inkula carefully increasing the speed to a steady forty miles per hour. Kane kept watching the pressure gauge and when the needle wavered too far below the redline, he fed the firebox more logs. Even wearing the shadow suit, he sweated profusely and every few minutes felt compelled to hang his head out the window in search of cooling breezes. He saw a pride of sleepy lions watching the train's passage from the shade of thorn trees and he briefly wondered if there were any mutated strains of African wildlife prowling around.

As the train rocked steadily toward the distant mountain range, more and more people dressed in bright native costumes appeared at the railway embankment.

They waved bouquets of flowers and feathers. On the passenger car, the approach of Pakari was heralded by a dramatic drumming and long, bass notes sounded by the horn made of an elephant tusk.

The princess stood on the garland-draped platform at the rear of the carriage, beautiful and regal, tossing handfuls of sweetmeats to the people who responded with shouting chants of *"Pakari atakupenda daima! Pakari atakupenda daima!"*

As the sun climbed toward its zenith, Kane guessed the outside temperature was 110 degrees and hovered around 130 in the cab of Old 88. The heat didn't seem to bother Inkula, and Kane wondered how the old man kept from passing out at the pilot wheel.

"Do you want some relief?" Kane asked him. "You can go sit back with the princess for a little while if you'd like."

"No, thank you," the priest replied. "This is my final journey aboard the Old 88...I do not wish to give up any second of it, if it's not absolutely necessary."

Kane narrowed his eyes. "Why would it be?"

Before Inkula answered, Grant's voice echoed in his head. "Bogey at three o'clock."

Chapter 27

For an hour and a half Grant flew without altering his course or seeing anything but blue sky and grassy veldt. There wasn't much in the way of interesting features to look at either above or below.

Now and then he saw herds of wildebeest and cattle, and once there was a group of black men in long skirts and round red caps, walking single file. They stopped and, their faces completely blank, stared upward solemnly as the Manta winged overhead, but they didn't run.

Looking toward the foothills of the mountain range, he saw buzzards wheeling but he wasn't inclined to find out what they might be circling. He felt a deep weariness. His thigh burned where the bedouin bullet had creased it and he wished he could catch a nap. But he felt a growing uneasiness, a disquiet that pinched at his nerves. He couldn't put his finger on the cause of his tension.

When his helmet resounded with an electronic buzz Grant almost chuckled with satisfaction. The sound was the radar-lock-on warning, piped from the forward sensor array into his helmet. Glancing out of the port side of the canopy, he glimpsed a brief flash of distant silver. It was high and moving as fast as the Manta. It grew larger until he caught the reflective glint of sunlight on the shimmering, domed surface.

Seeming to float in the air between his eyes and the visor, a column of numbers appeared, glowing red against the pale bronze. When he focused on a distant object, the visor magnified it and provided a readout as to distance and dimension. Now he focused on the aircraft soaring in from the general direction of the mountain range. It was a little under three nautical miles distant. Grant had expected airborne reconnaissance, if not a welcoming committee.

He knew from experience the Annunaki sky disks were good for high-altitude bombing and strafing runs, but he had often wondered how suited they were for low infighting or fast, tight maneuvering. He made up his mind to find out.

"Bogey at three o' clock," he said laconically.

"Bogey?" echoed Brigid and Kane almost simultaneously. "Utu's ship?"

"More than likely," Grant answered. "Of course, it's problematical if he's aboard, but the thing is on an intercept course."

Brigid said tersely, "He probably just wants to observe us."

"We can't take that chance," replied Grant. "For all we know, he could blow out the rails and while the train is stranded, Laputara and his troops could surround you and take the collar…after butchering everybody."

"That's a good point, but Utu could just be watching our progress," Kane commented reflectively.

"There's only one way to find out…I'll go say hi."

"You'll be out of comm range," Brigid argued. "Not a good tactic."

"Not knowing what Utu is up to is a worse one," Grant countered. "If there's any real shooting, I'll withdraw."

Without waiting to hear a response from his partners, Grant pulled back on the control stick and the lateral thrust smashed down on him, slamming him hard against the back of his chair. The speed-gauge icon scrolled with numbers.

He pushed the stick forward and then to the left. The Manta's velocity slowed and it banked to port. The LARC—or low-altitude ride control—subsystem fed him turbulence data. The controls automatically damped the effects of turbulent air pockets by the deflection of two small fins extending down from beneath the cockpit area.

The disk ship hovered motionless, looking like a featureless orb of alloy. Whoever was aboard it seemed unaware of the TAV's fast approach. Then, with a shocking suddenness it shot straight up, as if it had been jerked up by an invisible string.

The Manta whipped through the space the disk had occupied, and Grant tilted it starboard wing in a steep bank. A half second later, a stream of energy blazed through the air like phosphorescent threads and exploded against the ground.

Cursing, Grant put the TAV into a sharp climb. The disk zipped up and across his course. For the briefest of seconds, the TAV was outlined in his helmet sights, past the crosshairs, and he thumbed the trigger button on the control stick.

A missile flamed from its pod sheath on his starboard wing. He felt the craft shudder slightly with the explosive release of the projectile. The missile inscribed a fiery trail, bright against the blue backdrop of the sky. From the underside of the disk he saw the flare of incoming fire. The rocket exploded in midair.

Shoving the joystick forward, Grant dropped the ship in a sharp rollaway feint and came rushing up on the enemy craft from below and behind. The sensor scope targeted the disk and he launched two missiles. The sky was suddenly laced with a hellish web of pure energy, deadly beams stabbing out in a hellfire barrage. The missiles detonated in billowing clouds of orange flame and black smoke.

Grant jerked back on the stick, but the ship shook stem to stern as the pieces of the missile casing struck the fuselage glancing blows.

He barrel-rolled the Manta away from the disk just as its plasma batteries blazed again. He felt the TAV shudder beneath multiple impacts before he was able to whisk the craft out of range. A pattern of scorch marks appeared on the starboard wing.

Grant threw his vessel into a corkscrew spiral dive, and the blazing volley of plasma energy missed him entirely. The disk veered away, looped and returned to engage him again.

Grant forced the ship into a sharp ascent and executed perfect vertical reverse. He sent the Manta plunging directly back toward the maddeningly elusive disk.

It arrowed away, back in the direction it had come. Only the inertial damping field kept him from losing consciousness during the high-speed, high-stress maneuvers.

As the disk flitted away, seeming to shrink to the size of a silver pinhead, he growled between clenched teeth, "Not this time. *Not this time!*"

Engaging the pulse-detonation engines, Grant ignored how dangerously the craft vibrated as it slammed across the sky, trailing a sonic boom. He depressed the trigger switch, and a missile sprang toward the disk, but a swarm of plasma beams surrounded it and the projectile vanished in a billowing cloud of flame.

Grant saw the fireball spreading out toward him and there was nothing he could do but grit his teeth and plummet through it. A grid of CGI hairlines glowed inside the visor of his helmet and a tiny bead of light, a digital copy of the enemy ship, zipped to and fro through the computer-generated optics.

The terrain changed. The veldt rolled toward the line of mountains and became hillier. Beneath the two aircraft there were more outcroppings of rock lifting from the grassy plain like huge headstones, the stone gray and red and glittering with deposits of mica.

To avoid a thrusting spire of basalt, the disk climbed, putting itself directly in front of Grant's Manta. He didn't hesitate. Instantly, he lined up the ship in his helmet's crosshairs and thumbed the launch stud. The missile roared out of the starboard wing pod in a flare of flame.

It streaked in a straight line to impact against the

disk's topside dome, exploding in a bloom of flame and metal fragments. The disk flipped into a crazed sideways rim-over-rim tumble, trailing streamers of smoke.

Grant's snarl of bloodthirsty jubilation turned into a wordless roar of disbelief when the disk recovered from its roll. Wobbling, it put on a burst of speed as it dived toward the rock formations.

The disk ship swerved to port, entering a canyon. Grant hesitated, then biting back a profanity, he tipped the ship up on one wing to cruise through the cleft in the rock. Flying through the canyon was treacherous—the ramparts of stone bulged out several yards in some places, and sharp shelves of rock stabbed out like giant sword blades. Grant's hands were constantly busy with the pitch, tab and trim controls.

He gazed at the computer-generated image of the landscape on the HUD. Data scrolled down the side of the display, reviewing and assessing primary areas of danger beyond his line of vision. Each boulder, outcropping and curve in the gorge walls showed in detail as they whipped by in a blur. The disk was nowhere to be seen.

The canyon suddenly opened up into a broad basin, or series of basins surrounded by jagged bastions of granite. It was a barren wilderness, a jumble of broken rock. Mist rose in a fine spray from a waterfall and beads of condensation formed on the Manta's canopy.

The cascade poured over a hundred-foot cliff, crashing into a turbulent, foaming pool. Pulling back on the throttle control to reduce his speed, Grant realized the signature of the disk ship had disappeared from his HUD.

Cold fingers of warning inched up his spine to tighten into a fist at the nape of his neck. His scalp felt as if it were pulling taut, and he realized he had just blithely flown into a trap. He sensed it the way a seasoned old tiger could sense a snare.

He also experienced a surge of anger, but it was directed completely at himself. He had allowed himself to lose his temper, to become frustrated and take off in a thoughtless rage like the greenest Mag recruit. The disk had lured him into a cul de sac.

Directing the Manta in a wide, parabolic cross turn, he sent the ship barreling back in the direction he had come. Before he completed the maneuver, the radar-lock-on began buzzing like a hive of agitated bees. At the same time, his HUD flashed and crawled with a familiar signature.

Grant glanced out of the canopy and saw the silver disk ship bursting out from behind the cascade with an explosive spume of water, liquid glistening on the translucent hull. He realized the tactic employed by the craft and he muttered wearily to himself, "You're getting too old for this shit, pal."

Then he reached for the instrument panel.

Chapter 28

Brigid Baptiste studied the rolling landscape, noting the increasing rockiness of the terrain and the position of the sun in the sky. Red-tinged clouds shrouded it as it began its long descent. The foothills ahead were tinted a pale purple.

The railroad tracks inclined toward a gentle upgrade, wending toward a pass cut through solid rock. Signs of habitation sprouted from the veldt—irrigation canals, neat fields of crops, a scattering of huts and even windmills pumping up water from wells.

Old 88 had stopped at such a well an hour before to take on water. Following Inkula's instructions, Kane and several of Pakari's entourage formed a bucket brigade to quench the thirst of the panting locomotive.

During the twenty-minute procedure, Brigid scanned the sky in all directions for any sign of Grant's Manta or even Utu's disk. Peering through her binoculars, she saw only dark, distant specks she assumed were birds.

Coming to stand beside Brigid, Reba DeFore murmured, "Keep in mind that Grant—all of you—have been one second away from being declared dead a lot of times. So many, I can't even worry about it anymore."

Lowering the binoculars, Brigid favored her with a wan smile. "Liar."

The medic chuckled uneasily. "He'll be along... sooner or later, he'll be along."

Pakari had smiled at both women encouragingly, but not offered any words of comfort. Neither had Kane. He covered his concern with a facade of impatience, irritated that Grant had violated their security protocols but with the unspoken assumption he would return in short order to have vituperation heaped upon him.

Brigid supposed that both Kane and Grant had been through so many harrowing experiences both as Magistrates and after, that life-threatening situations no longer upset their emotional equilibrium. But she knew her assessment was a false one, despite the fact that they were hardened veterans of dozens of violent incidents. They had been raised to be killers, after all—to kill anything or anyone that threatened the security of Baron Cobalt. Most people who lived in the villes feared the Mags, but they relied on them to prevent a return to postunification chaos.

Now all of Cerberus relied on her, Grant and Kane, and although she wasn't entirely comfortable with the arrangement, she in turn relied on the two men.

Brigid Baptiste had always led something of a solitary life. The only person she had ever considered a friend was her mother, Moira. But when she inexplicably vanished from the flat they shared in Cobaltville some fifteen years before, Brigid had withdrawn into herself.

All her mother left behind as a legacy was a photo of herself taken when she was about Brigid's age, and of course, the unique sunset color of her hair. That was one reason she had never cut it.

For a while, Brigid had taken some comfort in the possibility that her mother was associated with the Preservationists and was off somewhere working to reverse the floodtide of ignorance. When she learned the Preservationists didn't exist as such, but were only a straw adversary manufactured by Lakesh, even that small hope had vanished.

After her mother disappeared, Brigid had withdrawn from what passed as a social life in the villes. However, to withdraw completely would have aroused suspicion, so she entered into shallow relationships with a few fellow archivists.

Like her, the men were ville-bred, raised much like herself—fed, clothed, educated and protected from all extremes. And their colorless, limited perspectives, their solemn pronouncements regarding their ambitions, had bored her into a coma. Centuries before they would have been classified as dweebs.

It wasn't until Magistrate Kane had stumbled half-drunk into her quarters and handed her a mystery to solve that she came to realize not all ville-bred men were the same. Of course, solving that mystery had earned her a death sentence and a new status as both exile and outlander, but she had long ago come to terms with it. She knew Kane still felt guilty about dragging her into his own private and illegal investigation, not to mention involving Grant in her rescue.

But she often wondered if that was the first time he had rescued her. She distinctly remembered the jump dream in the malfunctioning gateway unit in Russia that had suggested that they'd lived past lives, each of their souls continually intertwined with the other in some manner, never knowing romance. Morrigan, the blind telepath from the Priory of Awen, had told her that she and Kane were *anam-charas*. In the Gaelic tongue, it meant "soul-friend," but she was never sure what to believe.

As a trained archivist, Brigid knew misinformation often began with half truths, then grew into speculative transitions as someone worked to record the event. No information was sometimes better than half information. The primary duty of archivists was not to record predark history, but to revise, rewrite and often times completely disguise it, using misinformation as a springboard.

The political causes leading to the nukecaust were well known. They were major parts of the dogma, the doctrine, the articles of faith, and they had to be accurately recorded for posterity. The Cerberus database contained unedited and unexpurgated data, and having access to it was one of the few perks Brigid found in her life as an exile.

Life in Cobaltville had been predictable and she sometimes missed the monotony of routine. She knew Grant and Kane often longed for it as well. Their whole lives, from conception to death, were ordered for them, both at work and at home. Ville dogma, ville upbringing, convinced them how lucky they were to live on the bounty of the baron and not to have to scratch out a starvation existence in the Outlands. As long as they obeyed the maddening and contradictory volume of rules, they had security, medical and even retirement benefits.

It was the life Brigid had led, Kane and Grant had led, the only life they had known. Now they were forced to live with prices on their heads, which any so-called citizen could collect just by giving information about them. All because they had sinned by trying to learn a truth and develop a concept of a larger destiny. Reaching for the larger destiny had put them in the forefront of a covert war to free humanity, not just from the harness of slavery, but from the instilled belief they were no better than slaves.

After replenishing the boiler with water, Old 88 got under way again, with Kane still making the cab of the locomotive his duty station. The influence Inkula seemed to wield over him struck Brigid as odd, since Kane usually showed a marked disinclination to associate with self-professed holy men, especially if they were old and sarcastic.

The locomotive labored noisily against a steeper upgrade and at its crest Brigid saw the peak of Magebali Kwa Belewagi, the rim of the world, bulking up from a range of rocky foothills. She estimated it was only five miles or so ahead.

Old 88 chugged between bulwarks of stone, craggy outcroppings that formed a labyrinth bordered by huge boulders and low cliffs. Lizards, some over two feet long, stubbornly sunned themselves on the rocks, refusing to be alarmed by the passage of the train. The puff-

ing and chuffing of the locomotive's drivers echoed
and rebounded from the gorge walls as it navigated the
long narrow channel.

Leaning out from the side of the passenger car,
Brigid peered ahead, trying to see what lay beyond the
end of the pass. Raising the binoculars to her eyes
again, she saw the high spurs of rock rising from a
broad gravel plain that marked the base of Magebali
Kwa Belewagi.

Pakari joined her, saying in a reverential tone,
"There it is, the rim of the world. My pilgrimage is almost complete."

Brigid was not impressed by her view of the mountain. The treeless summit was only a dome of dark,
buttressed rock, slashed through with deep, shadowed
crevices. Squinting through the eyepieces, she barely
discerned a natural trail snaking up across its face. It
looked treacherous and dangerously steep, disappearing into a trough of shadows.

"I don't see any apes," Brigid commented offhandedly. "Or any reason why they would be hanging
around up there."

"That's just a legend," Pakari replied. "If you look
closely, you'll probably see rock formations that resem-
ble apes. I'm sure that's where the tale comes from."

Brigid did as she suggested, and to her mild surprise
identified a pair of rocks that roughly resembled apes
sitting in slouched postures just beneath the peak. But
then, she reminded herself wryly, they only looked like
apes after Pakari mentioned it.

Pakari continued serenely, "To the music of horn

and drum, we will make our way in a joyous procession to the rim and there—"

The girl's voice was abruptly drowned out by an eardrum-slamming detonation, easily audible over the clank and clatter of Old 88's progress. Just as the locomotive emerged from the pass onto the open plain, a blaze of hell-hued light erupted on the track less than fifty yards ahead. A geyser of yellow-and-red flames gushed out amid clods of earth. Smoke boiled upward in a black, mushroom-capped column.

Brigid recognized the explosion of a mortar round and hauled Pakari away from the side. Almost at the same time, metal clashed loudly and the drive wheels locked as Old 88 braked. Sparks flew from the rims like the fiery tails of crashing comets. The royal entourage went sprawling, one of the guardsmen pitching headlong over a bench. They raised their voices in screams and shouts. The goat bleated in outrage.

The entire train shook violently in a series of bone-jarring impacts. Old 88 plunged into the blinding cloud of smoke. Only when the front wheels hit the smoldering crater, the shattered ties and the twisted rails did the locomotive crash to a full halt, tipping over to the right. Crying out, several people tumbled out of the car to sprawl on the ground.

Brigid grabbed a crossbar and managed to keep on her feet, but both Pakari and DeFore fell to all fours. Kane's voice, transmitted over the Commtact, declared breathlessly but with unmistakable grimness, "This is what I was afraid of—Grant was lured away so Laputara could get the drop on us."

Brigid looked to the left and saw two open-bodied trucks speeding over the rocky plain toward them. Gun barrels protruded from the high sides, pointing in their direction like a collection of accusatory fingers.

Jumping down from the carriage, Brigid dragged the long, flat ordnance case from beneath a bench, shouting, "Everybody off! Take cover!"

As she undid the latches, Kane and Inkula sprinted up, both men soot stained and breathing hard. A thread of blood inched from Kane's right nostril, and Inkula held a hand over a raw red abrasion on his forehead.

Moving to the rear of the car, he unleathered his Sin Eater and fired a long, stuttering fusillade at the bouncing, jouncing trucks. A constellation of sparks flared from one of the vehicle's grilles, then a cloud of steam jetted from the punctured radiator. Both of the trucks veered away from their headlong charge, giving Pakari and DeFore time to clamber down from the carriage and take cover behind it.

There came a distant crump from a gorge wall, and a second later, rocks and dirt gouted in a flame-wreathed column only a few yards from the prow of Old 88.

DeFore quickly examined Kane and Inkula, but they waved off her ministrations.

"Sneaky bastards," Kane growled in grudging admiration, scanning the ramparts from beneath a hand. "They set a mortar emplacement up there, probably last night. Utu lured Grant away so Laputara could do his dirty work."

Brigid lifted the lid of the case and removed the long

hollow cylinder of a LAW 80 rocket launcher. She said, "There's dirty work and there's dirty work."

Expertly, she pulled the two sections to their full extended length and unfolded the reflex collinator sight on the smooth upper surface.

Kane eyed it and her dubiously. "Are you sure this is the time and place for your first official launch? You've only taken practice shots before—"

She shrugged. "No time like the present, is there?"

Kane reached down and lifted a sleek, two-foot long RPG-4 rocket from the case. Three more lay nestled within beds of foam rubber. "I guess not."

The truck with the punctured radiator had braked to a halt, steam boiling and hissing all around the cab. The men in the back fired from behind the high, metal-reinforced sides.

The range was too great for their handguns, but a volley of bullets fired from autorifles stitched ragged holes in the flower-bedecked platform upon which Pakari had stood, sending splinters and blossoms flying in sprays.

Brigid and Kane crept to the front of the car, kneeling down between it and the fuel tender. Brigid placed the launcher on her shoulder, and Kane inserted the rocket into the rear, giving it a twist so the fins locked into place and said, "Loaded."

Squinting through the sight, she carefully tracked and centered the crosshairs on the truck, exactly where she figured its fuel tank would be. Calmly, she announced, "Fire in the hole."

Flame and smoke spewed from the hollow bore of

the LAW 80. Propelled by a ribbon of spark-shot vapor, the RPG-4 round lanced from the tube accompanied by a ripping roar. Kane recoiled from the searing heat of the backblast.

The projectile impacted squarely against the fuel tank. The warhead detonated, followed a fraction of an instant later by an earsplitting explosion. The truck kicked over sideways, driven by the detonation from beneath that instantly gutted the cab and incinerated anyone within. The vehicle rose up on all four wheels and crashed down, strewing the ground with engine parts. Flames covered every inch of the chassis like a blanket.

A rain of debris filled the air, jagged pieces of metal banging and clattering down all around, mixed in with chunks and hunks of men's bodies.

Brigid lowered the LAW and gazed dispassionately at the carnage. After a moment, Kane said, "Like you said...there's dirty work and there's dirty work."

Chapter 29

Led by Brigid, Pakari and her entourage sprinted across the stone-littered ground to the shadowed foot of Mage-bali Kwa Belewagi. One of the men slung the goat over his shoulders and ran with it. For once, the animal didn't bleat in protest.

The troopers in the second truck abandoned their vehicle and took shelter behind a granite outcropping. They rightly assumed it was impervious to rocket fire. A quick head count showed there were only five men, one of whom Kane guessed was probably Laputara himself.

Though burdened by a pair of Copperheads, DeFore led Inkula toward a jumble of boulders. Automatic fire crackled and gravel spouted at their heels. Bringing up the rear, Kane fired a triburst at the distant troopers but he knew the shots missed. A Waziri guardsman stumbled, clutching at his chest. Dropping his spear, he kept on trying to run. Then he fell, blood welling from a gaping hole in his left pectoral. He convulsed briefly and made no movement afterward.

Pakari screamed in rage and grief. She spun around, running back toward the fallen man. Sweeping her up in the crook of an arm, Kane bore her to the cover provided by the boulders. Although she was tall, she weighed very little.

"He's dead," he told her flatly. "There's nothing that can be done for him."

Nostrils flaring, eyes bright with fear and fury, Pakari spit, "We will all be killed!"

"No," said Inkula calmly. "Not until Laputara has possession of the collar."

"Speaking of which," Brigid said, testing the actions of her TP-9 and Copperhead, "I hope somebody remembered to bring it along. Otherwise, this whole enterprise will be about the biggest waste of time and lives I've ever been involved with. And that's saying something."

Kane, DeFore and Pakari gazed at her with troubled eyes, then looked over at Inkula. The blind man sensed the weight of the stares and his lips twitched in a barely repressed sly smile.

"Well?" Kane challenged impatiently.

Inkula pulled aside his beard and tugged open his loose-fitting robe. Rubies glinted as bright as freshly spilled blood against his dark brown skin. "I have been wearing this since before dawn. It is heavy and I am anxious to give it over to its rightful owner."

Kane frowned. "I thought the collar had a euphoric effect on the mind."

The old man's smile broadened into a grin. "It does. Why else do you think you were so willing so help me run Old 88, to protect me and do whatever I asked of you without argument?"

For a second, Kane's face registered only confusion.

Then comprehension and anger flashed in his pale eyes. "You've been influencing my mind all damn day?"

Inkula pinched the air with a thumb and forefinger. "Only the tiniest bit, Kane. I would not have been able to sway you at all if you had not already been predisposed to help the Waziri."

Struggling to tamp down his mounting rage, Kane snarled, "You sneaky old son of a—"

The report from the mortar launcher sounded like the bursting of a wet paper bag, but all of them crouched, leaning into the boulders. The round fell short by several yards, but they still flinched away from the explosive concussion. Pebbles and grit pattered down all around.

Peering carefully over the top of the rock tumble, Brigid said, "We're just barely out of range."

"That works both ways, right?" DeFore inquired sourly. "But if we start walking up the trail, Laputara and his boys will move in and put us *in* range."

Pakari's face twisted. She looked like a small, frightened child. "What can we do?"

Inkula rested a hand on her arm. "You can talk to him."

The girl stared at him in shock. "He'll kill me!"

"Not before he has the collar," Brigid interjected.

Pakari drew a deep, uneasy breath. "He won't listen to anything I have to say."

"Maybe not," said Kane, cutting his eyes over to Inkula. "But maybe he'll listen to the collar."

Inkula nodded, gnarled fingers touching the gems. "It's worth a try. But he has to be much closer to feel its effects…so close in fact, he might as well be wearing it."

"We'll lure him to us, just like Utu did with Grant," Brigid stated.

Kane nodded, hooking a thumb over his shoulder. "We'll start up the trail. He'll damn sure follow, but the trick is to stay out of range of his men's guns. Princess, have your guards ever used firearms?"

The question took Pakari by surprise. After a thoughtful moment, she said, "Not that I recollect. But they learn very fast if the task is simple enough."

Gesturing to DeFore and Brigid, Kane said, "Give them your Copperheads. There's no more simple a task than pointing a gun and shooting. They don't have to be accurate to keep Laputara and his jolt-brains from overrunning us."

"They won't shoot Laputara," she objected. "If he orders them to cease fire and turn over their weapons, they will have no choice but to do so."

"Don't let them know Laputara is among the attackers," DeFore said, unslinging her Copperhead.

"Tell them to just keep the soldiers pinned down until we're out of sight up the mountain," Brigid suggested. "Then they can run or surrender or whatever they choose to do."

Pakari nibbled at her underlip, her eyelids drooping over eyes dull with weariness and grief. After a moment she said, "Mr. Grant is missing, possibly dead, Old 88 is destroyed, my loyal followers will probably die and it's all because of me and a ridiculous tradition."

"It's not because of you *or* tradition," Inkula said

softly. "It is because of your mad half brother and an arrogant pretender to godhood."

Pakari swallowed hard. "I'm scared to death."

DeFore gave her a jittery smile. "Join the club, sweetie."

THE TRAIL LEADING up from the base of the mountain was rugged and steep, but there was no other option but to follow it. The sky darkened quickly and Kane estimated less than hour remained before sunset. He had no desire to still be picking his way up the face of the mountain once night fell.

The rocket launcher bumped in an irritating rhythm against Kane's right hip as they climbed. Once more he brought up the rear. Ahead of him trudged Pakari, Inkula, DeFore and a male member of the retinue who had been charged with carrying the goat. Brigid walked beside him. The rest of the entourage had remained below with the guardsmen. The trail itself was a narrow fissure gouged knee-deep in the face of the mountain, overhung by crags of black stone.

Kane grimaced at the searing touch of the hot wind whining around his face, blinking against the grit that stung his eyes. He paused to put on his dark-vision glasses. The light-intensification feature of the electro-chemical polymer allowed him to see clearly in shadow for approximately ten feet as long as there was some kind of light source. The lenses also protected his eyes.

He looked up at the sky, squinting as blurry, amoebalike distortions swam across his vision and he rubbed them with thumb and forefinger. Glancing down the slope, he saw the tiny specks of Laputara and his men creeping across the gravel plain. They were spread out to present more difficult targets, but they assumed they faced only spears. Kane hoped the Waziri guardsmen lying in wait behind the boulders would not act until they were sure their enemies drew closer and then catch them in a triangulated cross fire.

Even as the notion registered, one of Pakari's guards bounded atop a rock and began firing the subgun from shoulder level, wildly spraying the plain with a full-auto burst. The staccato hammering floated up from below and everyone turned to watch. The troopers ducked behind any available cover and went to ground, returning the fire with their AK-47s.

Kane turned away, shaking his head in disgust. Briefly he considered launching a rocket to add more discouragement to the troopers, but decided to save the three remaining projectiles for a more immediate and formidable threat. At the moment, he couldn't imagine what form that threat might take, but his pointman's sense was on the verge of bursting into full alarm.

The farther they climbed, the more signs of ancient construction they encountered—fragments of a blue-tiled reinforcing wall and a small, faceless, winged statue, eroded out of recognition by the scouring of wind and sand.

Brigid pointed to them and said, her voice hoarse with strain, "Those artifacts predate the accepted time period of Prester John."

"Annunaki?" Kane asked.

She shook her head. "Not that far back. Abyssinian, maybe."

The party continued climbing, the distant crackle of gunfire accompanying their ascent. Because of the way the path curved beneath ribs of rock, they could not observe the events down below.

Three quarters of the way to the summit, the trail abruptly ended, flowing into a declivity in the face of the mountain, almost like a valley nestled within a fold of rock. The dim track led deeper into the depression.

A pair of shapeless statues squatted atop pedestals on either side of the crevice. Their featureless heads were bent forward, as to sniff out interlopers. The general outline of the sculptures suggested apes, but the merciless hand of time and the elements had blurred individual features.

"This is the threshold," Inkula called back. "This is where we will hold the investiture ritual."

Kane stepped forward, peering into the black mouth of the passage. Just looking at it made him feel very wary, as though he stared into the maw of some ravenous monster. In fact, he felt more than wary, he felt scared, but he stomped down on the fear, crushing it. His pointman's sense shrilled sharp warnings in his mind.

Pakari cast an anxious glance around her at the grim landscape and hugged herself. "I don't like it. I feel like we're being watched."

Old Inkula patted her shoulder. "We must begin the ceremony while there is still some daylight to see the threshold."

"Threshold?" echoed DeFore. "Threshold to what?"

A low grating sound, like a wire-bristled brush being dragged over jagged metal, reached their ears. The hair prickled on the nape of Kane's neck. He looked around but nothing moved. The strange noise continued—then the man carrying the goat howled with terror. His eyes bulged wide, fixed on a point behind Kane.

Skipping around, Sin Eater springing into his hand, Kane searched for a threat—and found it. All the moisture in his mouth dried to a bitter-tasting film of fear.

For a split second, he felt trapped in the mire of a nightmare as he tried to convince himself he looked only at a trick of the light that confused the eye and confounded the mind.

With a shimmer like quicksilver sliding over glass, the outlines of the pair of amorphous statues seemed to writhe, acquiring detail and features. Within a moment, two gorilla forms sat stooped on the pedestals, leaning forward on their long, coarse-furred arms, resting their massive weight on doorknob-sized knuckles. Lipless mouths gaped to reveal tusklike fangs, and broad nostrils flared wide.

Eyes wide with fear, Pakari shrilled, "The legends are true! The mountain is guarded by flesh-eating apes!"

The bestial faces turned toward them and deep-set eyes of red fire blazed from beneath jutting, overhanging brows.

"You're about half-right," Brigid snapped, raising her TP-9 in a double-fisted grip. "*Synthetic* apes."

Chapter 30

Kane wasn't certain of the implications of Brigid's declaration, and at the moment he wasn't inclined to question her. He stared at the two creatures as they swayed on the pedestals, eyeing their swag bellies and the huge pectoral muscles swelling in giant arches over their chests.

Their large heads, sunk between solid lumps of shoulder muscle, were topped by sagittal crests for the attachment of the massive jaw muscles. The apes looked identical with heavy, supraorbital ridges shadowing their eyes, the protruding muzzles and long yellow canines. He guessed that once they stood up, they would reach or exceed his height.

Brigid said quietly over her shoulder, "Reba, get everybody back, deeper into the tunnel."

DeFore did so, stepping back into the cleft, pulling Inkula and Pakari with her by the arms. The man holding the goat was too shocked to move, paralyzed with fear.

The apes made snuffling grunts in reaction to the movement of the people.

"They look like real gorillas to me," Kane whispered to Brigid.

"They very well may have been," she replied in the same low tone. "At one time. They served as the template for—"

Both creatures uttered thunderous roars and leaped down into the fissure, swinging wide their hairy arms.

Kane's finger depressed the trigger stud of his Sin Eater, and Brigid began firing her autopistol. The impacts turned the apes this way and that, but they remained on their feet. No blood spurted from the wounds. Snarling, they swatted out for the guns.

Brigid and Kane leaped aside, backpedaling toward the dark passage, avoiding the keglike, black-nailed hands by fractional margins. One of the gorillas thrust out a long arm and a leathery paw closed around the fear-frozen man's face, completely covering it. There was a sound as of pottery being crushed underfoot.

The ape opened his hand and the man collapsed to the ground, his limbs slack, his head pulped and squeezed horribly out of shape. The terrified goat went bleating and cantering deeper into the cleft. The ape stood over the corpse and bellowed in triumph, drumming on its chest, tiny eyes glowing crimson.

Brigid rose up from behind a small outcropping and, taking a double-handed grip on her weapon, fired the autopistol in a steady roll at both of the bestial shapes. Several bullets passed through their squat bodies, the rounds chiseling dust-spurting notches in the stone behind them.

As she fired, she shouted over the cracking reports, "Kane! The rocket launcher!"

Kane stared at her in disbelief, gauging the distance

between them and the gorillas. Brigid squeezed off another round, then the slide of the TP-9 popped back into the locked and empty position. The apes opened their mouths and roared deafeningly. They lumbered forward, listing from side to side, balancing themselves on their knuckles.

Instantly, Kane dropped to one knee, flipping the LAW up and over his shoulder in the same motion. A rocket was already in the tube and he expended less than a second establishing aim. He squeezed the trigger, caught only a fragmented glimpse of a flaming, smoking projectile skimming from the mouth of the launcher, then flung himself backward and down over Brigid. He covered her body with his own, cupping his gloved hands over the back of his head.

The RPG-4 exploded in a blazing fireball right between both apes, spreading a blanket of flame over their bodies. The concussion shook the cleft, and shards of stone clattered loudly all around. Compressed air crowded Kane and Brigid against the rock and they felt the blast of withering heat right through their shadow suits. He jerked in reaction to a jarring blow against his lower back but didn't otherwise move.

Neither person stirred, waiting until the echoes of the explosions faded or the clatter of falling debris became a series of sporadic thumps. Kane heard more than one clang of metal bouncing off rock.

The sound confused him, but he knew what had happened to the apes when the rocket's warhead exploded at such close range—razor-keen slivers of steel, impacting at over eight hundred pounds per square inch, would have penetrated their bodies like hot needles through soft wax. Their skeletons would splinter like rotten latticework, their flesh cook right off the bone.

In a breathless whisper, Brigid said, "You can get up off me now, Kane. Please."

Slowly, he pushed himself to his feet, setting his teeth on a groan as pain stabbed through his back muscles. He glanced around, looking for the object that had struck him. He found it and gaped in dumbfounded silence at the gorilla hand lying on the rock at his feet. Severed at the wrist, the thick black fingers still flexed but no blood streamed from the ragged amputation. Instead, he saw a gleam of filaments.

Brigid stood up, raking her disheveled mane of hair out of her face. Nudging the paw with the toe of a boot, she said, "I figured as much."

She didn't sound happy about it.

Kane squinted through the curling wreathes of smoke, wrinkling his nose at the stench of scorched hair. Retrieving the LAW, he stepped toward the impact point of the rocket, absently noting that referring to the range as point-blank was being liberal. If not for the shadow suits, he and Brigid would have been killed.

Dimly he made out the mutilated bodies of the gorillas but only one of them still resembled a creature that had ever lived—and even that was debatable. He peered down and recoiled, biting back a startled curse.

Its burned features locked in ferocious grimace, the ape stared up at him with glassy eyes. He heard an almost inaudible whining, and blue skeins of electricity crawled over the maimed face of the gorilla. Oily black smoke seethed from the gaping bloodless wounds and the red glare faded from its eyes.

Stunned by the sight, Kane husked out, "It's a robot. A goddamn ape-bot."

Brigid fanned the air in front of her face, clearing away the smoke. "It's a little more advanced than that. Utu blended the Annunaki smart-metal process with his own developments in bionics. Like his jinn, he turned these poor animals into mindless automatons."

Kane stared unblinkingly at the smoldering corpses. "Is that really possible?"

Brigid shrugged. "It's basically a system of nano-technology, like we've encountered before. Surface nanocomposites embedded in a host matrix can morph into new forms using ion implantation and thermal processing. I'd judge the smart-metal constituents of the apes were in a dormant state, which suspended their organic processes, encasing their bodies in a kind of protective glaze. They picked up layers of dust and dirt over the years…that's why they looked like rocks or statues. If you hadn't fired the rocket, we wouldn't have been able to stop them with our pistols. Their constituent parts had to be separated."

"Blown to pieces, you mean."

Brigid nodded grimly. "That was the general idea I was trying to convey."

Kane felt a surge of pity for the creatures. He inhaled a bit of the acrid smoke and coughed. "How long have the apes been standing here, do you figure?"

Shrugging, Brigid turned away. "There's no way to

tell or even estimate. A very, *very* long time. Centuries, I'd estimate. Certainly long enough to become folk-lore."

They walked back along the fissure into a low-ceil-inged cavity punched into the face of the mountain. In-kula, Pakari, DeFore and the goat huddled together.

"We heard what you said," Pakari murmured in tones of horror. "The apes weren't real?"

"They were real enough," Kane replied flatly, ges-turing toward the dead man. "One of them killed your goat-tender."

"Are you two all right?" DeFore asked anxiously.

Gingerly, Kane probed his lower back. "I could probably do with a soak in a hot tub, but I'll wait until we're back in Cerberus."

"Provided we manage to get back," said DeFore gloomily, reaching up to touch her right ear. "I've been trying to raise Grant on the Commtact every few min-utes for the last hour. If he's gone—"

"Nobody's gone until we see a body," Kane broke in, speaking more harshly than he intended. "Let's drop the subject."

Inkula stepped forward. "I agree. We haven't much time to complete the ritual. The Moon wanes tonight so we must begin now."

Brigid arched an eyebrow. "Here?"

Inkula made a strange, intricate gesture with his hands. "Where else? We stand upon the rim of the world, in the very the shadow of the threshold."

"I asked this before," DeFore said crossly. "Thresh-old to what?"

Inkula frowned at her disapprovingly. "You're very impudent for a healer. Your question will be answered if the ceremony is successful."

He swept a hand toward DeFore, Brigid and Kane. "I charge you three to act as witnesses."

Kane barely managed to refrain from muttering, "Anything to get this day over with," and obligingly moved to Pakari's left. DeFore stood on her right and Brigid took up a position behind her.

The outlanders watched in respectful silence as Inkula steepled his fingers at his lips and began murmuring a prayer. When he was done, he nodded to Pakari, who undid the clasps of her jerkin and unwrapped the leopard-skin belt from her around her waist. She handed the belt to Kane and the jerkin to DeFore.

All was hushed within the rim of the world. Pakari stood proudly, her shoulders straight, her carriage ramrod perfect. The angle of her head showed self-possession, serenity and an awareness of an inner power.

Inkula chanted in a feeble singsong voice, reciting a long epic poem about old kings and great battles, of splendid palaces and of queens and kings and the mysteries of a young Africa, long forgotten by the world.

He spoke of the great days of Prester John, relating the heroic age of his nation, when every man was a warrior and hunter, every woman wise and beautiful.

When the incantation was over, Inkula took a knife from within his robe and holding the goat firmly by its head, drew the blade swiftly across its throat, just under the hinge of its jaw. Although the animal died quickly and quietly, Brigid cast her gaze away. The old priest's lips moved in silent prayer as he placed small brass bowl beneath the goat's wound, catching the flow of blood.

"God has spoken," he intoned. "The path is clear. The Collar of Prester John returns to the House of its Birth."

Dipping forefinger into the bowl, he drew on Pakari's forehead and between her bare breasts a bloody cross. "I seal thee," he proclaimed, "queen of Prester John's people. I call thee to the inheritance of John. When he ascended on high he left to his kin the sacred snake, the ark of his valor, to be God's dower and pledge to the people whom He has chosen."

Kane could barely discern the words that followed. He guessed Inkula recited the long list of kings and conquerors who had worn the collar, the snake. He caught the names of Shaka, Arjuna and Iskander and a dozen others of whom he had never heard.

Opening his robe, the priest thrust his bony hand beneath. When he brought it forth again, he gripped a cascade of red, living fire. The glare of the gems was dazzling, as if they burned from within.

"Behold the collar," cried Inkula, and Pakari bowed her head reverently. "Behold the snake. In the name of God, I deliver to the heir of John, the Collar of John."

Inkula took the necklace and twined it in two loops round Pakari's neck. Taking her right hand in his, he drew the edge of the knife across the ball of her thumb. She endured the cut without so much as narrowing her golden eyes. Carefully, in studied, measured moves, he manipulated her thumb, pressing it against the largest of the rubies, smearing the surfaces with little droplets of her blood.

The strands of the collar burned and flickered on the girl's bosom, like fire that didn't burn. The old man knelt before her and pressed his forehead against her insteps and chanted in a guttural language.

Above the bloodred shimmer of the necklace, Pakari's face held the passive pride and dignity of an empress born to the role. Laying a hand on Inkula's bald head, she said, "Rise."

Slowly, the old man climbed to his feet, his seamed cheeks wet with tears that spilled from his eyes. "Now for the final measure," he wheezed.

Inkula led her forward by both hands, taking three, slow deliberate steps back. Light suddenly flared beneath her feet as she rested her weight on a hexagonal plate inset into the ground. As if in response, the Collar of Prester John glowed with an eerie luminescence. The shadowy murk lit up with a swimming sea of star specks. They swirled around Pakari like a swarm of miniscule fireflies.

"What the hell is going on here, Baptiste?" Kane side-mouthed.

"Some kind of sensory apparatus has been activated, I'd guess," Brigid responded in an enthralled tone. "Analyzing her DNA, matching her blood sample on the gems against files in a database, checking to ascertain if she does indeed carry the blood of the Waziri monarchy."

"Why the hell would Utu set up something like that?" Kane demanded.

"I'm betting he didn't."

"What if there's no match?" DeFore asked, lines of worry creasing her forehead. "Would all of this be a waste?"

Before Brigid could respond, a funnel of light splashed down from a lens in the stone ceiling, casting a halo over a freestanding archway of dull metal, pressed up almost flush with the rock wall. Kane and Brigid had seen a similar arch before. In general shape, height and width, it resembled the linteled door frames in predark cathedrals.

As the frame flashed with miniature lightning throbbing with rainbow hues, Brigid uttered a short, relieved laugh. "There's the answer to your threshold question, Reba. It really *is* a Threshold, and Pakári is keyed to its activation."

DeFore cast her a confused glance. She didn't speak because an amplified voice thundered down from above, "Yes—and its activation is what we've been waiting for."

Kane and Brigid heeled around, hearts pounding, looking out of the cleft. For a second, they saw nothing but the darkening sky. Then, with a shimmering effect they might have appreciated under other circumstances, a section of the sky rippled, like water sluicing over a pane of dusty glass.

The silver disk of Utu's ship hovered barely two yards above the path. Standing directly beneath, as if it were a gigantic umbrella, was Laputara. He panted heavily, as if he had just sprinted straight up the face of the mountain. His face was sheened with sweat and blood oozed from lacerations on his arms, legs and chest.

Laputara didn't look exhausted, happy or even angry. He looked insane.

Chapter 31

Kane saw little reason to react to the appearance of Utu and Laputara with gunfire. He had expected the overlord's arrival, realizing now the blurred distortion he had glimpsed in the sky wasn't due to grit in his eyes but the disk hovering overhead, employing its low-observable camouflage screen.

The TAVS were equipped with a similar feature—within the hulls were microcomputers that sensed the color and shade of the background and exactly mirrored the background image.

He also knew that even if he managed to drop Laputara dead, Utu could easily incinerate them all where they stood. He assumed that since Pakari had already inserted the key into the lock, even she was not safe.

The Cerberus exiles watched as the underside of the disk twisted, flowed and morphed into a short ladder. The armor-clad Utu climbed down it through an aperture that opened and closed like a mouth. He descended alone, without the company of any of the Nephilim.

During the procedure, Pakari hastily pulled on her jerkin, leaving the collar hanging over it. Against the white silk, the rubies looked like frozen clots of blood. By the time Utu and Pakari marched up to them, she had recovered some of her poise and regarded them with haughty eyes.

"My brother," she formally, "I have been invested as the rightful heir of Prester John, but I have no objection to sharing the Waziri throne with my kin. You and I must be united."

Laputara's eyes fixed hungrily on the collar, his lips twisting as if he meant to spit at her. In a voice so thick with hatred it was nearly unintelligible, he growled, "I am Prince Mubijika Muki Laputara. The Waziri nation is mine to rule alone!"

He reached for the collar, and Pakari said softly but firmly, "You have no right to touch it, brother. So do *not*."

Laputara's hand stopped moving, the tips of his fingers inches away from the rubies. His brow furrowed as if he were trying to work out a knotty problem. He seemed confused by Pakari's quietly worded command, as though his first inclination was to disobey, but then he experienced an inhibition. Brigid watched the exchange intently.

Utu reached out and pushed Laputara's hand down. He gave the collar only the most cursory of glances. "I agree, Princess. You and your brother should not be enemies. Both of you are young and misguided. I can counsel you both on how to rule jointly."

"You really mean that Pakari and Laputara will be puppets to do as you tell them," Brigid stated matter-of-factly.

"They need to be taught," Utu said smoothly. "Kingship is a skill acquired through many lessons."

Kane made a scoffing sound of disdain. "The first lesson will be the correct way to crawl on their bellies before you. The second lesson will be how they should convince the rest of Africa to crawl on their bellies to you."

Utu turned toward him, the basic cruelty of his nature apparent in the smirk that lifted his lips away from his teeth. "If not me, then one of the Supreme Council. That is an inevitability. All humanity, not just Africa, will eventually crawl before the overlords."

Kane rolled his eyes in exaggerated weariness. "Can't you lay off that melodramatic crap for one minute?"

"You are not only a fool, Kane—you're a doomed fool."

"What did you do to Grant?" DeFore demanded stridently.

Utu glanced at her contemptuously. "What makes you think I did anything to him?"

He strode past her dismissively, stepped to within a few inches of the archway. "Prince, Princess, this is a device my people created hundreds of thousands of years ago. We called them Thresholds…they are portals between great distances or through obstacles."

There was a low, soft, thrumming sound, like a plucked harp string that continued to vibrate just at the edge of audibility. Within the frame of the Threshold, variegated hues of color shifted and wavered. An image strobed, rippled, then coalesced. Beyond them lay a dark chamber. It was like looking through several feet of silt-clouded water.

The outlanders knew the Thresholds had been used by the Annunaki during their first occupation of Earth. Lakesh had opined the devices served as the templates for the mat-trans units of Project Cerberus.

"Once we step through it," Utu continued, "we will be within the fabled treasure vault of Prester John."

"I thought we'd be in your private toy store," Kane said. "Are there more wind-up monsters like those poor apes you mutilated?"

Utu chuckled. "Honestly? I really do not know. It's been over two thousand years since I last visited. I was barred from entering by the pact between the Annunaki and the Tuatha de Danaan."

"Speaking of wind-up monsters," said DeFore, "where are those walking dead bodyguards of yours?"

"I did not think I needed them." Utu eyed her challengingly. "If you feel otherwise, I can certainly summon a party of them to escort you and your friends."

"I don't think that will be necessary," Brigid interposed smoothly. "If anything happens to you, I'm sure you've given the Nephilim orders to make sure we don't leave this mountain alive."

Utu showed his teeth in a predatory grin. "Actually, if that eventuality does arise, I've given them orders to make sure there's no mountain, period. But I would be more comfortable if you did not bring weapons into the vault. There could be a number of fragile items in there, and I'm certain you'd hate to see them damaged."

When none of the three outlanders responded, Utu extended his right arm and an ASP emitter popped out from atop his wrist. He demanded, "Wouldn't you?"

After exchanging glances, Kane, DeFore and Brigid disarmed, dropping their weapons to the ground.

Utu nodded in acknowledgment and made an "after you" gesture to Pakari. "Your Highness, shall you precede us or do you and I travel together?"

The venomous glare Princess Pakari directed at Utu should have shriveled his heart, but he only sneered in response. Taking Inkula by the hand, Pakari stepped through the archway. The image within the frame of Threshold rippled slightly, like a pebble dropped into a pond.

"You and Baptiste next," Utu said to Kane. With the way the viper heads of the ASP emitter pointed at them, the overlord was obviously not making a request.

Kane took Brigid's hand, warily eyeing the energy fluctuations within the frame. "There's nothing to it," she whispered to him. "I traveled through one before."

"I remember," he replied gruffly.

"I traveled from Iraq to Tiamat in Earth orbit," she continued reassuringly. "We're only going a few feet."

"Yeah…through solid rock."

"You can close your eyes if you want."

Kane shot Brigid a resentful glance, inhaled a deep breath, held it and they stepped through simultaneously.

Their ears popped, his vision smeared, his belly turned over sickeningly. There was no shock of impact, merely a strange, cushioning sensation, as if they jumped into a wall a compressed air that yielded before them. They were conscious of a half instant of whirling vertigo as if they hurtled a vast distance at blinding speed.

Then they stumbled slightly across a solid, slick floor. Pakari and Inkula stood nearby, looking around their dim surroundings in wide-eyed apprehension. Kane turned to look behind him, seeing a duplicate of the archway only a few feet away. The Threshold disgorged DeFore, then Utu and Laputara. Only the prince showed any discomfiture, eyes rolling, teeth bared, like a trapped animal, still perspiring heavily.

A wavery light blinked on overhead. They stood in a great chamber with four walls slanting upward to an apex, like a hollow quarried out of a pyramid. Inset into the apex Kane discerned a huge, metal-collared iris hatch, over twenty-five feet in diameter. Below it, several large objects bulked up from the floor.

Utu pushed past them, marching purposefully into the man-made cavern. "Follow me," he snapped imperiously.

The six people fell into step behind him. They didn't walk far before they reached a pair of giant stone dragons, horned heads held high on curved serpentine necks, clawed forefeet joining to form a crescent curve. From within it rose a high-backed chair.

"Dragons," Kane muttered. "Always with the dragons."

"The *sirrush,* in this instance," Brigid responded, eyes darting back and forth. "They were Abyssian guardian creatures."

The chair and the statues faced a titanic sphere, at least three times Utu's height. It rested on an arrangement of plinths sunk deep into the floor. A mesh of fine wires stretched from tiny sockets sprouting from the outer curve of the globe to the arms of the chair, terminating in four crystalline thimbles. The substance of the sphere itself reminded Kane of tarnished, dull gray base metal.

Utu marched between the stone claws and sat down in the chair with a triumphant flourish. He gestured for Pakari and Laputara to join him. The young man did so, standing on the overlord's right side, but the princess hesitated, not moving until Inkula whispered into her ear. She took up a position beside the left arm of the chair.

Without preamble, Utu announced, "The Mirror of Prester John. That's not what I originally called it, of course, but the term will suffice. It was the first of the masterpieces I created, one of my greatest accomplishments. My step-father, grand and glorious Anu, loved it. Through the mirror he gazed at events taking place in any part of the world, no matter how remote or hidden. No walls could resist its probing eyes, no councils were so secret that he did not eavesdrop upon them and thus further his own plans."

Brigid examined it visually and said, "Like a crystal ball…or a discipline called 'remote-viewing.'"

Kane eyed the sphere dubiously. "How does it work? Like a television or something?"

One corner of Utu's mouth lifted in a blend of sneer and smile. "I thought you'd never ask…but I doubt you'll be able to understand the principle at work."

He inserted his fingers into the thimbles of the chair arms. With a prolonged squeaking, and clashing of metal against metal, the overhead hatch irised open.

Rust, dirt and grit sifted down in little showers. The sky above showed dim, dark gray sky glowing vaguely with the light of the rising moon.

"Your analogy to a primitive television receiver is correct in only one regard," Utu said. "For the mirror to work properly, it requires an unobstructed channel for the ultrawave to travel."

Brigid swiveled her head toward him. "Ultrawave?"

"The term means something to you?"

"Ultrawaves were a theoretical superluminal—faster than light—carrier form that could make possible instantaneous communication, anywhere in the universe. They were also called Dirac transmitters, named after physicist Paul Dirac, who initially proposed the theory. But because of the time dilation involved in faster-than-light communication, his theories were never fully explored."

Utu nodded in grudging agreement. "I'm impressed that you know that much about the principle, as superficial as it is. Yes, the Mirror of Prester John was constructed much like the Dirac transmitters, but using the energy of the mind as a propagation medium."

"If I recall the theory correctly," Brigid said musingly, "Dirac transmitters could hypothetically send messages that could be picked up by any Dirac receiver—past, present or future."

Utu chuckled and inclined his head toward the mirror. "Behold."

Milky light swirled over the smooth face of the sphere. It throbbed brighter and brighter until it formed a whirlpool of iridescence. The colors wove together into a blurred tapestry, then abruptly sharpened into an image so sharp that Kane, who stood by the nearest, took a startled step back.

"The present," Utu said laconically.

It was like looking down upon the blue-green-white globe of Earth from bridge of an orbiting spaceship. Even as the concept registered, the perspective changed in a blur of rainbow colors. The next image was still a view of the planet from space, but a new element appeared in the vision.

Sleek, deadly and dark with pinnacled towers silvered by moonlight, a vast craft sailed majestically over the blue oceans far, far below. From its hull rose spires and minarets tipped with glittering points, reminiscent of the dorsal fins of a mind-staggeringly enormous sea creature—or dragon.

"Tiamat," Brigid blurted fearfully.

Chapter 32

DeFore bit back a startled murmur and Kane repressed a shudder. The ancient, mile-long vessel that served as a starship and the birthing ward for the reborn Annunaki still evoked a sense of dread and awe, even though he knew Tiamat continuously orbited the Earth, as a watchful and even vengeful mother.

"With the power of the mirror," Utu continued, "I also learned many ancient secrets. As you speculated, it also acts as a recorder of the past."

Flickering fragments of scenes flashed across the surface of the mirror—mushroom clouds of incandescent yellow towering above the North American continent, flashing arrow shapes of missiles, a jumble of dim and misty images that made the eye ache—then a panorama of knights in mud-splashed cloaks and blood-smeared armor.

Their faces were pale and tense beneath shaggy beards and layers of dirt. Awe and terror shone in their eyes as they bowed humbly before a very tall, very slender figure who wore a simple drapery of a saffron hue. Hairless, his flesh held a blue-white tinge and his face consisted mainly of two huge eyes set beneath a smooth, domed cranium. His ears were small, almost vestigial and his small mouth seemed pursed in an eternal gentle smile.

"Do you recognize that creature?" Utu asked.

Kane nodded. "Lam, father of Balam. Last of the First Folk."

"One name of many he adopted while among the human societies he influenced." Utu's tone quavered with barely repressed disgust. "He was also known as Osiris, Tsong Kaba and here he is passing himself off as Zarathustra."

"Zarathustra?" echoed Brigid in surprise. "Of 'Thus Spake' fame?"

"The very one," Utu replied sullenly. "It was Lam who permitted the slouching barbarians led by the poseur who went by the name of Prester John into this very vault. Lam instructed him in the use of the mirror and the collar and other items that no longer exist. As Zarathustra, he was revered as a prophet. In reality, Lam was a common thief who gathered about him other common thieves."

"If he'd been hanging out with the overlords," DeFore observed sarcastically, "it was probably a step up for him."

Brigid shot her a surprised stare and DeFore cast her eyes downward in sudden embarrassment. "Sorry," she muttered. "I've been hanging around Kane and Grant too long."

Utu ignored the medic's jibe. "Through Prester John, Lam established an African empire, selecting the Waziri and the Zulu tribes to act as his chosen people."

He paused, frowned, and added, "Lam always had

a weakness for educating barbarians, the more primitive the better."

Brigid said confidently, "Lam educated the barbarians so they wouldn't be so inclined to worship frauds like you and the other Annunaki."

"Yeah," said Kane, a challenging smile crossing his face. "He also knew that the toys left behind by your people and the Danaan would be rediscovered one day. So he arranged matters so he would have an influence on the people who found them and the uses to which they were put."

DeFore nodded. "Like making sure the Collar of Prester John could only work in conjunction with a Waziri or Zulu DNA signature."

"There is a point to all of this?" Pakari asked impatiently.

Utu threw her a slit-eyed stare. "Like all barbarians, you have a short attention span."

"Hardly," Pakari shot back. "Just a low tolerance of more of your bullshit. Like all egomaniacs, you flaunt old knowledge but refuse to learn anything new. You think my people are the same as they were when you cowed them as Butu, and that mistake will cost you. But I know you didn't go to all the trouble to reclaim the Mirror of Prester John just so you could show us how he ended up with it in the first place."

"Surprisingly perceptive, Your Highness," Utu said with a sardonic smile. He inclined his head toward the sphere. "Look, and you will see why I went to all the trouble."

The mirror flashed, then showed a flat and barren

plain, swept by an endless desert even more desolate than that of the Nubian. The only feature in the wasteland was a pitted, wind-eroded statue, a Sphinx half buried by drifting sand dunes. In the far background, the vague outline of pyramid could be discerned rising from the horizon.

"Egypt," said Brigid. "The Great Sphinx. Is this the present, past or future we're seeing? Or is this an altogether new chapter in remote voyeurism?"

Utu didn't answer. His face was drawn tight in concentration. The image shifted, smearing across the sphere. When it coalesced, a dark and cavernous room, lit by a cold glare from a naked light fixture, swam into focus.

Kane received the unmistakable impression that the chamber was far underground. A gaunt figure sat alone at a huge table of black wood. He was garbed in a dark robes, fold after fold hanging from his frame as he turned the yellowed leaves of a massive book that lay open before him. The pages were inscribed with hieroglyphics and Sumerian cuneiform symbols.

At first the man's face could not be seen, obscured by bands of shadow. When he leaned forward, tension knotted like lengths of wet rope in the bellies of Brigid and Kane.

The man's skin was tinted a pale shade of gold, drawn tautly over the strong, high-arching bones of his face. A crest of long spines slanted back along the curve of his skull, gleaming like wires made of burnished steel.

Scales glistened with a metallic luster as if his flesh

were dusted with silver. The outer layer of his epidermis was like finely wrought mesh, an organic equivalent of chain-mail armor.

His eyes gleamed like molten brass, seething with a restless energy and the hot banked fires of unholy, ruthless ambition. They seemed ageless yet at the same time old beyond memory.

"Enlil," whispered Brigid.

"Yes, it is Enlil." Utu's voice was pitched to a low, gloating croon. "Lord of the Earth and the Air. I have found him at last."

Kane tore his gaze away from the mirror. "You didn't know where he was?"

"We of the Supreme Council are by blood related," Utu replied. "But we do not trust each other. Each of us maintain our own hidden lairs on Earth, our own little secret pockets of conspiracy, of bolt-holes."

"And whoever knows all the locations of those bolt-holes," DeFore said loudly, "has a tactical advantage over the others. You can spy on the other overlords, learn their plans, find out if any of them are moving against you and your territories."

"Or," interposed Kane, "you could sell that very same information to the other members of the council."

"Or blackmail them with it," Brigid declared, fixing a penetrating stare on Utu.

"Exactly," Utu replied with satisfaction. Then he frowned, took a deep breath and sighed heavily. "The mirror has an unfortunate limitation, however. Unless the operator has a personal frame of reference with the target he wishes to locate, the mirror will not function. I can find Enlil and the rest of the council, obviously."

He paused, lips creasing in a smile. "But I will not be able to isolate Balam or Ninlil in a specific time or place...but the three of you can."

Comprehension rushed through Brigid, Kane and DeFore simultaneously. Kane clenched his fists. "You want us to locate the baby for you? Why? So you can turn her over to Enlil and become his favorite snake-face flavor of the month?"

"No," Brigid declared, voice thick with loathing. "He wants to kidnap her and use her as a tool to bend Enlil to his will. That's the only reason he kept us alive...he thinks we may have an idea where to find her and Balam."

Utu chuckled, a rattlesnake rasp that caused Kane's flesh to crawl. "Not to mention that learning all I can about the layout, weaponry and personnel of Cerberus would be exceptionally advantageous, as well. I'm sure once I connect each one of you to the mirror, I'll be able to find all sorts of places and things of utter fascination."

A floodtide of memories washed through Kane, visions of the *Parallax Red* space station, of the subterranean cities of Agartha and Ultima Thule, of the Operation Chronos installation on Thunder Isle.

Accompanying each of the mental images came nightmare flashes of the ghastly and even perverted consequences of the overlords learning of their existence.

Inkula surprised everyone by proclaiming loudly, "You would defile the Mirror of Prester John to once more enslave humankind."

Utu waved at him negligently. "Silence, ju-ju man."

"Monsters will never rule the chosen of John," Inkula declared pridefully. "Not even those who dress up in the skins of gods."

Utu turned his head toward him, eyes seething with rage. He extended his right arm and the viper heads of the ASP emitter began to spark. "Your presence is no longer a requirement, you old bag of elephant turds."

Pakari instantly insinuated herself between the ASP and Inkula. She shouted defiantly, "You will not harm him without harming me!"

Utu's lips peeled back from his teeth. "You arrogant little savage, prancing and dancing around a fire. How dare you dictate terms of anything to me, particularly matters of your survival? You opened the way into my vault and thus I no longer need you."

"My people need me," she stated flatly. "And if you need my people, you need me."

Utu snorted. "All your people know is that you undertook a pilgrimage so you may legally wear the collar. Perhaps they know you left with it, but it is Prince Laputara who will return with it around his neck."

Pakari stared unblinkingly at Laputara, who tried to return her stare. In a measured, deliberate tone, Pakari said, "My brother, you and I must be united if we are to unite our nation. We will share the power, the collar of inheritance. Yes, we have both done many foolish things, but now we must think of ourselves as personifying the entire Waziri tribe."

She extended her right hand toward him. "Us, my brother. One nation. Imagine our power."

Laputara narrowed his eyes. For a moment, he looked as if he were on the verge of exploding into violence. Then, by jerky degrees, he lifted his hand, reaching out for hers. His face was curiously blank.

Kane guessed that Pakari was consciously channeling the mind-altering energy of the stones, exerting an influence over Laputara's drug-weakened reason, appealing to the remnants of his patriotism and his voracious ambition.

Snarling, Utu levered himself up from the chair. He pointed the ASP emitter directly at Pakari. At the same instant, Laputara bounded forward, shouldering Utu aside as he reached for his half sister.

None of the Cerberus exiles were certain if he intended to throttle the princess into silence or if he was trying to push her to safety. All they could be sure of was that the bolt of crimson energy lancing from the ASP struck Laputara directly between the shoulder blades.

A sharp crackling sound filled the chamber and the man's field jacket shed a flurry of blue sparks. He toppled sideways without an outcry, limbs contorting and twisting even as he fell.

Pakari screamed and Utu stared with angry, astonished eyes first at Laputara then at the princess. A sibilant hissing issued from his lips and he thrust out the ASP emitter again, the trio of serpent heads on a direct line with her face.

A cavity suddenly burst open in the floor at Utu's feet. The exploding, sharp-edged bits of rock pelted his legs and the overlord danced backward, face registering shock and confusion.

Grant's voice roared into the heads of Brigid, Kane and DeFore: "Get away from the mirror! Everybody down!"

No one hesitated. DeFore wrestled Inkula sideways and Brigid leaped across the floor, clutching Pakari and bearing her backward and down. Even as Kane tucked, rolled and then went into a belly slide, he heard a swishing whisper that almost instantly became a booming pressure against his eardrums.

Twisting around he, glimpsed of a pattern of sliding, shifting light near the ceiling. Dark, ambient waves shimmered, then revealed the bronze tones of a Manta's hull as it materialized just below the iris hatch.

Overlord Utu screeched in wordless fury and extended his arm upward. Buds of light burst from the ASP emitters and impacted against the Manta's prow. Smoke puffed and tongues of flame lapped along the fuselage.

Grant triggered the nose cannon, the jackhammering roar sounding like stuttering thunderclaps. The burst of tungsten-carbide shells struck sparks from his armor and spun Utu around in a clumsy pirouette. Fountains of dust erupted all around him as he hurtled backward, catching himself on the claw of a *sirrush*.

The rounds pounded into the Mirror of Prester John, smashing it into fragments, tendrils of energy coiling out from the network of splits that spread over its surface.

With a deafening crack, like the sound of a tree branch breaking, but amplified a hundred-fold, the mirror exploded from within. A fierce flash of white flame cascaded out of it in a torrent and engulfed Utu. For an instant he was sheathed in a chrysalis of dancing fire.

Staggering blindly, Utu shrieked, clapping his hands over his blackened face and burnt-out eye sockets. Droplets of superheated, molten metal sizzled their way through his flesh. He collapsed into the chair and his hands fell away from his face, revealing a raw, red mask of crisped flesh. He breathed in whistling gasps, through cooked sinuses and seared lungs.

Ignoring the sickening odor of burned meat, Kane slowly rose, staring at the Manta hovering overhead, listing slightly from side to side. "I guess it's like they say—better late than never."

Grant's voice over the Commtact was studiedly nonchalant. "Actually, I've been around ever since you were halfway up the mountain."

DeFore, helping Inkula to his feet, speared the Manta with a glare of fury. "What? You've been floating around invisible all that time? Why didn't you respond when I called?"

"I didn't know if Utu's ship could monitor our communications. As it was, I wasn't sure if he could spot me while in LOC mode while he flew around using his own low-observability camouflage system." Grant paused, then added blandly, "Guess not."

Kane shook his head and said in an admiring tone, "You're getting really sneaky in your old age."

"You know how it is," Grant replied modestly. "I learned from the best."

Pakari and Brigid rose to their feet. The sad eyes of the princess passed over the dead body of Laputara, then rested on the form of Utu, slumped over and smoldering in the chair.

"It's almost a pitiful thing," the princess said regretfully.

"What is?" asked Brigid.

Pakari sighed, absently fingering the Collar of Prester John. "To have lived as long as Utu and seen all that he has…and yet learned so little."

JAMES AXLER

DEATH LANDS

Shatter Zone

In this raw, brutal world ruled by the strongest and the most vicious, an unseen player is manipulating Ryan and his band, luring him across an unseen battle line drawn in the dust outside Tucson, Arizona. Here a local barony becomes the staging ground for a battle unlike any other, against a foe whose ties to preDark society present a new and incalculable threat to a fragile world. Ryan Cawdor is the only man living who stands between this adversary's glory...and the prize he seeks.

Available September 2006 wherever you buy books.

SENSOR SWEEP

Four freighters, armed with missiles to be launched
from mobile systems at four unidentified targets,
have left port in South Africa. The payload is a lethal
chemical agent and the death toll is incalculable.
For Stony Man, it means the speed, skill, intelligence
and righteous fury of those who place a premium
on human life will be pushed to the limits in a
race to stop those who would see the innocent
burn in the fires of fanaticism.

STONY MAN.

*Available
August 2006
wherever you
buy books.*
